A recorded voice overrode the next words spoken by the man. "This is a call from a California state prison."

It had come in on Hamlin's main firm number. The caller had asked for Donnally by name, and Takiyah Jackson had routed it to him in Hamlin's office. Donnally was relieved that he had enough of her cooperation for her at least to do that.

Unless the murder was a gang-related execution, which the condition of Hamlin's body suggested it wasn't, Donnally wasn't sure how someone in prison could have any credible information.

"Who did it?" Donnally asked.

"Pay me a visit and I'll tell you the story."

The man's voice sounded as though he was in his fifties or sixties, maybe older.

"How do I know you're not a lunatic?"

The line beeped, indicating that the call was being recorded.

"Look at my file. It's somewhere in the office. Five years ago. My name's Bennie Madison. A murder case. There's no psych report in there and no trips to the loony bin. I'm as sane as anybody ever is in here."

By Steven Gore

Graham Gage Thrillers

FINAL TARGET
ABSOLUTE RISK
POWER BLIND

Harlan Donnally Novels

ACT OF DECEIT
A CRIMINAL DEFENSE

STEVEN GORE

A CRIMINAL DEFENSE

A HARLAN DONNALLY NOVEL

HARPER

An Imprint of HarperCollinsPublishers

This book is a work of fiction. The characters, incidents, and dialogue are drawn from the author's imagination and are not to be construed as real. Any resemblance to actual events or persons, living or dead, is entirely coincidental.

HARPER

An Imprint of HarperCollins*Publishers*
10 East 53rd Street
New York, New York 10022-5299

Copyright © 2013 by Steven Gore
ISBN 978-0-06-202507-4

First Harper premium printing: August 2013

HarperCollins® and Harper® are registered trademarks of Harper-Collins Publishers.

Printed in the United States of America

Visit Harper paperbacks on the World Wide Web at
www.harpercollins.com

10 9 8 7 6 5 4 3 2 1

*For my dear cousins, Julie Quater, Bruce Kaplan, and
Bobbie Chinsky:
kind hearts, great minds, and doers of good deeds*

A
CRIMINAL
DEFENSE

CHAPTER 1

Since matter is neither created nor destroyed, in one way or another the world isn't done with Mark Hamlin.

The words had come to Harlan Donnally as he disconnected the call that wrenched him from sleep at four in the morning. And others had followed as he walked from his bungalow near San Francisco's Ocean Beach through whorls of fog and mist toward his street-lit truck.

Under ideal conditions, bodies in motion remain in motion and bodies at rest remain at rest.

But it was only now, gazing at the criminal defense attorney hanging by his neck from the Fort Point lighthouse, that Donnally realized these thoughts were reverberations from the last case he'd cleared as a homicide detective a decade earlier. They'd echoed not only in his unease about the uncertainties and entanglements awaiting him in the shadow of the south anchorage of the Golden Gate Bridge, but in his musings about the mechanics of life and death that had accompanied him on the drive through the wooded Presidio to the redbrick garrison and during his three-story climb to the top.

Except the conditions weren't ideal and Hamlin wasn't at rest.

Although the fifty-five-year-old lawyer hung just fifteen feet away, Donnally had to squint hard into the darkness to make him out, his mind registering the parts, but not the whole, as an onshore gust spun and rocked the body.

Head tilted down.

Hair matted.

Mouth twisted.

Shirttails fluttering.

Slacks and underwear collected around his ankles, shoe tips scraping the concrete.

Footsteps approaching Donnally from behind emerged out of the rush of swirling salt air. He glanced over at Ramon Navarro as he came to a stop. The homicide detective was cinched inside a trench coat, his head covered by a sheepskin crown cap, his brush-cut hair and rough-cut features familiar enough to Donnally that they didn't need to be seen to be perceived.

Navarro turned on a flashlight. Donnally grabbed for it, keeping the beam focused down. "Turn it off."

Navarro waved his free arm toward the diffused and haloed headlights of a patrol car parked a hundred yards away, sealing off Marine Drive and blocking access into the parking lot. "Why's everybody grinning and telling me to keep the—"

A foghorn blast obliterated his final words.

"You'll see it in a minute," Donnally said. "Just wait until your eyes adjust."

The light died. The wind let up. The duck-squawk of car tires hitting the bridge's ribbed expansion joints grew louder and a distant siren yelped on the Marin County end of the span.

Navarro looked over at Donnally. "What else did his assistant say other than that he was hanging out here?"

"Just that the call she got was anonymous and muffled."

"And she reached out to you because . . ."

"Hamlin told her to if something happened to him."

"Such as . . ." Navarro lifted his chin toward the dead lawyer.

Donnally shrugged. "He didn't say. She said he was a secretive guy, even with her, so she hadn't pressed him."

"And maybe because it would've been too long a list since he had so many things to be afraid of."

"And people."

"Yeah. Lots and lots of them."

Navarro glanced over at a fog-shrouded container ship sliding from ocean to bay, then surveyed the thirty-foot lighthouse, from its skeletal legs up to the squat iron tower, then to the dark lantern room, the whole an iron and glass palette of pre-dawn grays.

"Nobody's paid attention to this thing since the bridge was built," Navarro said, "except to keep it from turning to rust." His eyes settled again on Hamlin's body. "I don't think this is what they were preserving it for."

Donnally looked down at the news crews stationed along the rock seawall and then up at a television truck descending Battery East Road, heading toward a spot on the hillside under the anchorage, overlooking the fort.

"What about some crime scene screens to block the view?" Donnally said, and then pointed up at the early morning walkers and joggers gathering along the railing, backlit by the yellow bridge lights and peering down into the shadows. "It'll be bright enough in a half hour for them to get a good look at him."

Donnally's concern was less that they would recognize Hamlin, for they'd watched him over twenty years of nightly news programs and sidewalk commentaries during media-frenzied trials, and more that they and the press would fixate on just one thing and that thing would live forever in Internet videos and in jokes told over cubicle walls and inside police squad rooms.

The wind rose again and rotated Hamlin's body toward them.

"Son . . . of . . . a . . . bitch."

Navarro had just spotted it: the dead man's erection.

"I'll get the forensic people here as fast as I can," Navarro said, reaching for his cell phone, "but they've been tied up on two gang murders. And I can't have anybody walking up close or wrapping up the body until we can record whatever is there."

Navarro made the call and again turned on his flashlight, pointing it down and away from Hamlin. He directed the beam at the feet of a uniformed officer five yards away and then at the television truck, now coming to a stop.

The officer spoke into his radio, and a minute later a patrol car appeared on Battery East, red and blue flashes reflecting off the low clouds and headlights jittering over dips and potholes. It swung in next to the truck and herded it back out.

"He have a wife?" Donnally asked.

"As far as I know he was never married and didn't have any kids. He had kind of a Boston accent, so his family probably lives back East. I've got somebody trying to track them down to let them know before the media does."

Donnally ducked and reached upward as a gust tore at his baseball cap. He sensed motion to his left as he shoved it into the pocket of his windbreaker, then turned to face San Francisco District Attorney Hannah Goldhagen as she walked up next to him, her neck turtled inside her overcoat collar against the cold and her hands driven deep inside her pockets.

He wasn't surprised to see her. While some prosecutors wearied and softened by middle age, she'd hardened like hot lava cooling into rock. Donnally knew it would've been easy for her to hand this off to an underling who could later be second-guessed and sold out, but he'd called it right. She'd taken it herself.

Goldhagen's eyes tracked up and down as she scanned the fifteen-foot rope extending from the knot tied at the lighthouse railing to the one at Hamlin's neck. "I take it it's too much to hope it's a suicide."

The word pushed Donnally's thoughts back again toward his final homicide investigation at SFPD. Everyone in the Stanford physics department had assumed the professor's life would end either in murder at the hand of a colleague or in suicide at his own. And after examining the facts and the probabilities, the chains of causation and the body at rest, Donnally had concluded it was the latter.

Donnally pointed at Hamlin's bound hands as they spun into view. "Not very likely."

"And a drop that far would've snapped his head off," Navarro said, then looked over at Donnally for confirmation. Their careers in the homicide unit overlapped for a few years before Donnally was shot at thirty-eight and retired out because of his injuries, but Navarro still deferred to Donnally as his senior even though he now had twice as many years in the job.

Goldhagen directed her long, thin arm at Hamlin's erection. "What do you make of that? Before or after he died?"

Donnally and Navarro shrugged. They'd seen both.

"We'll have to wait to hear what the medical examiner says," Navarro said, "but unless there's Viagra or something like it in his blood, I'm not sure the ME will know for certain."

Goldhagen turned toward Donnally.

"I spoke to Hamlin's assistant as I was driving over. She's saying a week ago he told her to call you if anything happened to him. You know why?"

"Why me? Or why did he make the comment then?"

"Both."

Donnally spread his hands. "I don't know the answer to either."

And Donnally didn't, at least in any way he could yet articulate. He'd spoken to the man only once since his forced retirement from the department and his moving north to Mount Shasta ten years earlier.

"I heard you helped out a client of his a while back," Goldhagen said.

"Inadvertently. I needed to find out something that his client knew. Hamlin hired me—"

Goldhagen's brows furrowed. Hamlin was as warped as Donnally was straight, and he knew she couldn't imagine him making the kind of moral compromise required for him to work for Hamlin.

And he hadn't.

"It was only in order to keep what his client told me privileged. The information got me where I needed to go, and also led me down a trail leading to evidence that cleared his client of participating in a murder conspiracy."

Goldhagen squinted at Donnally, facing him head to head, matching him at five-eleven. He could see the buoy and beacon lights flash in her dark eyes and tint her graying hair red.

"That mean you're a private investigator now?"

"No. I was just helping out a friend."

She turned her gaze back toward Hamlin. "You take any money from him?"

"A dollar I later dropped into the employee tip jar at my café."

"And you haven't spoken to him since?"

"No reason to. I'm just a guy who flips burgers these days. I was only in town to do some work on my house. My girlfriend still lives there."

Goldhagen fell silent, her questions answered, her cross-examination ended.

A maverick wave broke hard on the rocks below. Shrieking gulls rose from the top of the lighthouse, then wheeled and fled inland.

"Damn," Goldhagen finally said, watching a TV satellite truck joining the others parked along Marine Drive. "This is going to be a mess."

Donnally understood she was speaking past him and to Navarro. None of them needed to say aloud why Hamlin was so hated by law enforcement and why both the public and the legal community would distrust an investigation into his death by SFPD or the DA's office. Hamlin didn't win cases so much as sabotage them, all the while accusing the district attorney of judicial fascism and the police of blue-on-black terrorism.

A week earlier Donnally had seen on the news that Hamlin had lined a courtroom hallway with gang members, forcing a rape victim to walk a tattooed gauntlet on her way into court to testify against their leader. Despite her having identified the defendant in both photo and standup line-ups during the previous weeks, when the moment came to point him out in court, her hands remained clenched in her lap.

"SFPD starts going through his files," Goldhagen said, "not only the criminal defense bar, but the state bar, will go haywire." She pointed at Hamlin.

"And not because they had any respect for that asshole."

Navarro took in a long breath and exhaled. "Give me just ten minutes in his office . . . just ten stinking minutes."

"You know that's not going to happen," Goldhagen said, "as much as I'd like to be in there with you."

"Then what *is* gonna happen?" Navarro asked.

"You'll know as soon as I do," Goldhagen said, then pulled out her cell phone and walked a few yards away.

The forensic team came striding across the rooftop carrying screens to surround Hamlin's body. They photographed the scene, collected cigarette butts and food wrappers damp-stuck on the surface around the base of the lighthouse, and then began fixing the barriers in place.

As they worked, Donnally could feel the weight of the city behind him, not just the bluff onto which the bridge was anchored, but the neighborhoods into which Hamlin's professional roots reached: the politically powerful Castro, the drug and prostitution ground zero of the Tenderloin, the gang-ridden Bayview–Hunters Point, and even downtown into the financial district and out to City Hall and deep into the yuppified Noe Valley and high into the mansions of Nob Hill.

As a cop, Donnally had borne that burden, had never struggled against it, had even sought it, but standing there in the muted dawn, he found he didn't miss it. Sure there were things he still needed in life and things he was still puzzling out, but he'd learned in the last decade that he didn't require the gun and the badge to get at them. Even more, the city that had once struck him as a maze or a labyrinth spread over its seven hills now seemed like a web.

Goldhagen returned as Donnally and Navarro were about to step inside the enclosure to examine Hamlin's body.

"I talked to the presiding judge," Goldhagen said to Donnally. "He's appointing you special master. You'll station yourself in Hamlin's office and figure out how to pursue leads without jeopardizing attorney-client privilege and you'll be the public face of the investigation."

Donnally shook his head. He was still embarrassed to have taken Hamlin's dollar, viewing it at the time as an evil necessity made for the sake of a greater good. And he wasn't about to have it made public, an inevitable consequence of his accepting the role as special master. The press would demand to know why he'd been chosen, what his relationship with Hamlin had been, and what motivated Hamlin to ask for his help in death.

Even more, Donnally knew he'd be compromised from the start. Reporters would focus not on the facts relating to why Hamlin had been murdered, but on what it was that Donnally knew—or the press suspected he must know—that intersected with what Hamlin feared in the days before his murder.

Donnally himself didn't know. And the fact that he didn't worried him.

"The judge and I will both give you cover," Goldhagen said.

"I don't see how that's possible. You'll be too busy trying to give yourself cover. I'll look tainted from the get-go and it'll slop back on you and the investigation."

Goldhagen gestured toward the enclosure. "Without you jumping in now, we may not be able to get to the heart of this investigation for days and days." She glanced at Navarro as if anticipating his disagreement with what she would say next. "I don't believe in the so-called forty-eight-hour rule. I think it's bullshit. Especially in this case, with Hamlin's history and the number of enemies he's made over the years. But I do believe it's foolish to give a killer time to wipe away his tracks."

"Nice try," Donnally said, "but you'll have to find someone else. Ask the attorney general to send somebody from Sacramento. I'm not indispensable."

"No, you're not," Goldhagen said. "You're convenient. His assistant said he left a letter in his desk drawer authorizing you to look at his files. And the shortest distance between two points is a straight line. It would be idiotic to go the long way."

"Look, man," Navarro said, turning to face Donnally. "The one thing we know is that Hamlin brought this on himself."

"That's a helluva leap," Donnally said.

Navarro ignored him. "And evidence about how he did it is probably in his office."

"Probably," Goldhagen said. "That's the operative word. And 'probably' is not probable cause, and without probable cause there's material relating to his death in there, we don't have the basis for a search warrant. Sounds to me like Hamlin trusted you to develop that basis in a way that protects his clients."

Donnally glanced over at Goldhagen. "You've got me confused with somebody else. I have no interest in protecting his clients."

"Maybe you don't, but I have to and so does the court—at least until I can get them convicted. Unless we do it by the book, some of them will walk. And the public will rightfully crucify me."

Navarro made a show of peering at his watch by the diffused light of the cloud-curtained daybreak showing itself behind the East Bay hills.

"The clock is ticking."

But Donnally knew that's not what he meant.

The fact was that like Goldhagen, Navarro understood that from this moment, in the small town that was San Francisco, his name would be forever connected to Hamlin's. And the detective dreaded heading into an investigation into the death of a man he despised while straitjacketed by rules that man had abused in life.

CHAPTER 2

Dr. Youssef Haddad pointed down at Mark Hamlin's naked body lying covered by a plastic sheet on the stainless steel gurney in the medical examiner's autopsy lab.

The two gangsters whose overnight murders had delayed the forensic team's arrival at Fort Point flanked him. Neither the humming exhaust fan nor the odor of disinfectant could suppress the stench of excrement and urine released from the bodies in death.

"*O propheta, certe penis tuus cælum versus erectus est.*"

"Sorry?" Donnally glanced over at the pathologist.

"O prophet, thy penis is erect unto the sky."

"A prophet or *the* Prophet."

"The. According to the historian Abulfeda, the Imam Ali proclaimed it upon seeing the corpse of the Prophet Mohammed."

Donnally had never heard the quote before, but he'd seen the condition a few times while he was with SFPD and the name came back to him. Priapism. In homicide investigation training it had been described as a persistent erection. He couldn't watch Viagra television commercials without thinking of its other names. When produced after execution by hanging or by strangling, it was called a death erection or angel lust.

Although the Latin words were spoken in neither irony nor sarcasm, Donnally was surprised a Muslim doctor would even mention Mohammed in this context. Maybe he was only trying to say it was so natural even the Prophet was subject to it.

The doctor pursed his lips and said, "Saints and sinners alike can be humiliated, even after death."

Haddad was one of the few pathologists Donnally had ever met who hadn't lost or repressed his tragic sense, neither fearing it nor wearing it like a hair shirt.

Donnally nodded toward Hamlin's body, the sheet tented by his erection. "Premortem or post?"

"The fact that it may be post doesn't exclude the possibility it began before he died. He might've taken an erectile dysfunction medication. The tox results will tell."

Haddad exposed Hamlin's head and shoulders.

"But that's not why I asked you to follow the body over here."

The swishing double doors announced the arrival of Detective Navarro, now dressed in surgical scrubs. His protective goggles and respirator mask, hanging by elastic straps around his neck, bounced against his chest as he crossed the room.

Navarro nodded at Donnally as he walked up, and then grinned and said to Haddad, "Nothing like a little slice and dice in the morning."

The detective hadn't rubbed his hands together, but had nonetheless sounded to Donnally as though he was about to sit down in front of a Denny's Grand Slam breakfast.

Haddad looked over at Navarro. The doctor wasn't smiling. His tight mouth communicated his disapproval of those who chose to escape from the horror of violent death into macabre linguistic dances of irony or burlesque.

"That line is getting old," Haddad said.

In Navarro's continuing grin, Donnally saw Navarro hadn't grasped the comment wasn't directed at the line as much as at Navarro himself.

Haddad gestured with his scalpel toward two ligature marks around Hamlin's neck. One ran just above his Adam's apple and circled his neck like a collar. The other looped under his chin and angled upward behind his ears and disappeared into his black hair.

Haddad pointed from one to the other.

"You can tell from the lack of blood in the abrasions in this diagonal one that it occurred after death."

"You think he was strangled from behind?" Donnally asked. "Then strung up?"

Haddad nodded. "That's my theory, but we'll only know for certain after I shave off his hair to look for bruising and after I open him up and examine the back of his head and neck."

Donnally leaned down to inspect the marks. An undercurrent of lavender flowed beneath the churning stench of cleaning fluid. He glanced at Navarro.

"Smell that."

Navarro bent over and took a sniff.

"Soap. Some kind of scented soap." Navarro looked at Donnally as he straightened up and said without a smile, "Smells like somebody washed him off before they hung him out to dry."

Donnally considered that crack to be Navarro's second strike. He'd never met a competent homicide detective who made a habit of gallows humor. He'd always found it was the outward expression of a counterproductive kind of imagination, one that tended to take the detective off course, diverting him away from a mental cause-and-effect recreation of the events that led to the death.

He'd been willing to give Navarro a break because, at least for the moment, sarcasm had been better than his expressing outright the hatred cops felt toward Hamlin, something that might be quoted later and would cast doubt on the integrity of the investigation.

But twice was enough, and he didn't want to fight Navarro all the way through the case.

Donnally glared at Navarro while holding up two fingers and shaking his head. The detective spread his arms as he raised his eyes toward the ceiling, then looked back and nodded in surrender.

At the same time, Donnally was grateful for that hate, even though it had been sublimated into humor, for it seemed better than the brute reductionism of the medical examiner's office by which still-warm humans devolved into mere fields of evidence.

Now conscious of the war between the odors of the lab and the aroma of lavender surrounding the body, Donnally realized something didn't make sense.

"There seems to be a contradiction," Donnally said. "Someone was rational and methodical enough to destroy evidence by washing him off, but irrational enough to think that the dead could be humiliated by being left hanging half naked in a public place."

Donnally tensed, ready to be annoyed when Navarro took another sarcastic swing, but he didn't.

"Unless the humiliation was directed at someone else," Navarro said. "Maybe as a warning."

There was a new seriousness in Navarro's voice, as though he worked his way past the filter of how he'd despised Hamlin in life in order to analyze the manner in which he had died and had been left to be discovered.

"His being dead ought to have been warning enough," Haddad said. "But then again, my part in the process has less to do with the psychology of homicide and more to do with the pathology of death." He gestured toward the body. "I only interrogate the dead."

Donnally looked from Hamlin to Haddad. "And you're sure it's saying homicide?"

Haddad pulled off the sheet and pointed at abrasions on Hamlin's right wrist.

"It certainly crossed my mind that he tied his own hands to keep himself from changing his mind," Haddad said. "But at least one factor mitigates against that." He cocked his head toward pieces of a mountain climber's rope bagged up on top of a utility table. "The knot was in a spot where he couldn't have tied it."

"You mean, by himself?"

"Exactly. By himself."

"So there's no way it's suicide?" Navarro asked.

"Not based on this."

The following silence told Donnally their minds were leading them to the last possibility, that Hamlin's death might have been a sexual homicide, an unintentional erotic asphyxiation at the hands of a partner.

And when Donnally finally said, "Either he had an enemy or he had a helper," they all knew what he meant.

As they stood looking at the body, Donnally felt as though Hamlin's history, outside of just the mechanics of how he'd come to this place, was now catching up to him and was verging on a future that lay in their hands.

Who Hamlin would be in the public mind and how he would live on in his family's memories might be determined in the next few minutes.

Donnally thought of the reporters waiting in the medical examiner's lobby, with voice recorders and video cameras ready, waiting to draw conclusions about Hamlin's life and character from the manner in which he died. Donnally wasn't a Buddhist, but, for the moment, an anonymous death leading toward eternal oblivion seemed a more preferable route to travel than the path someone had chosen for Hamlin.

Donnally felt Navarro's eyes on him, as though the detective was saying, *You do it. You release it to the press. Tell them about the condition of his body, his angel lust. Prove to the public you have no interest in protect-*

ing Hamlin, or at least that saving his reputation wasn't the reason Hamlin chose you.

He stared back at Navarro, as though to say, *You do it. You couldn't expose Hamlin in life, so take a shot at him now, when he can't answer, when you'll have the last word. Prove to the public Hamlin was reckless beyond just the immorality and illegality of his law practice, and all the way beyond the limits of life itself.*

Haddad cleared his throat.

Donnally and Navarro both blinked. Neither one was willing to play that game.

CHAPTER 3

We need some ground rules," Presiding Judge Raymond McMullin said as he leaned forward in his high-backed leather chair and hunched over his desk.

Donnally and Navarro had observed the autopsy just long enough to confirm Hamlin had been strangled from behind rather than asphyxiated by the rope by which he was hanging, and then walked over to the Superior Court to meet District Attorney Hannah Goldhagen in chambers when the judge arrived at 8 A.M.

During his detective years, Donnally always liked bringing search and arrest warrants to McMullin, always learned something new about the law and about the gap that too often separated the form of justice from its substance in practice, and the ideal of justice from the institutions in which it was supposed to be accomplished. For McMullin, the tragedy of the law and the heartbreak of his life as a judge was his inability to close all those gaps and to prevent the free fall of victims, witnesses, and defendants into them, and he'd never been afraid to admit it, even to a cop half his age.

It had always seemed to Donnally that McMullin was a throwback, reincarnated from a world that existed early in the previous century. He was a judge because someone in his family always had to become a judge, like an old Irish family in which one son always had to become a priest. And since Donnally had been retired out of SFPD, McMullin had aged into the most senior, the monsignor to the Hall of Justice's priestly class.

McMullin pointed at Goldhagen. "I don't want you to use this investigation as a fishing expedition, a device to reexamine and reopen all of Mark Hamlin's old cases."

Goldhagen sat up, her back arched as though about to protest.

McMullin held up his palm toward her.

"It's not that I wouldn't want to do it if I were in your place. There are countless times when I wished I could've gotten him prosecuted for obstruction of justice. But he was too slick and always found ways to slip by."

Goldhagen sat back.

The judge gestured toward the hallway. "The stunt he pulled last week was disgusting, but none of those gangsters would admit he put them up to it."

"What if he"—Goldhagen glanced at Donnally—"comes across evidence of crimes that can still be prosecuted, like against some of the private investigators Hamlin used to do his dirty work?"

"That's a hypothetical you won't have to face. He"—now McMullin looked at Donnally—"won't. Hamlin wasn't stupid enough to leave that kind of trail."

Donnally didn't like being talked about in the third person, as though he was a dog or an Alzheimer's patient incapable of exercising his own judgment.

"That gives us rule number one," Donnally said. "Based on what I find, I'll decide whether something should be referred for prosecution."

Now all eyes turned toward him.

"And rule number two, I'll take Detective Navarro along whenever I can." Donnally glanced over at Goldhagen and pointed with his thumb toward Navarro. "He'll work with you to get whatever search warrants we need."

"So far, so good," McMullin said, then smiled. "Don't I get to . . ."

Donnally nodded and spread his hands to take in the wood-paneled chambers. "You're the one in charge."

McMullin shifted his gaze toward Goldhagen. "I'm very concerned about the appearance of a conflict of interest. The public might view your office as more interested in getting even than seeing justice done."

Goldhagen reddened, and they all understood why. After a series of district attorneys that had been perceived by the press as defense attorneys in the guise of prosecutors—who never sought the death penalty in murder cases, who never moved to deport immigrant felons, who never prosecuted marijuana grow operations—she'd run as a prosecutor's prosecutor in what had been, since the Barbary Coast days, a lawless and disordered town.

The police officers association supported her, but not with enthusiasm, as they weren't ready to wean themselves from the political cover of always having someone else to blame for their low case-closure percentages and the court's low conviction rates.

It wasn't that San Francisco was the murder capital of California, just that it was the city in which murderers were most likely to get away with it.

And for those times when there was neither the district attorney nor the police department to blame, there was always Mark Hamlin and others like him in the defense bar.

"There's nothing we can do to Hamlin that's any worse than what was done to him this morning," Goldhagen said. "But whether or not his death is connected to any of his clients, we'll kick down any door to get to whoever did it."

"That's rule number three," McMullin said. "You'll refer any potential cases arising out of this investigation to the state attorney general for prosecution."

Goldhagen folded her arms across her chest. "You can't force—"

"Aren't we getting ahead of ourselves?" Donnally said. "For all we know, his death has nothing to do with his work and all to do with his private life. I don't know all the things Hamlin was up to. The condition of his body suggests some possibilities, but no more than that. Maybe we can narrow them when we open up his apartment."

Donnally saw Navarro look down. He noticed Goldhagen had also spotted the motion. They both turned toward him.

"Don't tell me you've already gone inside?" Donnally said. "You led me to believe your people just checked for forced entry and looked in through the windows."

"We had to make sure there weren't other victims in there," Navarro said, looking first at Donnally, then at the judge. "I promise, Your Honor"—he raised his hand as though swearing an oath—"the officers didn't touch anything. Just glanced around and sealed up the place."

The irony of SFPD's breaking into Hamlin's apartment rose up before all of them. It was exactly the sort of illegal search Hamlin had exploited a hundred times to force courts to dismiss otherwise provable crimes. And now that same violation might taint the prosecution of Hamlin's own killer.

Donnally heard Goldhagen mumble a few words.

"What did you say?" Donnally asked.

"I said it's poetic justice."

Donnally pushed himself to his feet. "And I don't want to have anything to do with it."

"Look," Navarro said, his voice rising, "if we didn't go inside and there was a victim bleeding out in there, we'd look like idiots for not doing it."

"By that logic," McMullin said, "you'd have the right to search every apartment in San Francisco." He pointed at Donnally, now sliding back his chair in order to make his way to the door. "Hold on." He then asked Navarro, "Have officers also broken into Hamlin's office?"

"His assistant opened up the place and let them do a sweep." Navarro looked up at Donnally. "You would've done the same thing when you had my job." Then at the judge. "Until you issue the order making him special master, it's my case and I'm responsible. I didn't want it on my conscience if somebody died on Hamlin's kitchen floor waiting for that to happen."

"Consider the order issued."

"Don't I have anything to say about it?" Donnally asked, knowing he had a choice, but also now understanding that he probably wasn't going to exercise it.

When he left police work, he'd taken some unanswered questions with him. Some had come to him while he was on the job, but the more fundamental ones he'd brought with him from a nightmarish childhood in Hollywood, ones he'd hoped a career in the world of brute fact and rough justice would answer.

And he wasn't going to deceive himself about it. He understood the reason he'd accept the appointment wasn't because he cared all that much about who killed Hamlin, except in the abstract sense that killers must be caught. It was more that he'd never understood lawyers like Hamlin, and maybe this was his chance to get an understanding of what was satisfied in them by corrupting the criminal justice process. To understand why the kind of deceit that would've outraged Hamlin, if he had been a victim, was just a harmless game when he inflicted it on others. To understand why his deceptions seemed to justify all other deceptions, by judges, by police, and by prosecutors.

Or maybe he'd get an answer to another question, one that asked whether Hamlin was a product of a system he'd joined or one of its creators. A chicken-both-before-and-after-the-egg scheme of organized deception that already had Navarro lying to him about searching Hamlin's apartment.

McMullin pointed at Donnally's chair. "Sit down. It's no harm, no foul."

"You sure?"

They all looked at Navarro, who hesitated a beat, then said, "I'm sure."

"I think we need a rule number four," McMullin said. "Just to make sure there is no harm in the future and we risk no more fouls." He looked at Donnally. "No dipping into Hamlin's attorney-client privileged materials unless you have very strong reason—"

"Probable cause?" Donnally asked.

"That's too high a standard. Just a strong reason to believe one of his clients or other people involved in his cases are connected to his death and that evidence relevant to that reason might be contained in his files."

The judge looked from face to face.

"Can we all live with that?"

CHAPTER 4

Mark Hamlin's assistant gazed dead-eyed across the conference table at Donnally and Navarro in Hamlin's tenth floor office near San Francisco City Hall. Takiyah Jackson held her fifty-year-old face firm, fortresslike. Only her forefinger tapping the legal pad in front of her betrayed emotion. To Donnally, she looked like Angela Bassett in the Tina Turner movie, facing Ike at the divorce trial, ready to take what would come and prepared to walk away with nothing.

A dozen framed courtroom sketches hung on the plaster wall behind her, all depicting Hamlin in action. More were spaced on the other walls. With Hamlin dead, the room seemed to Donnally to be more like a makeshift shrine than a meeting place.

In one drawing, his arm was raised in a frozen jab at a witness.

In another, fists braced against his hips, Hamlin glared at a prosecutor standing with his palms pressed against his chest in a plea to the judge.

Donnally tensed when he recognized two scenes from his days at SFPD. The chalk one on the left showed Hamlin standing in front of a jury and pointing at Donnally sitting in the witness box.

People v. Darnell Simpson.

A twenty-year leader of the Black Guerilla Family, Simpson had murdered a Mexican Mafia member in the county jail where they were both awaiting trial. It was a dead-bang-caught-on-video-slash-the-victim's-throat-from-behind-willful-premeditated-just-like-the-penal-code-says-first-degree-murder—except that Hamlin had paid off a psychologist to say that due to Simpson's history of childhood abuse, confirmed during trial testimony by his guilt-ridden, weeping mother, he mistakenly thought he was about to be attacked and therefore struck first.

Under California law, a jury's factual conclusion of mistaken self-defense requires a verdict of voluntary manslaughter, not murder, because there can be no malice involved. And that was the jurors' factual conclusion. Simpson received a sentence with a parole date, seventeen years, instead of life with no possibility of release that he deserved.

A year later, Donnally learned the weeping mother had actually been Simpson's aunt, recruited to play the role by a private investigator working for Hamlin. By that time, she'd been murdered in a drug deal gone bad. The PI then pled the Fifth during the grand jury investigation, Hamlin professed innocence, and the law of double jeopardy meant the defendant couldn't be tried again.

That was the last time Donnally handed a case off to the DA's office and walked away. From then on, he stayed with them all the way through trial and checked out every defense witness himself.

Donnally watched Jackson's red-painted nail pound the legal pad as Navarro did the preliminaries and showed her Judge McMullin's written order appointing Donnally the special master.

"The ground rule is any information that might bear on attorney-client privilege goes through Donnally," Navarro said. "If he's uncertain in any way, he'll run it by the judge, and he'll decide whether it should be shared with me."

Jackson's gaze moved from Navarro toward a row of file cabinets behind him, and then to Donnally.

"But we may not even have to go down that road," Donnally said, "depending on where the investigation leads us."

Jackson nodded. Her finger stopped moving, but the agitation seemed to vibrate up her arm and into her blinking eyelids.

If the eyes are the window to the soul, Donnally thought, *hers are a view into a troubled one.* And he suspected that over the years it had become a repository of Hamlin's crimes and secrets, and was now occupied by a chaos of motions and emotions, of anticipated attacks and defenses, of alternating currents of grief and fear. Her fidgeting made him wonder whether she was there in Hamlin's office twelve years earlier, as Hamlin pretried Simpson's aunt and taught her the script for the role she would play in the trial.

"Do you know where Mark was last night?" Donnally asked.

Jackson averted her eyes for a moment, then shrugged. "I don't know for certain."

Donnally recognized it was a lawyer's answer, an

evasion. He imagined an opposing attorney's objection to the form of his question and Judge McMullin ruling, "Lack of foundation."

He dropped back a step. "Did Mark tell you whether he was going somewhere other than to his home last night?"

She nodded. "He said he had an appointment to meet a new client." Jackson half smiled, more of a smirk. "And no, he didn't say who he was."

"He?"

"He."

"Where?"

Another shrug.

"Did he get any calls that you can connect with the appointment?"

"They could've come in on his cell phone."

"Which means no?"

"Which means no."

Donnally looked at Navarro, who dipped his head, acknowledging he'd get a court order from Judge McMullin to obtain Hamlin's cell phone records for the last few weeks.

It had been a long time since Donnally had worked with someone who was as good at investigating crimes as Navarro, and realized he'd missed it. There was a fluidity of movement and unspoken cooperation up at his café in Mount Shasta, but hamburgers and omelets didn't carry the moral weight of life and death and justice.

"What's his cell number?" Navarro asked. Jackson reached into her suit pocket and handed him Hamlin's business card. The detective accepted it and rose from his chair. "I'll be back in a minute."

After the door closed behind him, Donnally asked, "Why the change in attitude from this morning when you called me?"

"Dawn shed some light on the subject."

"Which means?"

"I want immunity before I answer any more questions."

"You didn't kill him, so you don't need it."

"How can you be sure? How do you know I didn't call you as a dodge, a kind of misdirection?"

"You want it because you're concerned about what may come out about what's been going on around here for the last twenty-some years. You figure a grant of immunity in the homicide will cover all your other sins, too."

Jackson looked away. "Maybe."

"Then you should ask yourself something else first. Like why Mark wanted me to do this. If he trusted me, then maybe you should, too."

Jackson snorted. "At this point Mark's got nothing to fear. And I don't think it was a matter of him trusting you, but him not trusting the SFPD and the DA's office and him not wanting someone to get away with killing him." She smirked. "I have no doubt you've already heard the words 'poetic justice' spoken by somebody on their side."

Donnally locked his expression on his face, trying not to reveal how accurate she was.

"But that's not the kind of justice you're worried about," Donnally said. "You know the investigation into his murder—successful or not—poses the risk of exposing you to prosecution." He gestured toward the outer office where Hamlin's two paralegals waited in their cubicles to be interviewed. "And everybody else connected with Hamlin, too."

Donnally had seen her type before—private investigators, paralegals, junior attorneys—in court hallways or behind defense tables, underlings of lawyers like Hamlin, with a cops-versus-cons mentality they'd adopted from their clients in which the cons were the victims and the cops were the persecutors. And this framing of the world provided both the logic and the justification for their acts of war against the integrity of the criminal justice system.

Donnally had learned that lesson while he was still a patrol officer. It was a delusional kind of thinking only matched by that of corrupt narcotics cops for whom the war on drugs justified planting evidence and framing those they believed—based on little more than a feeling in their gut—were guilty anyway.

But what explained the mentality of the underlings in their war against the system didn't necessarily explain the Hamlins themselves. Donnally had long recognized there was more to them than that, more motivating them than that, but he'd never understood what it was.

Jackson didn't respond right off. Her blinking accelerated and her hands formed into fists. "I always thought a sense of mission and loyalty went together. Driving over here I realized that they don't. Mark was ready to throw us under the bus."

Donnally could also see that Jackson now felt herself facing the prospect of no longer just playing the part of a con in fantasy, but of living the reality in state prison.

Suborning perjury: two to four years.

Destroying evidence: two to four years.

Concurrent: as few as two years.

Consecutive: as many as eight.

In her immunity demand, Donnally heard a disguised confession to all the police and prosecutors suspected Hamlin and his crew had been up to throughout his career.

Donnally looked up again at the second of the framed courtroom drawings he'd recognized when he first sat down.

People v. Demetrio Arellano.

Hamlin was pictured standing below the bench staring at his wristwatch, his right hand raised in the air, as though counting down to the dropping of the flag at the Indy 500. Except zero didn't mark the start of a race, but the end. The killer went free because the single prosecution witness hadn't appeared to testify.

It had been Navarro's case.

On the night before he was to testify, the witness took a cab to the airport and caught a plane to El Salvador. Later, Navarro and Donnally searched the man's Tenderloin District apartment and recovered an answering machine message.

Hey man, this is a friend. You show up in court and you're gonna get busted for that thing you did in Texas. You know what it's about and you're in the crosshairs. They say scarcity is a bad thing. They're wrong. It's a good thing, a really good thing, if you know what I mean.

Navarro had suspected the caller was a private investigator hired by Hamlin. Who else would've known how to find out about an out-of-state warrant, and who else but Hamlin would've known how to phrase a threat solely out of statements from which the sense of menace could be parsed away in a sharp cross-examination.

In the end, no parsing was required because the witness never showed up again in San Francisco.

Demetrio Arellano walked on the case for lack of evidence.

Hamlin walked on the witness intimidation charge because no one could tie the tape to him.

And the private investigator, who Navarro later identified through a pretext call to his office, walked because the witness wasn't around to authenticate the recording and testify that it hadn't been altered.

Donnally looked back at Jackson.

"If I get you immunity," Donnally said, "you'll have to answer every question I ask. Every single one. That's how immunity agreements read. It's a contract. A trade. And it's absolute."

Jackson's eyes widened and her jaw clenched. "Then I'll take the Fifth on everything."

"I know you think that sounds like something Mark would've said, but in the real world you can't do that since not every answer will implicate you in a crime. Some may only implicate others. I'll have Goldhagen put you in front of a grand jury, you'll pull your stunt, and Judge McMullin will hold you in contempt and lock you up."

Donnally paused and let a picture of San Francisco's crowded, gang-ridden county jail form in her mind.

"You sure you want to be brushing shoulders with Hamlin's old clients? Them all looking at you funny, wondering when you're gonna crack and spill everything in order to get yourself sprung."

Jackson's finger started tapping again. It seemed to Donnally like a private sign language for spelling out her fears.

Donnally heard the door open. Navarro signaled him to come outside.

"And you will crack," Donnally said, rising to his feet. "You know it and I know it. You're not going to throw your life away living out Hamlin's fantasy all the way to the end."

He walked outside and swung the door closed behind him.

As the latch clicked into place, Donnally flashed on her face and her fidgeting hands and realized he was seeing more than just fear of potential accusations. He was seeing terror at her failing resistance against dissolving self-deceptions that were once held firm by Hamlin's force of will.

The immunity she wanted was more than just strategic, it was existential, and there was no way to give it to her.

"Three things," Navarro whispered. "One, beat cops found Hamlin's car parked along Ocean Beach."

"They towing it in?"

Navarro nodded.

"And two?"

"Hamlin's cell phone was on the pavement next to it. Smashed. Nothing recoverable in it."

"And three is . . ."

"The news radio station is reporting Hamlin did a David Carradine right out there at Fort Point."

Donnally felt a rush of anger.

Navarro raised his hands. "It wasn't me. I haven't talked to the press—and I'm not that stupid. Auto-erotic asphyxiation means do-it-yourself. And you can't do it yourself with your hands tied behind your back. The damn reporter should've figured that out himself."

"Go down to the station and make sure Hamlin's car stays sealed until I get there." Donnally tilted his head toward the conference room. "I've got to work out some kind of deal with her."

Navarro headed toward the hallway and the elevators beyond.

Donnally opened the door. He spotted Jackson standing next to an open file cabinet drawer, her hand under her suit jacket. He jabbed a forefinger at her.

"Put it back."

CHAPTER 5

I got nothing," Donnally said to Navarro as he walked up to Hamlin's Porsche in the police garage. "Jackson claims Hamlin didn't tell her who he was afraid of, or why."

"You have to give up anything to get her talking?" Navarro asked.

"She wanted immunity, but I explained to her why that wasn't a possibility." He smiled. "I caught her trying to sneak off with a file. It showed Hamlin had been paying part of her salary under the table out of cash retainers he'd received from clients. He wasn't reporting the fees to the IRS and she wasn't reporting the income."

"Tax fraud and money laundering." Navarro smiled back. "I see why you took immunity off the table. There's no way of knowing all the crimes she's committed. What about the other two in the office?"

"No immunity demands, but no one will admit to knowing what Hamlin was worried about or where he went last night—if they even know. They're little ferrets. Neither one has the guts to do anything more dangerous than steal Post-it notes from the

office. I sent them home and told them to stay there
until we need them again."

Navarro nodded toward two evidence technicians, who then opened the doors of the car and
began dusting for prints.

"The cell phone records?" Donnally asked.

"In an hour. They'll e-mail them to me and I'll
get printouts to you."

Donnally shielded his eyes and looked through
the back window.

"Man, what a mess. Who spends a hundred and
twenty thousand dollars on a car like this and treats
it like a garbage dump."

Navarro bit his lower lip as he stared at the passenger seat and floor. On both were scattered court
filings, fast-food wrappers, sheets torn from legal
pads, balled-up clothing.

"This'll take hours."

Donnally thought for a moment. Anything that
Hamlin had left in plain view in his car couldn't be
considered confidential. Whatever attorney-client
privilege he might have claimed for any document
had been waived as soon as he let the sunshine fall
on it, at least as far as Hamlin's part of the privilege
was concerned.

If his clients had a beef on their end with him
leaving case documents where anyone could see
them, they could sue Hamlin's estate. But it wasn't
Donnally's problem. Preserving Hamlin's money
for his heirs wasn't part of his job.

Donnally waited until the evidence techs finished
dusting for prints, did a quick check of the glove
compartment, console, and trunk without finding

additional case files or notes. He pointed at the two techs, and said to Navarro, "Have these guys bag up everything. Let's go check out Hamlin's apartment."

Navarro gave the instruction and then led Donnally to his car, parked in a lot under the freeway behind the Hall of Justice.

"You're a little more flexible than I remembered," Navarro said, as he turned the ignition.

"Not really, I've just learned to draw finer lines. I'm not going to do any more to protect Hamlin than he deserves and the law requires."

Navarro drove out from the thin shadows next to the police department into the late morning sun. He skirted downtown as he worked his way toward the Panhandle, a narrow arm of Golden Gate Park running along the north side of the Haight-Ashbury District.

Donnally's cell phone rang as they passed the steep-sided Buena Vista Park, trees rising up from the otherwise house- and apartment-covered heights.

"I came home to pick up a file for work and found a television satellite truck driving away."

The caller was Janie Nguyen, Donnally's girlfriend, a psychiatrist at the Fort Miley Veterans Hospital. Donnally had come down from Mount Shasta a few days earlier to visit her and replace the roof gutters on the house they shared a few blocks from the ocean. He drove down two or three times a month, usually for three or four days. He always brought his tool chest in the bed of his truck to repair damage to the shingled bungalow inflicted by salt air driven hard by onshore winds.

"One of the neighbors told me they knocked on the door, then took a video of the house. You up to something?"

"The call that got me out of bed this morning and put that grumpy look on your face was about Mark Hamlin."

Donnally felt Navarro's eyes on him. He covered the phone and said, "Janie."

Navarro raised his eyebrows. "Still?"

Donnally nodded.

Navarro reached up and tapped the wedding ring on his left hand, gripping the steering wheel.

Donnally shook his head, and then said into the phone, "I'm helping out Ramon Navarro on the Hamlin investigation."

"I saw it on the news," Janie said, "and the first word that comes to mind is 'byzantine.'"

"And the second?"

"Whichever one means you should have your head examined. Any route that took Mark Hamlin from wherever he started last night to the end of a rope at Fort Point this morning had to have been very unpleasant, and it will be unpleasant to relive it."

Donnally understood what she was saying. The only other investigative work he'd done since he left SFPD, looking into the thirty-year-old murder of the sister of a deceased friend, had devolved into weeks of agonized confusion that had enveloped her, too, and almost shredded their relationship.

But he wasn't sure how to respond with Navarro listening.

Before he found an answer, Janie said, "I know why you're doing this."

"It's because Hamlin asked for me and Judge McMullin appointed me to be the special master."

"You could've turned it down. I suspect you're less interested in who murdered Mark Hamlin than in how a guy like Mark Hamlin became a guy like Mark Hamlin, lived the life he lived. For you, it's kind of like a physics problem, what bent Hamlin toward corruption and how he bent other people whose life trajectories brought them near him, and this is your chance to find out."

He felt himself cringe. She'd already gotten inside his head and figured out what he'd been thinking earlier, even repeating his own half-spoken words to him.

He now wondered whether his puzzlement was less a carryover from his own past, and more just residue from the resignation he'd felt, that every San Francisco cop felt, after they'd spent a few years in the investigations bureau, especially in homicide, where he had been assigned when he first met Janie.

Early in their careers, anger defined cops' attitudes toward the Hamlins of the world. Later it transformed into outrage that neither the judges nor the DAs were willing to take them on. Finally, they just got beaten down and felt themselves reduced to note takers, surrendering their role as law enforcement officers after coming to accept that the enforcement of the law was out of their hands.

Donnally had sometimes felt queasy when he looked at the words "Hall of Justice" as he walked up the wide steps and into the building, for it seemed to proclaim a fact when those inside had yet to prove it up, and never would since they had allowed lawyers like Hamlin to corrupt the process.

"You're right," Donnally said. "I've never understood these guys. Maybe I'll learn something."

And maybe I'll learn why I'm doing this. And why I couldn't walk away.

He knew it wasn't just curiosity. There were lots of things in the world to be curious about.

It was—

He felt his body push back against the seat as Navarro began a twisting ascent up the hill on which Hamlin's house sat. Then again as the car downshifted.

Donnally surprised himself when the answer came. It was an old anger, an old outrage, not only at the death of Hamlin and at whoever murdered him, but at Hamlin the man.

But he wanted to think through what that meant before expressing the thought to Janie.

"Be sure to take good notes," Janie said, "and maybe you can explain him to me."

She paused for a moment, then said, "But don't kid yourself, pal. Whether you solve the enigma of Hamlin or not, now that you're in it, you won't be walking away until you figure out why his life ended this way. And it's not that I think you'll like doing it. You won't. You'll despise every minute of it, but your world will seem disjointed until you get the answer."

Donnally's thoughts continued moving after they disconnected the call, first returning to those that had begun the day, the ones about matter and motion, and then toward Hamlin's body at rest in the medical examiner's office, and finally toward Jackson's terror. And he wondered whether he had it backward. Maybe he'd been wrong and Janie only partially right. Maybe it wasn't just whether the world was done with Hamlin, but whether Hamlin was done with the world—for the momentum of the lawyer's existence—the chains of causes and effects, of things done and suffered—hadn't ceased with his death.

And Donnally wondered whether that was the real source of his anger.

CHAPTER 6

The uniformed officer standing on Mark Hamlin's porch raised his hands as though in a protestation of innocence as Donnally and Navarro climbed the stairs of the three-story Victorian duplex facing Buena Vista Park and overlooking the distant downtown.

They'd just pushed their way through four reporters from local television and radio stations, two from national cable channels, and five from newspapers, all jabbing video cameras and microphones toward their faces and asking nonsensical who, where, how, and why questions that if they already had the answers to, they wouldn't be bothering to search Hamlin's residence.

"I didn't do it," the officer said, "I didn't touch a thing." He turned and opened the front door of the multimillion-dollar property and gestured toward the interior. "It's just the way we found it."

Donnally and Navarro drew on latex gloves and slipped on polyethylene shoe covers and crossed the threshold into the foyer. Straight ahead was the hallway leading to the kitchen. They turned left and examined the living room. The plaster walls were eggshell white and pristine, looking as though they'd never felt the impact of a child's ball or a bicycle tire, seeming as though never touched by life at all. The couch, chairs, and tables, on the other hand, were as strewn with trash as the passenger seat of Hamlin's Porsche. Books, pleadings, and files were also piled on the Oriental rugs covering the parquet floors. The only unlittered furniture were the bookcases standing along the wall opposite the fireplace and framing the television and DVD player. These bore dozens of Asian artifacts, from pottery bowls to brass statues to a collection of long-stemmed clay pipes, all spaced and positioned as if part of a museum exhibit.

"Try not to focus too long on paper you're not supposed to be looking at," Donnally said to Navarro as they walked through the living room.

"Unless there's blood spatter on it or it's a signed confession from the killer, I won't be paying much attention."

Navarro stopped and glanced at the chaos of half-used legal pads and scattered folders lying on the dining room table. Interleaved were misfolded newspaper sections, legal journals, and flyers announcing political events.

"I know Goldhagen was playing like she wants to leverage this investigation into a way to reopen a bunch of Hamlin's old cases," Navarro said, "but I don't see her doing it. I suspect that his closet has got a few bones from her skeleton in it, too."

Donnally looked over at Navarro. "What do you mean?"

"A lot has happened since you moved north.

Hamlin and a bunch of his pals did some fund-raisers for her reelection campaign."

"You've got to be—" Donnally remembered Goldhagen's aggression—apparent aggression—toward Hamlin and his practice, and realized it was an act for his benefit, or maybe for the judge's or Navarro's as a way of demonstrating her independence.

"It's true," Navarro said. "He'd done enough posturing over the years about civil rights and lesbian and gay rights and transgender rights and immigrant rights and dog and cat rights that he could deliver up to any politician any group that devoted itself to playing the victim. It's like a . . ." Navarro flicked his fingers next to his head like he was flipping through note cards in his mind. "What do you call it where two people share the same delusion?"

Donnally guessed that Navarro assumed he'd know the word because the nature of Janie's work—and he did.

"A folie à deux," Donnally said.

"That's it. That's what he has with the LGBT groups. They act like we live in a Jim Crow world, but they control who gets elected in this town, who gets appointed police chief, and who gets the big city contracts. Whenever something bad happened, Hamlin would undergo some kind of mind meld with them in their fake victimization. Some transgender idiot would get his ass kicked, and Hamlin was on TV declaring a hate crime. Never considered the possibility that the asshole might've deserved it. Lot of rough stuff happens in the Castro and most of it people bring on themselves."

"Sounds like you've joined the Log Cabin Republicans," Donnally said. "I wouldn't have expected it."

"Being gay doesn't mean I have to follow the party line and wiggle my ass in a conga line at the pride parade. I moved out here in order to fit in and live a normal life, not to keep drawing attention to myself." Navarro tapped his chest. "I'm a cop. Not a gay cop, or a fag cop, or a ho-mo-sex-u-al cop. A cop. If I hear somebody yell one more time, 'We're here. We're queer. Get used to it,' I'll rip out his vocal cords. Everybody in San Francisco is already used to it."

"How about just give him a bus ticket out of town?"

Navarro half smiled in embarrassment, realizing that his rant was irrelevant to their task, then said, "That'll do, too."

Navarro turned and led the way into the kitchen.

"Doesn't seem to be part of the same apartment," Donnally said, as they stood looking at the clean granite counters, the bare butcher-block island, the slick Sub-Zero refrigerator, and the polished walnut table and chairs. "Either he's got a cleaning service or somebody did a helluva job destroying evidence." Donnally pointed through the doorway toward a bathroom across the hall. "Check that one for anything that smells like lavender. I'll take a look upstairs."

Donnally walked back to the foyer and climbed the stairs to the second floor. He glanced into two small bedrooms as he made his way down the carpeted hallway and then turned into what appeared to be Hamlin's master suite, shadowed within closed curtains. The blanket and spread were draped off the side of the bed and both pillows showed depressions. He resisted the temptation to conclude that they had been used the previous night. That was a fact not yet in evidence, and might never be.

The only illumination in the room came from a shaft of sunlight spreading out from the bathroom. He followed it inside and sniffed the air.

Lavender.

He spotted a bar of soap on the shower floor, then opened the glass door and kneeled down to inspect it. A brown hair was stuck to it and partially wrapped around. A curled black one lay on the tile next to it. At least two people, or one with dyed hair, had used it. He suspected that the black one was from Hamlin, but only forensic testing would tell.

Donnally pushed himself to his feet and returned to the bedroom. He flicked on the overhead light and checked the visible portions of the pillows and sheets for hair or semen stains. He found none. He figured he'd leave it to the evidence technicians to do a more thorough search.

After he walked back downstairs, he found Navarro talking on his cell phone in the laundry room beyond the kitchen, reporting their address.

Navarro pointed at a frayed length of rope lying on the floor, visible in the inch-wide gap between the washer and dryer, and then said to the person on the other end of the call, "I think we may have found the crime scene. Let's get some people over here."

CHAPTER 7

Donnally didn't know whether Hamlin's apartment was the crime scene or not, but needing the techs to go through it freed him to return to Hamlin's office.

A uniformed officer was waiting for him at the building entrance on McAllister Street with a printout of Hamlin's cell phone calls for the last two weeks.

"What did Mark use to keep track of contacts?" Donnally asked Takiyah Jackson as he walked into the reception area.

Another officer sat along the wall opposite her desk with views both into the conference room where files were stored and into Hamlin's private office. Donnally wanted all the cabinets guarded until he could install locks to keep Jackson out of them.

Jackson pointed at her monitor. "His e-mail program and his cell phone."

"Were they synced?"

She nodded.

"How about getting me into it?"

Jackson leaned back in her chair and folded her

arms across her chest. "Don't you need a search warrant for that?"

"What do you think?"

She chewed at her lip. Donnally could see that she was torn between what Hamlin would've said to protect a client—whether it was well-founded in the law or not—and what Hamlin would've said in order to help catch his own killer.

Donnally then remembered what Navarro had said about a folie à deux and what Janie had once told him about how it operated. When the dominant person is gone, the submissive one tends to break free from the grandiose or persecutory delusion they had shared and that had bound them together.

"I guess you don't need a warrant," Jackson said, then rose and led him into Hamlin's office, where she turned on his monitor and activated his e-mail program. She returned to her desk as he sat down in Hamlin's chair.

It took Donnally half an hour to compare the telephone numbers from Hamlin's call log with his contacts. He found matches for only about a third. He wondered whether any of those whose names he'd identified so far would turn out to be the source—or sources—for the hairs he found in Hamlin's shower.

Now he was ready to question Jackson about who Hamlin might have been talking to or meeting with during the last days. He hadn't wanted to start that line of questioning until he had something to compare her answers with. Her knowing he'd looked at both Hamlin's contact list and his calls would make it harder for her to lie. She'd assume that he knew more than he actually did, a mistake witnesses with something to fear or hide nearly always made.

Donnally noticed the icon for Hamlin's appointment calendar and then drew another fine line. He didn't have any basis yet for invading privileged attorney-client material, for engaging in the fishing expedition that the judge had warned them all against. At the same time, the fact that Hamlin had met with someone couldn't be considered privileged, only the content of the consultation, the he-said, she-said of the case. Based on that distinction, Donnally accessed Hamlin's list of recent appointments and printed it out.

Donnally saw that Hamlin used his calendar to track not only client meetings, court appearances, and motion due dates, but also personal lunches and dinners and political meetings.

While looking through the names of the people Hamlin had met with, Donnally realized that his having moved north so many years ago was a disadvantage. A local might've recognized many of the names he had in front of him now and others that he would come across.

On the legitimate side, he didn't know who was now on the board of supervisors, who had the confidence of the mayor, who were the power brokers in the city.

On the underworld side, from where Hamlin drew most of his clients, Donnally didn't know who were the gang leaders out in Bayview–Hunters Point or who ran the Big Block gang in the housing projects, or even if it still existed, or which tongs were running the protection rackets in Chinatown, or which Russians had moved in to take over organized crime in the Richmond District.

To him, the names were inert, mere labels on imaginary stick figures. And instead of seeing live conflicts and connections, he was just seeing dead letters on a page—and he recognized Jackson would have an advantage on him. She knew the players and understood how the game was played in the city, at least those players and games that related to Hamlin. He now realized he'd have to rely on Navarro more than he wanted to, and share more with him than he had intended to, for the detective would see relationships Donnally couldn't and understand their meaning.

Jackson appeared at the office door. "Can I go to lunch?"

"You coming back afterwards?"

"What?" She smirked. "You think I'm starting my job hunting already?"

Donnally didn't like the sarcasm. "That's not what I meant." He rose from the desk and walked over to her. "We need to figure out some way to work together. I don't see me finding out who killed Mark without your help."

She stared at him for a long moment, then lowered her head and picked at her thumbnail.

"Shit . . . shit, shit, shit. I didn't sign up for this."

"What did you sign up for?"

"I don't know anymore." She looked up again, shaking her head. "All I know is that this place seems more and more like Jonestown on the night before they served the Kool-Aid."

CHAPTER 8

I know who killed Mark Hamlin." A recorded voice overrode the next words spoken by the man. "This is a call from a California state prison."

It had come in on Hamlin's main firm number. The caller had asked for Donnally by name, and Jackson had routed it to him in Hamlin's office. Donnally was relieved that he had enough of her cooperation for her at least to do that.

Unless the murder was a gang-related execution, which the condition of Hamlin's body suggested it wasn't, Donnally wasn't sure how someone in prison could have any credible information.

"Who did it?"

"Pay me a visit and I'll tell you the story."

The man's voice sounded as though he was in his fifties or sixties, maybe older.

"How do I know you're not a lunatic?"

The line beeped, indicating that the call was being recorded.

"Look at my file. It's somewhere in the office. Five years ago. My name's Bennie Madison. A murder case. There's no psych report in there and no trips to the loony bin. I'm as sane as anybody ever is in here."

"Hold on."

Donnally wrote out the name, then walked to the outer office and asked Jackson to retrieve the file. He kept watch on her as she pulled it from a cabinet in the conference room and brought it to him. He sat down and flipped it open.

"There's almost nothing in here," Donnally told the caller. "A police report, a detective's investigative log, a transcript of your plea, and a court sentencing form. Twenty-five to life."

"There should be a letter in there I sent last month saying I'm filing a motion to withdraw my plea."

"I don't see it. Did you want Hamlin to represent you?"

The man laughed. "Not a chance. It's the last thing that asshole would've done."

"Because . . ."

"Take a drive up here and you'll find out."

"Where's here?"

"The California Medical Facility in Vacaville. And I'll also tell you why someone wanted him dead."

"You're being a little too cryptic for me to spend the hours it would take to get up there and back at this point in the investigation."

"You're gonna have to see me eventually, might as well make it now."

"I'll think about it."

Donnally disconnected and called the SFPD homicide detective whose name appeared on the log. She told him that Bennie Madison had pled guilty to a robbery murder. He'd dragged the victim into an alley near her downtown office as she walked from an ATM to her car. He stabbed her, robbed her, and then flopped her body into a Dumpster.

Madison had been homeless at the time, living under an overpass. He was arrested for trespassing a couple of days later, and the arresting officer found the victim's wallet and credit cards in his backpack. Madison claimed he found it all in an alley. A city worker in the area of the bank around the time of the murder wasn't able to ID Madison, but gave a description of the killer's clothes that matched his.

The clincher in the case was a statement from a jailhouse informant that Madison had confessed to the crime and tried to get the informant to send someone to dispose of the knife, which was hidden inside his sleeping bag. Detectives went to the overpass, located it, and the lab later found traces of the victim's blood lodged between the blade and the hilt.

"The unusual thing," the detective said, "was that Hamlin volunteered to represent the guy pro bono and took the case over from the court-appointed lawyer."

"Why was that?"

"My guess? Grandstanding and money. A public defender proved that an informant in another case was making up stories in exchange for get-out-of-jail-free cards. I suspect Hamlin figured if he had a horse in the race he could ride the scandal to the bank a few times. I think the plan was that he'd prove that the informant in the Madison case was a liar, then get other convicts sending him retainers to reopen their cases."

"But Madison ended up pleading guilty anyway."

"Two weeks later, before he even had a preliminary hearing—and I still don't have a clue why. What kind of idiot pleads to a life sentence? The smarter move would've been to roll the dice. You never know what a San Francisco jury will do."

CHAPTER 9

Donnally looked at his watch as he hung up the telephone. An hour-and-a-half drive out to Vacaville in the Central Valley, an hour with Madison, and the trip back. A decade earlier he could've badged his way into the facility; this time he'd have to rely on Navarro to make the appointment for him and get him inside.

After a drive that took him over the spot where Hamlin's body was found under Golden Gate Bridge, up through the hills of Marin County, skirting the north end of the bay, and past suburbs and outlet malls spread out in a series of wide valleys, he pulled into a parking spot outside the California Medical Facility. He unclipped his holster and slipped his semiautomatic into the glove compartment.

Madison's correctional counselor met Donnally in the small administration building, a one-story, wooden structure set into the razor wire–topped fence surrounding the prison.

"Five years nobody comes to see this guy," Rich Taylor said after Donnally showed him the court order appointing him special master, "and now you're third in the last month."

"Who else?"

Taylor pointed at the order. "Hamlin was the first. Then a lawyer who specializes in getting convictions overturned. Not as sleazy as Hamlin, may he rest in peace, but close."

"Why is Madison in here rather than in a regular prison?"

"You'll have to ask him. That kind of medical information is covered by HIPAA." Taylor paused, biting his lower lip, then said, "But I can tell you this. We're moving him out of here in the next few weeks. He's about to start doing some really hard time in supermax. Maybe up in Pelican Bay."

Taylor pointed toward the security station. "Why don't you go through and I'll take you to him."

Donnally emptied his pockets, took off his belt and shoes, and put everything in a plastic tray. He waited until it got moving toward the scanner tunnel, then stepped through the metal detector.

Taylor met him on the other side and walked with him into the main building and up to his second floor office. A middle-aged prisoner with scraggly white hair sat handcuffed to a chair, a soiled manila envelope lying on his lap, a cane leaning against the wall next to him. A guard wearing a protective vest and a shielded riot helmet stood across from him.

Taylor introduced Donnally to Madison, then uncuffed him and led them inside.

"You guys can talk in here," Taylor said, then directed Donnally to his chair behind the desk and Madison to the one in the front. He pointed at the phone. "Call the operator and they'll page me when you're done. Just hit zero." Taylor then nodded toward a red alarm button on the wall next to the desk. Donnally got the message and nodded back.

Donnally waited until Taylor closed the office door behind him, then said, "I know who you are and you know who I am, so let's skip the preliminaries."

Madison smiled. "You're just as advertised." He tilted his head toward the window overlooking the rows of cell blocks. "Some guys remembered you from your cop days."

Donnally didn't respond, just stared at him.

Madison nodded. "Oh, yeah. That's right. No preliminaries." He hunched forward, resting his forearms on his thighs, looking up from under his eyebrows. "I'll start with the punch line. Hamlin hired me to ride the beef."

Donnally didn't know what to make of the claim. The problem with the truth and nothing but the truth is it sometimes sounded like a big lie.

And this sounded like a big lie.

"Why would you take the job?" Donnally asked. "Twenty-five to life would pretty much take you past retirement age, maybe even to an eternity in a pine box."

Madison leaned back, turned the side of his head toward Donnally, then separated the hair above his ear.

Donnally could make out a four-inch scar.

"Brain tumor. The doctors at the county hospital took it out and I did radiation and chemo, but it came back again. They said I had no more than a year to live. I figured, why not? I'd get better medical treatment in here than on the outside and

Hamlin said he'd keep me happy. Money every month. Nice TV in my cell. Any kind of drugs I want, prescription"—he flashed a grin—"or otherwise. Hamlin has a lot of old clients in here, guys with connections. They can smuggle in anything. Anything at all. It's just like being on the outside."

"But you're still alive."

Madison made a smacking sound with his lips, then said, "I hadn't counted on that. The law changed and the government started letting prisoners be in clinical trials. I hit a home run doing one of them and went into remission."

This was the only thing Madison had said so far that seemed credible. After accusations of reckless experimentation, the Department of Corrections had barred prisoners from participating in trials. The legislature had reversed the ban a few years earlier.

Madison slid the manila envelope across the desk.

"The report of my last PET-CT is in there. Clean as clean could be."

Donnally read it and handed it back.

"If you didn't do the crime, who did?"

Donnally guessed what Madison's answer would be, true or not, assuming that Madison knew the homicide statistics as well as he did.

"The woman's husband," Madison said. "She was cheating on him. And he's a hard guy. Real hard. Story was he grabbed her as she was getting cash out of the ATM to buy her boyfriend something. It was the boyfriend's birthday and she didn't want the payment for his present to show up on her credit card."

"What about your confession to the jailhouse informant?"

"He's the guy who recruited me and sold the deal to Hamlin. He got five grand out of it."

"And the knife?"

Madison smiled again. "You studied up. Hamlin's PI got it from her husband and hid it in my sleeping bag for the police to find."

The fact that the story sounded like something Hamlin would do, didn't mean to Donnally that he'd done it.

"How long have you been in remission?"

"A year and a half, but I didn't want to make a move until I was sure it was gonna stick." Madison's face darkened and he slapped the edge of the desk. "But then that asshole Hamlin tried to fuck me. He stopped putting the money on my books like he was supposed to."

"And so you sent him a letter threatening to file a motion to withdraw your plea."

Madison nodded. "A little sooner than I'd planned. I was hoping to wait until after my next scan. But I'd gotten used to the finer things in prison life, and doing without was pissing me off, so I made my move."

"How do you know it wasn't the husband who stopped paying Hamlin, so he had to stop paying you?"

"Because the deal was there would always be a hundred grand on account, in cash. I could draw out as much as I needed every month. The husband would add to it if it went under. Even if the guy stopped paying, it would've taken a couple of more years for the money to run out."

"I guess they didn't expect you to live so long."

"So what? That's not my problem. A deal's a deal."

"And you figure the husband killed Hamlin."

"Has to be. Only way for a surefire cover-up."

"Wouldn't it have been simpler just to take you out?"

"They tried." Madison pointed out the window toward the prison blocks. "I've been in isolation for the last month, after an Aryan Brotherhood guy tried to shank me. Since then, if hubby was gonna break the chain, he was gonna have to do it at the Hamlin link. Ain't no way they're getting to me again."

Madison pointed toward the door. "That guard outside? He ain't standing there to protect you from me, but me from them."

Takiyah Jackson was sitting at her desk when Donnally arrived at Hamlin's office.

Donnally had called Navarro while he was driving back from Vacaville and got confirmation his earlier theory had been right. Navarro knew the players in town. He'd recognized the name of the victim's husband, not because he'd worked on the Bennie Madison case, but because the husband owned a well-known biker bar in the mostly Hispanic Mission District. It now made sense that the husband could've sicced an imprisoned gang member on Madison.

Navarro walked in a few minutes after Donnally had taken Jackson into the conference room.

Donnally glanced over at Navarro, pointed at the two-foot-square safe in the corner, and said to Jackson, "I have reason to believe there is evidence related to Mark's death in that thing and I wanted a witness when we opened it up."

Jackson swallowed and twisted her hands together on top of the conference table. Her daunted gaze shifted between Navarro and Donnally.

"Why do you need a witness?"

"There may be money in there and I don't want anybody accusing me of stealing any."

She tilted her head toward the row of filing cabinets. "You tell him about the file?"

Donnally shook his head, hoping Navarro wouldn't react and give him away.

"It wasn't relevant to any of the leads we're working on."

"You have the combination," Navarro said. The sentence came out as a statement, not a question.

"Mark gave it to me only for emergencies."

Donnally understood her to be saying she wasn't responsible for what they would find inside.

"I'd say this was an emergency."

Donnally followed her over to the safe, where she kneeled and spun the combination right, left, right, and then pushed the handle down and pulled the door open. She then raised her hands and backed away as though trying to break her connection with whatever they would find inside.

"You got some latex gloves?" Donnally asked Navarro.

Navarro reached into his inside suit jacket pocket and gave him a pair and slipped ones on his own hands. He lowered himself to one knee, pulled out a digital camera, and took a couple of photos of the inside of the safe.

Donnally began moving the safe's contents onto the conference table. Financial records, checkbooks, file folders, and notes. On the third reach, he pulled out a rubber-banded stack of hundred-dollar bills, almost five inches high. He looked over at Jackson.

She shrugged.

"Does that mean you know where this money came from?" Donnally asked.

"There's always cash in there. Usually about a hundred thousand. Sometimes less. Sometimes more."

"And . . ."

"No, I don't know where that particular money came from."

Donnally reached in again and removed another stack and laid it next to the other. He estimated that each held between forty and fifty thousand dollars.

After emptying all the paper out of the safe, he felt around and discovered a small metal box against the back wall. He held it by the edges, pulled it out, and set it on the table. He used the end of a pen to open the latch. Inside he found diamonds, rubies, sapphires, and old gold coins.

Donnally suspected it might be stolen property Hamlin had taken in legal fees.

He glanced over at Jackson. Her teeth were clenched. He wondered about her psychological makeup since her only ways of expressing emotion seemed to be tapping her finger or clenching her teeth.

He took this clench to be anger.

"He told me he'd never do that," Jackson said, speaking through an unmoving jaw.

"You sure he didn't get this stuff from a relative's estate?" Navarro asked.

"He would've made me look at it. He was a showoff about money and shit."

"At least he had the good sense to keep this a secret from you," Donnally said. "It shows he was at least embarrassed."

She stared at the box for a few moments. "I don't think so. I don't think it was that at all," and then she turned away and left the room.

F uck that bitch," Rudy Rusch told Donnally from
behind the bar in the grimy and shadowed Hide-
away Lounge just off Mission Street, a few miles
southwest of the Hall of Justice. Rusch stopped
toweling the dark oak surface and leaned his hairy-
armed, six-four frame down toward Donnally and
lowered his voice. "If Madison hadn't killed her, I
would've done it myself."

Rusch's delivery had a practiced tone, almost
rhythmic. Donnally wondered how many times
he'd repeated those phrases since the night of his
wife's murder.

"He's saying you did do it," Donnally said, "and
you paid off Mark Hamlin to get him to plead to
the sheet."

"Sure I gave Hamlin some money. I don't deny
it. A lot of money. He came to me and said he could
make the case go away, and fast."

"Why the hurry?"

"Shit, man." Rusch surveyed the crowd, bikers
hunched over tables and talking low, and skinny
girlfriends with tangled hair and windblown faces
sipping beers and wine coolers in the booths and

waiting for the men's business to get done. "Hamlin was gonna try to frame me, expose the stuff that goes on in here to make me look like the kind of guy who'd kill his wife for cheating on him."

Donnally smiled. So far, his story made as much sense as Madison's.

"But you are the kind of guy who would kill his wife for cheating on him," Donnally said. "And I take it she was."

"Yeah. With some asshole in the office she was working in. Some fucking stockbroker. We were short on cash and she got herself hired on as a temp. It started out with her being his drug connection." He glanced toward one of the biker tables as though her source was sitting there now. "Then they started hooking up after work. Every fucking time I turned my back."

What he meant to say was that every time he turned his back they were fucking. Donnally wondered why he didn't just come out and say it. Maybe he wasn't as tough as he pretended.

Rusch reached down, filled a glass with beer from the tap, and slid it to Donnally.

"On the house."

Donnally nodded thanks and took a sip.

Rusch cocked his head toward the front window and pointed up the block toward Mission Street.

"I'd just bought this place when you got shot out there. At least ten years ago and I remember it like it was yesterday. People are still talking about it. You're a legend . . . a leg-end." Rusch smiled and made a trigger motion with his thumb. "Like at the O.K. Corral. Bam-bam, bam-bam-bam." He laughed. "All my customers go running out the back door like they didn't want to be anywhere near the Mission District when the cops showed up and started patting people down. Then sirens coming from everywhere. Whoop—whoop—whoop."

Donnally had gotten caught in a crossfire between Sureño and Norteño gangsters after he climbed out of his car to meet an informant at Morelia Taqueria. He put fatal slugs into both of them, and the Norteño put the one into him that ended his career.

"I ran out there. I could see by the way them EMTs were working on you that your cop days were done." Rusch pointed down at Donnally's hip. "All the blood coming out of there told me that's where you got shot. I didn't figure that you'd be doing much running and gunning after that."

Rusch rubbed his side as though in sympathy. "That joint back to working okay?"

In fact it wasn't. Donnally woke up to the stabbing memory of that day every morning and went to sleep with it every night.

But that was none of Rusch's business.

Donnally nodded and changed the subject. "I found some cash in Hamlin's safe."

"Not from me. I gave him thirty grand altogether. It's got to be gone by now. Long gone."

"Madison seemed to think that the deal was for life with a hundred grand always on deposit."

Rusch smiled again. "He should've taken up that little misunderstanding with Hamlin."

"He tried."

Rusch paused and pursed his lips, then squinted

at Donnally and asked, "What kind of bills did Hamlin have?"

"Hundreds."

"You won't find my fingerprints on that money." Rusch gestured toward the cash register. "Biggest bills I get coming through here are fifties and most are twenties."

Rusch didn't need to say that the denomination of choice in the biker drug trade was the twenty.

"Then why the attempted hit on Madison in prison?" Donnally asked.

Rusch's brows furrowed and he drummed his fingers on the bar. "Where's this information going?"

"You see me taking notes?"

"That's not an answer."

"In my head unless you're lying to me."

Rusch stared out into the bar until he got the attention of a biker wearing a black vest and a green T-shirt with a shamrock printed on the front, then he nodded at the stool next to Donnally.

Donnally recognized the shamrock as an Aryan Brotherhood emblem. One of the first homicides he investigated was an execution of a Hell's Angel named Irish by an Aryan Brotherhood member wearing a similar T-shirt, except with the words "When Irish Eyes Are Smiling" printed below it. He now wondered if this gang connection was the reason Rusch remembered his name and the day he was shot down. Donnally was known throughout the Aryan Brotherhood because he'd chased down scores of members, their wives, girlfriends, hangers-on, and associates and until he'd gathered enough leads to identify the killer.

The biker walked over and slipped onto the stool. He had a windburned, middle-aged face that had seen a lot of sun and grit, and teeth that had met a lot of cigarette smoke.

"You know anything about a stabbing in CMF Vacaville? Guy named Madison." Rusch looked at Donnally. "When?"

"Little over a month ago."

The biker rotated his chair toward Donnally and inspected him. "What's your interest?"

Rusch cut in. "My interest."

"He looks like a cop," the biker said, still eyeing Donnally, but not recognizing him due to the passage of time. "Who is he?"

"He was a cop. Now he . . ." Without lifting up his hand, Rusch flicked his forefinger at Donnally. "What do you do now?"

Donnally noticed that Rusch had avoided introducing him by name, probably fearing the biker would take a swing at him, with the rest jumping in, because he'd put a gang brother in prison for life.

Looking at bikers reflected in the mirror behind the bar, Donnally imagined that after the police cleared the scene on the day he was shot, some of these same men had returned to celebrate. Laughing, backslapping, high-fiving, and laying bets on whether he'd ever walk out of the hospital.

"I run a restaurant in Mount Shasta."

"Which one?" The biker asked the question like he'd been through the town enough to catch Donnally in a lie.

"You know it," Donnally said. "Lot of motorcycle

club guys stop in on their way up to Washington and Oregon. Lone Mountain Café."

The biker nodded, spun his stool around, and walked back to his table. Moments after he sat down and whispered a few words to the others at the table, one of them withdrew a cell phone and made a call. It rang a few minutes later and the biker returned.

He looked at Rusch. "Bennie Madison? The guy who—"

Rusch nodded.

The biker turned toward Donnally. "His nickname is Shitty. He refused to pay for some crystal meth he got from *somebody*." The biker emphasized the last word, then paused, implying the somebody was the Aryan Brotherhood. "He was supposed to hand over some Oxycontin tablets he got from the doc." The biker pointed at his own head. "He was milking some kind of brain thing. Scamming the hell out of it. Shitty claimed the meth was bunk—it wasn't. And *somebody* couldn't let that kind of disrespect pass."

CHAPTER 12

Donnally dropped into a chair across from Ramon Navarro in the Golden Phoenix, a shotgun Chinese café composed of six tables, two fish tanks at the back, and a cook who doubled as the waiter, halfway between the Hall of Justice and the Mission District bar of Rudy Rusch. It was long past sunset and they figured they owed themselves both lunch and dinner. Only one other table was occupied, by an old man hunched over a bowl of soup and watched by a lobster sitting shoulder-level behind the glass.

"A waste of time," Donnally said. "My guess is Madison knew he was dead on the case and figured he'd be dead for real in a year or two, so he sent Hamlin to threaten Rusch and extort some cash in order to cushion his fall. Maybe they split the money."

Navarro displayed an I-was-right-about-Hamlin smirk. "So it wasn't so pro bono after all."

"Looks that way."

Donnally reached for the menu standing between the napkin dispenser and the wall.

"You sure it wasn't Rusch who sent the Aryan

Brotherhood after Madison?" Navarro asked. "The rumor years ago was that they backed him in buying the bar."

"In a credibility contest between Madison and Rusch, I'll take Rusch. He still calls his wife The Bitch, even though saying it paints crosshairs on his forehead."

The cook walked up. Donnally ordered chicken chow fun. He'd missed Golden Phoenix's version of the dish, nutty, dry-fried, and spicy, during the years since he'd moved up to Mount Shasta. Since he was doing cop work, he felt like eating cop food, at least in San Francisco. Long gone were the days when officers limited themselves to a Norman Rockwell diet of burgers and fries and roast beef or turkey plate specials.

Navarro ordered the same.

"You get any prints off the money?" Donnally asked.

"Some." Navarro reached down and withdrew a file folder from his briefcase and handed it to Donnally, who passed over copies of his cell phone research and Hamlin's calendar. "We've dusted most of the bills and recovered a few prints so far. The techs are still going through them." He pointed at the folder. "Those are the people we've identified so far."

Donnally spotted Takiyah Jackson's name, along with Hamlin's and one he didn't recognize.

"How'd you happen to have Jackson's prints on file?" Donnally asked.

"She got arrested in a raid on a Black Prisoners Union hideout in the eighties."

"Which one?"

"The one in which Bumper was killed."

Donnally now understood why Jackson had been drawn to Hamlin. It had been one of the most notorious cases of the era. The medical examiner's autopsy had confirmed witnesses' testimony that the ideological leader of the Black Prisoners Union had been killed by police officers while lying facedown on his bed. Donnally guessed from then on Jackson's world was made up of cops and cons, and she saw herself as a con.

"What was she doing there?"

"A runaway from the East Oakland housing projects. Sexually abusive father. Heroin-addicted mother. She'd been in the BPU house for a couple of days. I pulled the file when we got the match. Her real name is Jeanette. They gave her the African name Takiyah. It means righteous."

Donnally read off the second name. "Who's Sheldon Galen?"

"Defense lawyer. Been around San Francisco for about eight years. Shares Hamlin's point of view, but doesn't have his brains. Hamlin would bring him in on codefendant cases. Hamlin always took the heavy and gave Galen the lightweight and expected Galen to make sure the client didn't turn snitch and roll on Hamlin's guy."

"He have a criminal history, too?"

"No. His prints were in the applicant file from when he tried to get a job in the public defender's office."

"If his prints were on the cash," Donnally said, "that suggests he must've been the bagman, col-

lecting the fees and bringing them to Hamlin."
He smiled. "I don't see Hamlin handing anybody
a hundred grand and then telling him to strip off a
couple as his cut."

Donnally leaned back and held the sheet against
his chest as the cook delivered their plates of chow
fun. The peanut-oiled noodles in brown sauce shimmered under the overhead fluorescent lights. He
could tell by the aroma that nothing had changed
in the kitchen of the Golden Phoenix since he'd last
eaten there.

"Homicides are usually about drugs, sex, or
money," Donnally said after he walked away.
"Maybe I should drop in on Galen tomorrow."

"Let me make a few calls first and see if any of
the courthouse gossips know if there was anything
going on between them. Maybe a fight over a case
or fees or something. Some kind of falling out. Give
you something to work with."

Donnally nodded. "It's tough to go after a witness cold, especially a lawyer."

Navarro grinned. "You mean a professional questioner like yourself has no chance against a professional liar like him?"

"My professional days are long over. Now I'm
just a guy who runs a café."

Donnally pointed at Navarro's plate, then took
a bite from his own. They didn't speak again until
they'd gotten a few mouthfuls down.

"What did you turn up from the apartment?"
Donnally asked.

"A few latents, but none from the kitchen. Somebody did a helluva clean-up job. The people in the other half of the duplex were out of town, and neighborhood canvass got us nothing at all. Hear no evil, see no evil. But we haven't given up. We're looking for some local kids who hang out in the park across the street at night."

"What's your thinking about the hairs in the bathroom and the rope left behind?"

"Maybe they got panicky or something made them rush at the end." Navarro smiled again. "Like you used to say, nobody gets murder right the first time. It takes practice."

"You sure this was a first time?"

"At least in terms of MO. I've never seen anything like it in San Francisco before." Navarro took a sip of tea. "It's so bizarre the loonies are all coming out. A couple of them called the tip line. Apparently a conspiracy of Martians and Scientologists did Hamlin in."

Navarro reached into his briefcase again. Donnally expected him to take out the legitimate leads from the calls. Instead, it was his department-issued iPad. He turned it on, tapped an icon, and handed it to Donnally. It displayed a story about Hamlin's murder on the home page of the *San Francisco Chronicle*.

"You'll love this," Navarro said, pointing at a second paragraph.

Donnally read it to himself.

"It is a monumental loss to the legal community of San Francisco," District Attorney Hannah Goldhagen said late this morning. "We'll miss his intelligence, his aggressive advocacy, and his humor that

informed as much as it entertained. I can guarantee
the people of San Francisco we will find and pros-
ecute whoever murdered him to the fullest extent of
the law."

Donnally passed it back. "She had to say something other than good riddance. It's Bay Area politics in its most perfect state."

Navarro's fists tightened on the table. "That
bitch has never prosecuted anyone to the fullest
extent of the law. She's spent her whole career oiling
the hinges on the revolving door."

"And somehow I get the feeling you're hoping
whoever did Hamlin in is one of those who slipped
through."

"Yeah. With him holding it open."

CHAPTER 13

Donnally noticed the letter-sized envelope protruding from under the doormat as he reached into his pocket to dig out his house keys. He bent down and rolled back the corner of the rubber pad, then squeezed the envelope by opposite edges and picked it up. The words printed on the paper inside showed through when he raised it up toward the porch light: "Follow the Money."

What do you think I'm doing? was his first thought. His second was *Who gave you the right to come to my house?*

He unlocked the door of the two-story bungalow and followed the distant light through the living room and into the kitchen where Janie was working on her laptop at the table. Handwritten case notes from her psychotherapy sessions at Fort Miley lay next to it. He set the envelope on top of the newspaper lying on his side of the table, then kissed her on the forehead.

"What's that?" she asked, pointing at the envelope.

"A love letter from somebody who's one step behind me, but who thinks they're one step ahead."

"Better for you than the other way around."

Donnally made a point of scratching his head. "I'm not sure I understand that one."

Janie smiled. "Ever since Freud and Jung, shrinks are allowed to be cryptic and nonsensical. It adds to our aura of enlightenment." She pointed at the chair across from her and closed the laptop lid. "Tell me about your day. All I know is what's been on TV." Her smile transformed into a grin. "I kind of like the title special master, especially since in San Francisco it sounds kind of sexual. Dungeons. Dominatrices. And special masters." She raised her eyebrows. "Did they give you a little whip?"

Donnally smiled back, holding up his empty hands, and then filled her in on what had happened since he'd climbed out of their bed at 4 A.M.

"I've got to handle Takiyah Jackson carefully," Donnally said when he came to the end of the story and began to think about next steps. "I'm convinced that folie à deux really does capture her relationship with Hamlin."

"Or maybe a folie à plusieurs," Janie said. "A madness of many. He had lots of people willing to work for him and lots of attorneys willing to work with him, like Sheldon Galen."

Donnally narrowed his eyes at her. "How do you know about Galen?"

"He was on the news. And not easily forgotten. He has a New York accent and a face like a greyhound."

Janie paused in thought for a moment, then said, " 'Madness' may be too strong a word, but I see why you'd latch on to it."

Donnally felt himself stiffen and his stomach

tighten. The problem with having a shrink as a girl-friend is the continuing risk of getting shrunk.

Janie stared at him. He knew she was waiting for permission to say what was on her mind. He nodded.

"It's because you can't accept that people like Hamlin feel morally justified in what they do."

He knew she was right.

"I think that's why you never really understood narcotics officers who planted drugs on gangsters and then committed perjury to make the cases stick. You always believed their motives were more basic, like it was only about power. Cons playing the part of cops. Same with Hamlin, you always thought attorneys like him were motivated by greed alone and they merely disguised their motives in moral language."

Donnally always thought one of his strengths as a detective was that he never believed either cops' or crooks' justifications for their criminal offenses. Rather, he saw the crimes graphically and abstractly, like moves in a game, or as forms of self-deception or as attempts to justify the unjustifiable.

Janie hadn't known him during those years. He had been referred to her after he was shot. It wasn't that the department thought he'd gone nuts and needed treatment. It was just a requirement of the general orders that an officer who killed a suspect in the line of duty undergo a psych evaluation. He considered it a sign of his sanity that at the first meeting he decided he'd rather date her than get shrunk by her.

She ended up doing both, starting with the dating.

"I think that's why you sometimes sound like you operate on a kind of mechanistic and reductionist theory of homicide and view them as motivated only by drugs, sex, or money."

It was like she'd been sitting at the next table in the Golden Phoenix listening in, but in truth it was that she'd paid close enough attention over the years to be able to tell him how he saw the world, and why he did so.

"But I'm not sure you really believe that. It's just that thinking in terms of power, of brute causes and effects, seems more honest to you than the way your father thinks about the world."

Donnally felt himself tense. Every time Janie started down this kind of analytic road, his past washed over him like a flash flood, the storm triggered by the mention of his father. It made him feel like he'd spent too many years circling in an eddy.

He'd become a cop as a form of rebellion, and he recognized it at the time. It had been against his filmmaker father, a man who treated fiction as more real than fact because it made possible the evasion from responsibility he'd sought for most of his life. For his father, justice had been no more than a kind of fictive irony, a subversion of cause and consequence, of effect and responsibility, because real-world justice would've meant facing up to what he'd done to his older son. Donnally's older brother had believed the propaganda his father had created as a press officer in Saigon during the Vietnam War. His father had falsely claimed that North Vietnamese regulars had massacred a group of Buddhist monks near the DMZ, and the lie not only provoked worldwide outrage, but persuaded his brother to enlist. He learned the truth—that the killers had been Korean mercenaries working for the U.S.— just days before he was killed in an ambush.

Years later, his father became a movie director, playing out his evasions on film, and liked to say that Hollywood wasn't a place, but an idea, while Donnally had always thought of it as no more than a patch of concrete and viewed the motives of those who worked there as more base than artistic—and his father was proof of that. After all, what was post-Vietnam Hollywood, the years in which his father first achieved fame, but an escape from reality into drugs, sex, and money.

Donnally pushed aside the memory and worked his way back to where their conversation had started, with Jackson and what had connected her to Mark Hamlin, where it began, how it grew, its character just before his death and whether it might have transformed afterward.

"What you're saying," Donnally said, "is that I need to understand Jackson's transition from victim of a police crime into . . ." He spread open his hands on the table. "Into what?"

"Someone whose identity was somehow tied to Hamlin's ends-justifies-the-means mentality."

Donnally had the feeling Janie was right. That could be the reason why Jackson could be terrified of being prosecuted for the illegal means Hamlin had chosen, but could still be loyal to him.

"Even though," Donnally said, "whatever ends were hers over the twenty years she was with him may not have been his anymore when he died."

"But I suspect that she doesn't quite see it yet. And if you push her too hard, she'll never let herself see it. It would be just too terrifying."

CHAPTER 14

The note on Donnally's windshield had read:

> We decided to flatten only one tire so you could use
> your spare to get yourself out of town. Next time . . .

Donnally hadn't noticed the listing right rear end of his truck when he walked out of the house and into the predawn shadows at 7 A.M. He felt a surge of anger as he examined the tire under the streetlight and realized that he'd overlooked a ground rule when he met with Judge McMullin. Who was going to pay for the damage.

The note was still pinned under his wiper blade. Four thoughts came to him as he retrieved it.

The first was that whoever left it probably wrote for a living. They didn't split the infinitive and they knew how to use an ellipsis.

The second was that he wished Hamlin's friends and enemies would stop leaving notes.

The third was that the absent words "Fuck you, asshole" meant that the author probably hadn't been one of Hamlin's clients.

The fourth was that the "we" was really an "I."

Twenty minutes later, Donnally had changed the tire and was driving toward Hamlin's office. He parked in an underground garage up the block, then walked over and waited for Takiyah Jackson behind a pillar by the building entrance.

Donnally spotted her coming down the sidewalk before she noticed him. He stepped toward the brass and glass door as if he was just arriving, then looked back as she made the turn, and smiled.

"Good timing," Donnally said.

Jackson didn't smile back. She pointed upward, toward the higher floors. "You setting up shop?"

"Might as well. Looks like I'll be in town awhile. Can I buy you some coffee?"

"I thought you cops liked to start the grilling cold, then offered coffee as a pretended act of friendship to fudge up a little warm feeling in the interrogation room."

"Crooks never fell for that except on television. I always relied on charm."

Jackson rolled her eyes. "I'll take the coffee instead."

They turned together and walked to the Starbucks on the corner. She ordered regular house blend. He ordered the same out of solidarity, otherwise he would've gotten the decaf. He'd learned over the years that it wasn't enough just to break bread, but you had to break the same bread, or to drink the same coffee.

Sometimes he didn't want to try to rely on charm alone, and this was one of those times.

Jackson raised her cup in what Donnally took to be a silent toast to Hamlin, then they both took sips and headed back out the door.

"Mark must have really trusted you," Donnally said as they headed back up the sidewalk.

"How do you figure?"

"We found your fingerprints on the cash in his safe."

"Maybe he shouldn't have trusted me. How do you know I didn't reach in and grab some for myself?"

Donnally glanced over at her and smiled. "A do-it-yourself severance package?"

"Maybe."

"You've been around long enough, seen enough screw-ups by crooks, to have learned how to cover your tracks by wearing gloves."

"You find anyone else's prints?"

"Yes."

Jackson stopped in the middle of the sidewalk, forcing Donnally to stop and face her. Office workers brushed by them, some making a point of bumping their shoulders. Donnally pointed toward the front window of a copy service and they stepped over to it.

"It really wasn't a yes or no question," Jackson said.

"How about you tell me whose prints they are."

"It's better if you take the lead. I'm not gonna snitch on anybody."

"Even if they did something wrong?"

"Who am I to judge? People make mistakes."

"Like Sheldon Galen?"

Jackson took in a long breath and looked past

Donnally up the sidewalk. He noticed part of what had made him think of Angela Bassett when he'd first looked at her. The severity of her nose and cheeks and her eyes, less windows than screens. He wondered whether over the years her face had become her or she had become her face.

Finally, Jackson exhaled and said, "That's a complicated one. Sheldon showed up a while back all tense and excited. Really pressured, like there was a lot on the line. Him and Mark talked in the office for a long time and then Mark cleaned out the safe and gave him all the cash inside. They were in such a tizzy I thought maybe they'd landed a big case and Mark was giving him his cut upfront."

"That matches what I've heard," Donnally said. "That Mark often hired Galen to work on cases with him. But I'm not sure how money with Galen's fingerprints ended up in Mark's safe. It should've been all outgoing, and none incoming."

"That's not the end of the story."

Jackson took a sip of her coffee. Donnally thought she was buying time to decide how much of the tale to tell. He didn't imagine he'd get the whole thing. Jackson wasn't there yet.

"A week later the money was back. I asked Mark about it. He told me it was some kind of loan. I flashed on how Sheldon acted when he came for it and realized what I was prepared to see as tension and excitement because of all the cases they'd worked on over the years might have been desperation."

"And when the cash showed up again?"

"I figured that Sheldon had returned the money, or at least part of it."

"How much?"

"I think about eighty thousand dollars."

"Why do you think it was Sheldon?"

"There were a bunch of conference calls the day before. Sheldon, Mark, and a bunch of the lawyers in The Crew."

"The Crew?"

"A group of old lefty lawyers from the sixties and seventies. I got the feeling they took up a collection so Sheldon could pay Mark back, because the money showed up right afterwards."

"Is that the same money that I took out of the safe yesterday?"

"Some." Jackson stared past Donnally again, but this time her eyes didn't seem to register the commuter traffic on the street or the office workers rushing by. Whatever she was seeing was playing out in her head.

After a few moments, she looked back at Donnally.

"Sheldon is a weasel. He graduated from NYU law school and worked as a court-appointed lawyer back there for a couple of years. Why he showed up in San Francisco, I don't know. But he knew how to talk the talk, how to pump up his credibility. It was all about how he'd represented terrorism suspects and about all his trial victories. It was all bullshit. He only represented terrorism suspects because they couldn't afford their own lawyers and the federal judges needed attorneys who'd work cheap."

"How'd you find out the truth about him?"

"Him and Mark did a heroin importation case back there a couple of years ago. They were brought in by a local lawyer. I talked to her paralegal. She told me all his money came from CJA."

Donnally cast her a puzzled look.

"Federal Criminal Justice Act. Indigent defense. Sheldon never had a paying client until he came out here."

"What kind of weaseling led him to need eighty thousand dollars all of a sudden?"

Jackson shrugged. "I told you. I ain't a snitch."

Donnally anticipated the dodge and had his answer prepared. As he readied himself to give it, he wondered whether it had been Jackson who'd left the "Follow the Money" note in the envelope under his doormat, a way of snitching without being seen to snitch.

Donnally backed off the idea of pressuring her; instead he said, "Then point me in the right direction so I can find out myself."

She paused, then aimed her finger down the street in the direction from which they'd come.

"Go see Warren Bohr. His office is in the Frederickson Building. He put some money in, so he must know why."

Donnally recognized the name. Bohr had been a defense lawyer who represented Black Panthers and other radical political groups in the sixties, then criminal defendants in big drug and racketeering cases in the seventies and eighties, and finally migrated into public interest law after he grew wealthy enough that he didn't need the money. The last time Donnally had heard his name was before he'd left San Francisco, when Bohr had filed a suit to stop the federal government from leasing part of

Alcatraz Island to the Marriott corporation to build a hotel. But that was fifteen years ago.

Donnally glanced at his watch. It was 8:25.

"What time does he get in?"

"You know how these old guys are. In at 7 A.M., and tell everyone they meet that they've never missed a day of work in the gazillion years they've been practicing." She gestured with her cup toward Bohr's office. "He'll be there."

CHAPTER 15

Donnally headed back up the sidewalk toward the Frederickson Building. Every cop in town knew the place, a three-story Victorian composed of tiny offices filled with aging sole practitioners. Most were so lousy at law that their mortgage payments depended on indigent defense cases, state and federal court appointments, for clients either without the money, or without the sense to borrow the money, to hire someone competent.

Donnally hated their pretense. The court-appointed attorneys swaggered around the courthouses like they had real paying customers. In the end, nearly all their clients pled out. The defendants were unwilling to risk trials with appointed help, and the DAs and federal prosecutors were willing to cut deals just to clear the calendar. The attorney who managed the Frederickson Building set the tone for the rest. Donnally had heard him praised by prosecutors as a clown with great client control, and they were willing to put up with his clowning because he never failed to find a way to make his client cave.

There were exceptions, good defense lawyers

who were bad at self-marketing or who were committed to defending the poor, but most of the appointed lawyers were less advocates than fixers.

The whole game of deal cutting had pissed off Donnally and the other cops in the department, at least with respect to the cases they cared about, because some victims needed their day in court, needed to have their suffering seen, not reduced to a penal code section entered on a form and passed from judge to clerk to file and then consigned into the dark eternity of a storage room.

Donnally suspected that were it not for Hamlin lifting him up, if only to use him as a tool, Sheldon Galen would have spent his career as one of those Frederickson Building lawyers. And Galen had to know and dread that Hamlin might someday decide he was done with him and drop him back onto the pile.

As Donnally approached the edge of the financial district, he wondered why Bohr still had his office in there. Bohr had to feel like the odd man out since he couldn't have much in common with the hand-to-mouth lawyers that worked out of the place. He wondered whether Bohr stayed there because he liked knowing he was the guy all the others wanted to be when they were young, and maybe having him around made them feel like they had made it. Maybe he was an artifact, or a totem, from a time when law was a mission in San Francisco, instead of the chiseling it too often revealed itself to be.

On the other hand, maybe he was still there only because he had always been there, like a backyard tree stump that was just too much trouble to haul away.

Donnally paused at the bottom of the front steps and called Navarro.

"You find out anything about whether there was any kind of problem between Hamlin and Sheldon Galen?"

"Not between them. Only between Galen and an old client that threatened to sue him. But it settled before the papers got filed, so I couldn't find out the details. His client was charged with beating up a security guard who wouldn't let him take his dog into a bank. Galen lost the trial. Maybe the guy wanted his money back. His name was Fisher except with a C, Tink Fischer. I'll text you an address when I come up with one."

Donnally heard the sound of papers rustling through the fine static on the line.

"We got a few more latents off the money," Navarro said. "I'll have the results later this morning. But no guarantee that we'll be able to ID them."

Donnally then told Navarro about the note telling him to follow the money and the slashed tire warning him to leave.

Navarro laughed. "Maybe somebody's telling you to follow the money all the way out of town."

"I hadn't thought of that," Donnally said. "You were always good at putting one and one together."

"I'll make sure it's not two and two. I'll have the beat cops do drive-bys for the next few days, see if they can snag whoever he is, or at least scare him away."

CHAPTER 16

Old-people smell. That's what it was called. Donnally recognized it at first breath when he entered Warren Bohr's reception area. It was the background odor of nearly every elderly suicide he'd ever investigated.

It wasn't just the dust on the desk and in the built-in bookcases, or the grime worn into the marble floor, or the months of legal newspapers stacked on the low table in front of the leather couch.

It was something else.

It was what it meant: the kind of cognitive impairment that always seemed to go with it. That had been the first sign that his grandmother was heading toward Alzheimer's, what the doctors called impaired odor recognition.

Bohr must have heard the door open, for he appeared at his inner office door.

"Can I help you?" Bohr asked, looking up from under eyebrows lowered by his hunched back.

Donnally recognized the middle-aged lawyer under the smudge and tarnish of old age. His wool suit draped his thinned body, his once angular nose had softened, his ears drooped like overgrown botanical specimens, and his once black hair had turned fungus yellow-gray.

"I hope so." Donnally crossed the room and shook his hand, saying, "I'm Harlan Donnally; Judge McMullin appointed me special master in the Hamlin case."

"I didn't expect someone would be coming by so soon."

"So soon?"

"You couldn't have run out of leads this fast, that you needed to start shaking the bushes to see what falls out."

Donnally pointed through the door and toward Bohr's desk. "Can we?"

Bohr nodded and led him inside his wood-paneled office. Donnally waited until Bohr shuffled his way around to his high-back chair, then sat down facing him. Hanging on the wall behind the lawyer were photos of him with former mayors George Moscone and Willie Brown, Harvey Milk, César Chávez, Carol Doda, and Eldridge Cleaver.

"I can save you some time and trouble," Bohr said. "I hadn't spoken to Mark in a year."

Donnally raised up his hands in a football time-out motion, then realized that it might have been preemptive.

The old-people smell. Maybe Bohr didn't remember.

"I understood you spoke to him within the last few months."

Bohr glanced over at his wall calendar. It hadn't

been turned in half a year. He sighed. "That keeps happening." He looked back at Donnally. "Refresh me."

"I was told that you participated in a conference call about money. Somebody needing money real bad and real quick."

Bohr nodded. "I remember. Sheldon Galen." He pretended to spit. "That putz. The idiot borrowed from a client, then couldn't pay it back. Could've lost his bar card for doing it."

"Why'd you help him out?"

"I didn't. Mark stepped in right away and paid the client to keep him from suing Galen. The rest of The Crew then put in money so Mark wouldn't be out on a limb alone." Bohr glanced at the calendar again. "I think Mark was supposed to pay me back by now."

"You may want to put in a claim with the probate court."

Bohr paused, thinking, then blinked. "It may be better to write it off. I'm not sure I want to be the one who explains to the court why Mark wanted the money."

No, Donnally thought, *you don't want to explain to the court why Galen needed the money.*

Donnally felt his phone vibrate once in his pocket. He pulled it out. It was the text message from Navarro with Tink Fischer's address.

"Can you think of anyone who might want to kill Mark?" Donnally asked.

"By anyone, you mean Galen?"

"Not just Galen."

"A thousand people."

"I think you'll need to narrow it down some."

"Mark was an aggressive lawyer. And aggressive lawyers make enemies." Bohr spread his hands. "How'd you like to be the father of a kid who was murdered by one of Mark's clients? Mark dummies up some reasonable doubt—which doesn't take much around here—and the killer walks."

"The odds of that being the reason are pretty slim. A winning lawyer has never been murdered before, at least in San Francisco."

Bohr paused and inspected Donnally's face. "What did you do before you started this special master business?"

Bohr said the words "special master business" like Donnally was in the same class as the court-appointed lawyers in the building.

"I was a homicide detective," Donnally said. "And it's not a business. It's a onetime thing."

"How many unsolved homicides have there been in San Francisco. Hundreds? Thousands?"

Donnally nodded. He knew where Bohr was going, but didn't get in his way.

"Then I guess you can't say whether it hasn't happened before." Bohr gestured toward the window. "Lot of the people getting killed out there are old clients of Mark's. Most of those murders don't get solved. People assume it's gang on gang. Maybe not."

The old man had gone off course. They hadn't been talking about clients being murdered, but their lawyers. He should've been arguing that some lawyers had been murdered over the years and not all of those murders had been solved. Donnally wondered whether there was some thought or memory inside Bohr's brain that was pushing him that way.

"That just means killers get killed," Donnally said. "It doesn't mean their lawyers get killed for getting them off. I don't recall any of those, even when there were serious criminal organizations involved."

Bohr leaned forward in his chair. "But if it was going to happen to one of them, my candidate would've been Mark." He leaned back again and squinted up toward the ceiling. "Where did we start with this? Oh yes. Sheldon Galen." He looked again at Donnally. "You're thinking that Hamlin's murder is a lawyer-on-lawyer crime. Galen kills Mark so he doesn't have to pay back the money?"

"I'm not thinking anything."

Bohr smiled. "But if you were about to think something, I'd make it that."

L oan? It wasn't no loan. That asshole Galen stole my money. *Stole . . .* it. A hundred thousand dollars."

The man standing behind the chain-link fence next to a fight-scarred pit bull didn't look to Donnally like a guy who'd ever seen a hundred thousand dollars in any form. Cash, check, or money order.

Having emitted a rapid first blast, Tink Fischer fell silent and then looked Donnally up and down as if only now having the thought he'd should've had when Donnally first walked up and set the dog to barking. *What's a white guy doing out here without a badge and a backup?*

"Where'd you park your car?"

"Truck." Donnally pointed his thumb over his shoulder toward the curb in front of the faded pink stucco bungalow across the street.

"The Big Block Boys have been fighting a turf war with Bay Side. You're in what you could call the line of fire. Lots of dope money to be made on the corner so there's lots to fight over."

Fischer glanced over at the mostly primer gray 1980s Caprice Classic in his carport. Donnally followed his eyes. The only shiny spots on the skin were the bent-in edges of the bullet holes.

"Maybe I should talk fast," Donnally said.

Fischer smiled. "I'll try to keep up once I know where you're headed."

Donnally smiled back. "I'm interested in Sheldon Galen."

"You a private investigator?"

"Let's just say I'm a dissatisfied customer."

Fischer snorted. "Been down that road myself."

Donnally looked down at the dog, guessing that it was the one that Fischer had tried to bring into the bank with him.

"Because he lost your case?"

Fischer waved the question away. "I wasn't gonna win it. The DA was offering a bullet in the county jail and I figured I could get it cut down if the judge heard some kinda sob story from me."

It was called a long sentencing hearing. Using a trial not to prove innocence, but mitigation. And a bullet was courthouse slang for a year in the county jail.

"I told them about how the dog was my son's and how the dog got all despondent after he got killed and didn't like being left alone." Fischer tilted his head toward the corner, implying that was where the murder took place. "It was true. That's what happened. Judge bought it and I got six months."

"But it really didn't have anything to do with why you punched the security guard."

"I hit him because he was a racist asshole. He had what I call a black-guy-with-a-pit-bull complex." Fischer spread his hands. "The dog is like a loaded gun. Like I was supposed to leave him tied up on the sidewalk so he could take chunks out of people's legs walking by?"

"Then what was your beef with Galen?"

"He represented me in a civil suit. A false arrest case. Cops beat the shit out of me. I was walking by a sideshow—just . . . walking . . . by—"

"A what?"

"Aren't you from around here?"

"I'm from up north."

"A sideshow is where the kids spin donuts in their cars in intersections. Look at the pavement when you drive on out of here. You'll see the skid marks. Big crowds show up. Sometimes the drivers lose control and jump the curb and people get killed. Cops always trying to stop them."

Donnally nodded his understanding.

"I'm walking by one last year and the cops come squealing up and everybody scatters. Me and the dog are the last ones there. Next thing I know, I'm facedown on the sidewalk bleeding from out my broken nose and my neck all twisted up."

Something of Donnally's incredulity must have shown on his face.

"It's true. I didn't know what happened until I saw the cell phone video somebody took from their second story window. When the city attorney got a look at it, they couldn't wait to get the case settled. Galen got me a hundred and forty grand. He was supposed to keep forty for his fees and expenses, like for the chiropractor treatments to help build up the damages, and give me the rest."

"But he was slow to give it to you."

"Damn slow. A month goes by, then two, then four."

Donnally figured out right then what Hamlin must have. The settlement check from the city would've been made out to the Sheldon Galen trust account, separate from Galen's own money, where it would be held for the benefit of the client—and Galen had embezzled it. And to do that he would've had to falsify accounting records and launder the funds into a form in which he could use them himself. He might even have had to forge checks to make it appear that the payments were made to Fischer when they were actually made to himself. If caught, not only would he have lost his bar card, but he would've ended up as a real jailhouse lawyer, doing his own bullet in the county jail.

"Finally, I go over to Galen's office and he says he'll have it in a week. A month goes by. I head over there again. I tell him to have it tomorrow or he's gonna have a long meeting with the dog."

"I heard you threatened to sue him."

Fischer laughed. "By then, I'd had enough of lawyers. He must've come up with that tale to go along with his Fischer-loaned-me-the-money story. I go back the next day and he's got it. In cash. Two stacks."

"He tell you where he got the money to pay you back?"

"Didn't stay around long enough." Fischer reached down and patted the pit bull's head. "Me and the dog grabbed it and got out of there."

CHAPTER 18

Donnally's cell phone rang as his truck tires rolled over the circular sideshow skid marks in the intersection at the end of Tink Fischer's block. The dope dealers playing dice on the corner glanced over as he passed. Through his rearview mirror, he watched them return to the game.

It was Takiyah Jackson.

"I need to know the rules."

"About what?"

"Sheldon Galen called, said he wants to pick up some files so he can make Mark's court appearances for the next couple of days."

"Has he filled in like that for Mark before?"

"Yeah. He's the guy Mark always called, but only when he was sick or had a calendar conflict and needed to have a case put over. Galen never needed the files for that. Just an e-mailed copy of Mark's calendar so the judge could set a new hearing date."

Donnally turned onto Third Street, which ran through the industrial district toward downtown. It wasn't worth the risk of getting caught in a backup on the Bayshore Freeway.

"What do you think is going on?" Donnally asked.

Jackson laughed. "The same thing you do. He's trying to poach Mark's cases."

"I take it he wants to study up fast and then convince the clients he's up to speed and ready to go."

"Especially with the in-custodies. A lot of them were waiting for Mark's calendar to clear so they could get their full day in court. And the ones Galen wants are all in-custody."

"How would the money work if Galen substituted in?"

"If there's a retainer balance in Mark's trust account, it would get transferred to Galen. He'd make the client come up with the difference between what's there and the amount of the original retainer."

"So he starts out fresh with the same up-front money Mark began the case with."

"The three files he wants are probably worth fifty grand altogether," Jackson said. "I checked. There's about twenty left in Mark's trust account from these clients."

Donnally thought of Bohr pretending to spit upon hearing Sheldon Galen's name.

"I don't get why the clients would go with Galen," Donnally said. "For the same amount of money, they could get someone good."

"It's because Galen is known as Mark's go-to guy. Say Mark gets hired by the main defendant in a codefendant case. If there were just two defendants, Galen would get the call. If there were three or four or five, Mark would work down his list, usually drawn from the folks at the Frederickson Building. What these other defendants never realized was that Mark brought in attorneys not to advocate for them, but to control them, to keep them from rolling on his client."

"What happened to loyalty to one's client . . . what do they call it?"

"An attorney's duty of zealous representation," Jackson said. "Around here, it was what you might call situational. It was situated with whoever's paying the bills. And that whoever was Mark's client."

Donnally felt too many thoughts crisscrossing. Galen had motive. In one quick move he could both get himself out from under the embezzlement hammer and take over Hamlin's practice.

Beyond Galen, who knew how many defendants had realized too late that Hamlin had corrupted their lawyers and set them up to take falls, and which of them might've wanted to get even after they did their time, or reach out and touch him from prison.

And finally, and maybe most important, why was Jackson telling him things she might not have even admitted to herself when Hamlin was alive? After all, she profited from those betrayals and ethical violations every month when she accepted her wages.

Instinct told him not to press her any further.

"Set up a time for Galen to come by," Donnally said. "I'll be there. And make copies of the files, except Mark's notes or any defense investigation, that way he can't learn enough about the cases to do anything more than just kick them over."

"But how you gonna keep him from looking at the files before he leaves and notice what's missing?"

"Don't worry." Donnally hit the accelerator. "I'll take care of that."

CHAPTER 19 ═══════════════

Sitting behind Mark Hamlin's desk, Donnally noticed Sheldon Galen's face harden as he walked into the office and spotted Detective Ramon Navarro sitting on the couch. Galen flinched at the metallic click when Takiyah Jackson closed the door behind him, then came to a stop and glared at Donnally.

Janie's description had been dead-on. Galen looked like a greyhound, maybe a whippet. Narrow shoulders. Dark eyes. Prematurely gray at forty. So stiff and skinny Donnally felt like he was looking at a manikin.

"Your appointment as a special master doesn't authorize you to disclose attorney-client privileged matters to the police," Galen said. He pointed a forefinger at Navarro. "He shouldn't be here."

Donnally patted the three file folders he centered on the desk. "I haven't talked to him about these." He opened his hand toward one of the chairs facing the desk. "He's here for another reason."

Donnally watched Galen glance back and forth between the chairs and files, as though evaluating the risks. He imagined Galen was asking himself

whether it was worth subjecting himself to whatever Donnally had in mind in order to walk out
later with the files and the money they represented.

Galen rocked back and forth on the balls of his
feet, then took the four steps forward and sat down.

Navarro stayed seated where he was, didn't rise
and take the chair next to Galen. The plan was for
him to inflict a kind of side pressure to keep Galen
off balance, with Donnally pushing from the front.

Galen unbuttoned his suit jacket and tugged at
each pant leg to preserve the creases, and did so
with such flourish it seemed to Donnally to be a
performance, for reasons he didn't know, but for
whose benefit he did.

Contrary to what Galen might have had in mind,
what the theatrical gesture engendered in Donnally
was revulsion. He imagined Galen making the same
moves in court, each time with a different meaning.
One time to show annoyance at an adverse ruling,
the next time as a way of providing the jury with a
silent commentary on the testimony of a prosecution witness, and the time after that to impress a
client with his confidence even though he was out-
numbered in a hostile environment.

It reminded Donnally of what he hated about the
court system; it cherished theater over fact. He'd
watched it turn testifying police officers into actors
in order to compete with the professionals—the
lawyers—and it too often got them into a kind of
self-destructive verbal sparring they couldn't win
against people who did it for a living.

Even worse, the courtroom as stage made jurors
expect a show and left them bored and frustrated

when they didn't get one. It was bad enough that they expected television crime drama forensics, they also wanted to be entertained by popping dialogue and sudden plot twists.

Donnally wished he was back in his café kitchen. His burgers and fries were either done right or done wrong, and they couldn't pretend to be anything other than what they were. Meat, wheat, and potatoes.

"I'm interested in the theories you have about what happened to Mark," Donnally said.

Galen crossed his right leg over his left. "At the moment I don't have any."

Donnally leaned forward. "I'm not asking for conclusions, just theory, speculation."

Galen rocked his head side to side.

Hamlin's intercom buzzed. Donnally picked up the telephone receiver. It was Jackson.

"I just realized something," Jackson said. "Can you come out for a minute?"

Donnally didn't look up, but knew Galen was staring at him, suspecting the call was about him. It was like a ringing phone in those old black and white movies. There was never a wrong number. It always moved the story forward, and Galen's licking lips and fidgeting fingers told Donnally he understood he was at the heart of today's episode.

"I'll be right there." Donnally hung up and walked out to Jackson's desk.

"Galen's fingerprints shouldn't have been on any of the money," Jackson said. "I just realized that the cash from Galen was all paid out to The Crew. There shouldn't have been anything left."

"You sure? Warren Bohr didn't remember receiving his share back."

"I think that says more about Warren's mental state than about the money." Jackson tapped the side of her head. "He comes and goes. The Lawyers Guild had a dinner honoring him last month and he showed up at the hotel a day early."

"Then where did the money in the safe come from?"

Jackson shrugged.

Galen didn't look behind him when Donnally came back into the office, but tracked him with a stare as Donnally walked past him on his way to the desk.

Donnally watched Galen's eyebrows rise and the skin on his forehead wrinkle in expectation, as though waiting for Donnally to explain the call.

Instead, Donnally asked, "Where were we?" He paused. He knew exactly what the topic had been. "We were talking about any theories you might have."

Galen's face relaxed as though the call had been a wrong number, not one that might lead to the exposure of one of his secrets.

"Mark was an aggressive lawyer," Galen said. "Aggressive lawyers make lots of enemies."

It sounded to Donnally like Galen and Warren Bohr had been reading from the same book of evasive descriptions.

"Like who?"

Galen smirked. "How much time have you got?"

Donnally glanced at Navarro. "As much time as we need to figure who killed him." He folded his arms across his chest. "Let's narrow it down. Did Mark ever tell you that he was afraid of anyone?"

"He never used the word 'afraid.' He wasn't that kind of guy. Concerned? Sure. But not so he felt he needed to go into hiding. It was more professional stuff. Sometimes he'd pull a stunt and worry about it snapping back on him or his clients."

"Anything recent?"

Galen shrugged. "I guess it can't hurt now. Mark's gone." He pointed at the television on Hamlin's credenza. "You see on the news last month about that federal judge who'd been telling people for years he went into law after he saw his sister murdered on the street right in front of him?"

Donnally nodded. It was a big story since the judge had been nominated to head the FBI. The judge had used it to inspire law students to pass on offers to join big civil firms and to encourage them to become prosecutors, even though they'd make just a quarter of the salary.

"Hamlin found out it was bogus and went to the press," Galen said. "The judge never had a sister."

The judge had withdrawn his nomination the next day.

"Why'd Hamlin do it?"

"The judge was forcing him out to trial on a case he wasn't prepared on. Big, complicated securities fraud. I'm not sure Mark even understood the money flow, and that's most of what those cases are about. He'd expected the case to deal out, but the U.S. Attorney played hardball and it didn't. The day before jury selection, the story is all over the news.

The judge is afraid to show his face in court. The trial gets put over and Mark is off the hook."

"Why didn't Mark just call in sick?"

"That would've only bought him a day or two, not enough time to read fifty thousand pages of discovery and get all the forensic accounting work done. And there was a lot of bad blood between him and the judge that had built up over the years. That's why the judge was forcing the case. He could see by the lack of defense motions that Mark wasn't ready. Mark was hoping he could get even once and for all and get the judge drop-kicked off the bench."

"Didn't work."

"Didn't work. The Bay Area is a very forgiving place."

"Mark do that kind of thing a lot?"

Galen's eyes widened, then his brow furrowed. "Which kind of thing? Not prepare for trial or—"

"Get dirt on people."

"That's what defense attorneys do." Galen forced a smile. "It's not like we're going to win on the facts very often."

Donnally realized Galen could spend the rest of the day telling stories about Hamlin, all of which would make him look bad but get Donnally no closer to a suspect, other than the one who was sitting across from him.

"What about you?" Donnally asked. "Were you one of those people?"

"What have you heard?"

It wasn't true, but Donnally said, "Just some

rumors about why you came out to California from New York."

In fact, they hadn't even risen to the level of rumors, but were only questions that arose in his mind after he first heard about Galen's move West.

"Anybody could've found out about that just by looking at the New York state court Web site. So I got suspended, so what? Happens all the time and it was only for six months. I'm the one who told Mark about it and he suggested I come out to California and start over."

Galen straightened up in his chair.

"I don't see what this has to do with what happened to Mark. I didn't even know Mark then. I met him at a criminal defense conference afterwards." Galen pointed at the files. "How about just letting me have those and I'll be on my way." He glanced at his watch. "I need to be in court at 2 P.M."

Donnally ignored him. "But that's not the only thing he found out about you."

"Is that a statement or a question?"

"Call it a question. The statement would be that he figured out you embezzled Tink Fischer's settlement money out of your trust account."

Galen pushed himself to his feet. "I'm out of here."

"No you're not." Donnally pointed at Navarro. "He knows enough right now to get a subpoena for your bank account records and a search warrant for your office, and to get a criminal complaint filed by tomorrow morning. It's better not to provoke him."

"I . . . didn't . . . kill . . . Mark. He's the one that gave me the money to pay it back."

"Only so he could control you by having a hammer he could drop on you at any time."

Galen locked his hands on his hips. "You don't think I had my hammers, too? After almost ten years of working together. I knew everything. Everything."

Donnally thought of Galen's fingerprints SFPD found on the money in the safe—and guessed how they'd gotten there.

He rose from his chair and faced Galen straight on.

"Or maybe it was just so he could keep bleeding you."

Galen's mouth opened. He swallowed. "How . . ." He licked his lips. "How did you find out?"

CHAPTER 20 ═══════

The sounds were disgusting. They reminded Donnally of the two weeks early in his career when he'd filled in driving the wagon picking up street drunks to deliver them to the SFPD tank.

Donnally and Navarro stood outside the open door to Hamlin's private bathroom as Galen hunched over the toilet, retching, gasping, sobbing. His body shuddering, his once creased pant knees rubbing themselves flat on the tile floor. Positioned just feet away, Donnally and Navarro weren't going take a chance of him jumping out of the tenth floor window.

When it appeared that Galen was done, or at least empty, Donnally stepped inside and reached down with a couple of paper towels. Galen took them and wiped his mouth before straightening up. He washed his face and hands, then Donnally led him back into the office.

"I didn't kill Mark," Galen said, looking back and forth between Navarro now sitting next to him and Donnally across the desk. "And I can prove it. I've got witnesses."

"You throwing up sounded a lot like a confession," Donnally said. "And lawyers like you are experts at fudging up witnesses to say what you want."

"I had a court appearance in Monterey and stayed overnight. I hung out with the lawyer who brought me into the case until about 1 A.M., then went back to the hotel." Galen glanced at Navarro. "The desk clerk will remember me calling at about three because the people in the next room were making too much noise." He looked at Donnally. "The press said that you got the call at four and it's a two-hour drive."

"Which hotel?" Navarro asked.

"The Intercontinental. I don't remember the clerk's name, but he was a chubby Hispanic wearing rimless glasses."

Navarro rose and walked from the office.

Donnally tilted his head toward the bathroom. "Then why that?"

"Because . . ." Galen hesitated.

Donnally could tell Galen had just realized that it had been his mind racing toward a conclusion that had sickened him. If Donnally knew about Hamlin's extortion, he must've known where Galen got the money to pay it.

"Because you dipped into your trust account again?"

Even as he said the words, Donnally realized he'd made a mistake. He might have given Galen an explanation for the source of the money that couldn't hurt him any more than he was already going to get hurt.

Galen looked down and nodded. He looked up again and opened his mouth to speak—

Donnally cut him off. "Be careful what you say. We'll be checking your answer."

And the answer as to whether the money came from his trust account would show up in his bank records.

Galen leaned back in his chair, closed his eyes, and interlaced his fingers on top of his head.

He looked to Donnally like a defendant who shows up in court all geared up for trial, who'd fantasized for months about how the case would go, even convincing himself that despite the fingerprints and the DNA and the eyewitnesses, the DA couldn't prove his case—then just before the jury is seated his attorney comes to him with a deal offered by the prosecutor to make the case go away, and tells him he'd better cut his losses and take it. He's got only minutes to make a decision. And even though there's only the two of them in the interview room, it's like the whole world is watching—

"I need to think," Galen said.

"No," Donnally said, "you need to talk."

Galen lowered his hands and opened his eyes.

"I can handle a bar suspension, but not a felony," Galen said. He pointed at the chair in which Navarro had been sitting. "Will he cut a deal?"

"It won't be up to him, but to Hannah Goldhagen."

"Then I'm screwed. She hates me. Really, really hates me, almost as much as she hated Mark. She won't do it."

"Maybe she won't have to know it's you until after she makes the decision."

"Who'll pitch it to her?" He glanced toward Navarro returning to his seat. "You or him?"

"Me," Donnally said. "But not yet. I need to know how many felonies you expect to walk on and what we get in return. We have a homicide to solve."

Galen paused. "I'll tell you one thing now because I need the credit. The rest you'll have to wait for until I get a pass from Goldhagen."

"Is this one worth much?" Donnally asked.

"It's huge. I mean really huge."

"Galen was right," Navarro said as they sat in the office of the A&B Gas Mart on International Boulevard in East Oakland near the Sixty-fifth Avenue housing project.

Donnally remembered when the name of the wide commercial street had been changed from East Fourteenth Street. It had been done at the same time and for the same reason that garbage collection had been renamed waste management and budget cuts were called revenue recapture—and nobody had been fooled. There weren't fewer drug dealers on the side streets, hookers walking the sidewalks, or murderers hanging out on the corners and along the storefronts because the four lanes of litter-strewn blacktop had been relabeled based on some bureaucrat's melting pot fantasy.

It sometimes seemed to Donnally that more than the taquerias and Vietnamese noodle shops and Arab markets, what made the boulevard international was the same thing that made it territorial: the gangs that controlled it from Lake Merritt downtown all the way to the southern city limit. The Mexican Norteños, Sureños, and Border

Brothers; the Asian Bui Doi, V-Boyz, and Sons of Death; and the Salvadoran M–13.

Despite the name change, the street remained not merely mean, but wounded, like a victim of Tink Fischer's fight-mangled pit bull.

Donnally and Navarro were peering at a monitor displaying a soundless month-old video showing the market's gas pump islands and the front of Burger's Motorcycle Repair across the street. They'd just watched Mark Hamlin pull to a stop under a streetlight in his Porsche and knock on the door an hour before a homicide had been reported to 911 by the admitted killer, David Burger.

On the drive over, Navarro had relayed to Donnally what he'd learned from Oakland homicide. Burger and the victim, Ed Sanders, operated both the garage on International Boulevard and a meth lab in the Central Valley, but they'd had a falling out. Burger had claimed in his statement to the police that Sanders had come at him with a lug wrench. Burger had punched Sanders and he'd fallen back, hitting his head on a metalworking lathe.

Donnally and Navarro were only able to recognize Hamlin in the grainy video because Sheldon Galen told them what to look for and when to look for it. Navarro hadn't asked the Oakland Police Department to review their copy of the recording for fear they'd study it more closely and figure out why he wanted it. Neither Navarro nor Donnally wanted to risk losing control of the investigation.

They watched the front door to the garage open from the inside. A white male stuck his head out and glanced up and down the sidewalk, then stepped back into the shadow to let Hamlin in.

"That's Burger," Navarro said.

A homeless man pushing a grocery cart came into the frame a couple of minutes later. He peered into Hamlin's car and tried the passenger door handle. He then reached in among the cans and bottles in the cart, pulled out a brick, glanced around, and smashed the window. He yanked out what looked like a laptop case, hid it in the cart, and disappeared from view.

"Didn't the car alarm go off?" Navarro said.

The garage door opened. Hamlin came running out. He stared at the broken glass, then his head swiveled as he surveyed the street for someone running away. He started in the direction the homeless man had gone, then stopped and turned back and ran the other way.

"Something must have caught his attention," Donnally said. "Maybe the guy had a crime partner, a decoy to lead Hamlin in the wrong direction."

Donnally realized he hadn't seen a laptop or tablet in Hamlin's car, apartment, or office. This burglary must be the reason. He stopped the recorder, skimmed back to where the burglar was facing the camera, then walked to the front counter and returned with the owner.

"You recognize that guy?" Donnally asked.

The owner squinted at the figure, then said in a heavy Indian accent, "I am thinking he is coming by here often. A very smelly man." He pointed north. "He is always going to the recycling center with cans and bottles."

"You know his name?"

"No idea." The owner then straightened up and returned to the front counter.

Donnally started the video again. A minute later Hamlin reappeared. He opened the passenger door and pulled out his briefcase, apparently to keep someone else from stealing it. He glanced over as two motorcycles passed by, the riders wearing black leather vests and Nazi-like helmets, then went back into the garage. He left again a half hour later.

Two patrol cars arrived thirty minutes after Hamlin drove away. Burger opened the door and spoke with the officers. The officers gestured him outside, patted him down and handcuffed him, and then one of the two officers walked inside.

"Galen was right so far," Donnally said. He turned to Navarro. "Can you confirm real quick that Hamlin didn't report the car burglary?"

Navarro called the Oakland Police Department records section and asked whether a Mark Hamlin had ever reported his car burglarized in the city.

"Galen was right about that, too," Navarro said, after he disconnected. "He didn't report the break-in."

Donnally thought for a moment.

"The victim's family may have seen something in the condition of the garage that led them to believe Hamlin helped stage the scene to make it look like self-defense. Hamlin and Burger could've moved things around—chairs, tables, maybe even the lathe—to make sure all the blood spatter was in the right places. Who knows what else they could've done."

"And when they couldn't get to Burger in the county jail," Navarro said, "they went after Hamlin."

Navarro's cell phone rang. He listened for a few seconds, then said to Donnally, "You were right about putting a tail on Galen. He just let himself into Hamlin's place through the back door."

CHAPTER 22 ═══════════════

Galen was sitting on the living room couch hand-cuffed and guarded by uniformed officers when Donnally and Navarro walked into Hamlin's apartment forty minutes later. They passed by without speaking to him on their way to the stairs to the second floor bedroom, where he'd been captured by the surveillance team. One of the undercover officers stood next to the bed, now propped against the wall, and pointed down at a large screwdriver lying next to a pried-up floorboard.

"This is how it was when I walked in," the officer said. "Good thing he didn't try to shoot his way out."

Donnally kneeled down and peered into the opening in the floor. A .38 Special revolver lay on top of a stuffed lunch-sized paper bag. He looked up at the officer. "Was he putting these in or taking them out?"

"I don't know whether he was stealing or planting and I didn't know enough about where things stand legally with him to read him his rights and start asking him questions. I searched him. He didn't have anything on him he shouldn't have had. Keys and wallet and change."

Donnally rose and said to Navarro, "Let's see what he has to say before we monkey with this stuff."

They returned downstairs, and Navarro sent the uniformed officer to the front landing. Donnally and Navarro pulled chairs up to the couch and faced Galen, perched on the front edge of the cushion, hands still cuffed behind him.

"Aren't you supposed to be protesting the handcuffs?" Donnally said. "You had a key to this place. That alone suggests that Hamlin gave you permission to be here, so it's probably not trespassing or burglary." He glanced at Navarro. "Malicious mischief for damaging the floor?"

Navarro made a show of considering the possibility by closing one eye and staring up at the ceiling, then he looked down, shaking his head. "That would probably require Hamlin's testimony saying that he didn't okay it, and Hamlin is remaining silent."

Donnally snapped his fingers. "I've got it. Destroying evidence."

Galen swallowed.

"But evidence of what?" Navarro asked Donnally, but his target was Galen. "Something this guy did or something Hamlin did?"

"I wasn't destroying evidence," Galen said. "Or at least that wasn't the point of it." He swallowed again. "I just wanted to get my money back before I lost my license to practice. I've got a mortgage and car payments."

"How did you know it would be there?"

"Because I brought ten grand to Mark here three days ago. He took the money and walked upstairs and came back down without it. I knew about his hiding place. I guessed it was in there."

"So basically," Navarro said, "it's evidence of two crimes. You stealing from your trust account and Hamlin extorting from you."

Galen stared down at his feet.

"What about the gun?" Donnally asked. "That evidence, too?"

"I've never seen that one before. He had a 9mm semiautomatic in a drawer next to his bed."

Donnally looked over at Navarro, his raised eyebrows asking whether one had been discovered during the search of the apartment on the morning Hamlin's body was discovered.

"We didn't find it," Navarro said.

Donnally rose. "Time to go look in the bag."

He didn't want to put himself in the chain of evidence and risk complicating the case later, so he asked the surveillance officer to handle it.

The officer slipped on latex gloves and removed the revolver, then the paper bag, setting both on Hamlin's dresser. He separated the top of the bag, and gripping the edges, pulled out four stacks of twenty-dollar bills, and lined them up. It looked to Donnally like a total of about forty thousand dollars. He took a photo of the bills with his cell phone and checked the nightstand and confirmed the gun was missing. He returned downstairs.

"In what denominations was the money you gave Mark?" Donnally asked, remembering that Galen's fingerprints had been on a hundred-dollar bill.

"Hundreds. All hundreds."

Donnally showed the photo to Navarro, and then to Galen. "What's wrong with this picture?"

Galen's eyes widened at the sight of the twenties, then he looked at Donnally, "Maybe he . . ."

"Went to the bank and traded them in?" Donnally gave him a stern, parental stare. "You don't believe that."

Galen shrugged.

"Where do you think this money came from?"

"I don't have a clue."

Donnally pointed toward Galen's back, and Navarro removed the handcuffs. There was nothing they could charge him with, yet.

Galen didn't make a move to rise, acknowledging they weren't done with him.

"You're back to zero," Donnally said. "You got credit for giving us the lead to the Sanders homicide, but lost it by coming in here."

"I'll try to do better," Galen said. "Next time . . ." He ended the sentence with a sigh.

Donnally heard an echo in the trailing phrase, "Next time . . ."

He pointed down at Galen. "If you want to tell me something, just call. Don't slash my tire and leave a note on my windshield."

CHAPTER 23

Donnally went alone to try to interview David Burger at the Alameda County jail, a block of brown cement along the freeway near downtown Oakland. He hoped to ascertain whether there was a connection between Hamlin's murder and his visit to the garage crime scene.

On the one hand, he recognized it could be argued that with Hamlin dead, Burger was unrepresented, so there was no bar to law enforcement contacting him.

On the other hand, it was too much of a gray area to risk involving Detective Navarro, and he figured that his going in as a special master might make the contact light enough gray that he wouldn't get too much grief from a judge later.

Burger was already sitting at the table in the interview room by the time Donnally cleared security.

Mid-forties. Mid-height. Mid-weight. Mid-smirk.

Burger folded his tattooed arms across his chest after Donnally sat down, and said, "Special master, huh?" It was as if he'd singsonged the words "birthday boy." "Make you feel important?"

"It wasn't a job I wanted."

"What's it got to do with me? I didn't kill him." He spread his hands to encompass the jail. "I've got the best alibi anybody can have. Nobody's ever escaped from this place. And if I had, I wouldn't have broken back inside. I'd be in the wind."

"It's not about you, directly. It's about Sanders's people. I was told by an attorney who was close to Hamlin that they were threatening him."

"They been threatening me, too. Don't mean nothing. They'll get over it."

"But why Hamlin? They think he tampered with the crime scene?"

Burger forced a smile. "How could he have done that? Far as I know, him and his private investigator didn't get in there until two days after the cops cleared out."

"Which private investigator?"

"Dan something or Van something. I'm not sure. He's from SF. Has an office downtown."

"What did Hamlin do in there?"

"Took some photos and measurements, investigation shit like that."

"No." Donnally leaned forward and rested his forearms on the table. "I don't mean then. I mean after you killed Sanders and before you called the police."

Donnally watched Burger's body tense, but his eyes showed no change.

"I don't know what you're talking about."

"I saw the surveillance tape from the gas station across the street. Shows everything."

"Hamlin didn't touch nothing. Sanders was

tweaking and came at me with a wrench. One punch, that's all I hit him with. No reason to screw with anything."

"Then what was Hamlin doing in there?"

"We was talking. I needed to know whether to turn myself in or try to . . . uh . . ."

"Try to pin it on somebody else?"

"No need to go that way," Burger said. "Hamlin figured I could beat the case. I'd just have to do some pretrial time in here 'cause bail would be set too high for me to make. But not too much time. We figured on not waiving my speedy trial rights. We were gonna just jam the case and get it over in a couple of months."

"Then why didn't Hamlin wait for the police?"

"He thought it would look bad in the press. Me calling him first, instead of 911." Burger grinned. "Him and me are notorious guys."

Donnally decided he'd gotten as much as he was going to get and that he'd keep the door open for a return visit by not challenging Burger with the obvious. Maybe Sanders had still been alive and a quick call to 911 could've saved him. But instead of doing that, Burger had called his lawyer.

Donnally buzzed for the jailer, who escorted him back to the lobby. He called Navarro as he was heading toward the Bay Bridge.

"Stay on that side," Navarro said. "Meet me out at the Sixty-fifth Avenue Village. I've got a lead on Sanders's wife and brother."

Donnally made a U-turn through the toll plaza parking lot and headed east, first along the port and then out to the flatland avenues. He parked his truck in the housing project visitors' area and then waited for Navarro, who pulled up ten minutes later. After Donnally got into Navarro's car, they headed farther east.

When they neared the Seventies, Donnally said, "This was Freeman's old turf, wasn't it?"

Donnally could still remember the flash and swagger of the now-deceased Randy Freeman, a legendary East Oakland drug dealer. His name had come up in a homicide Donnally had worked on early in his career, but Freeman was insulated from the heat because the lieutenant who handled the contract had been snuffed out in retaliation a day afterward. Donnally last saw Freeman coming out of Esther's Orbit Room in what was called Harlem West when Basie and Coltrane played there, but became Ghost Town when players like Freeman showed up. He was climbing into a black Range Rover with gold rims and Vogue tires and bullet-proof glass, N.W.A.'s "Fuck tha Police" throbbing the sheet metal and blasting louder than the BART train passing on the tracks above. Freeman was later convicted in federal court of racketeering. Eleven months into his fifteen-year sentence, he decided to try to work off some time by rolling on his lawyers.

Donnally remembered all this now because one of those lawyers was Mark Hamlin.

Freeman contacted the U.S. Attorney who had prosecuted him and told him that despite a court order freezing all his assets, he'd paid Hamlin's fee in the form of a 1956 Mercedes Gullwing. Freeman later testified that a week after the order was issued, his father-in-law had taken Hamlin to where the car was hidden in the Central Valley and gave him the keys. The U.S. Attorney produced a catalog displaying the car up for auction at the Dubai Classic Car Show three years after Freeman's conviction, its sales history made untraceable by a series of offshore transactions.

The case became a credibility contest, and the weight of Freeman and his father-in-law's felony histories tipped the scale in Hamlin's favor. No one in the legal community knew whether Hamlin did it, but most agreed it was the kind of thing he would do if he had the chance. In the end, and as always, the hearings were less about facts of what happened and more about evidence and the rules of evidence, and about what would stand up on appeal.

Freeman was murdered six months after he finished his federal prison sentence and returned to Oakland. He fell to the sidewalk below the bulletproof driver's side window of his Range Rover that had been hidden in storage while he served his sentence. For a couple of years afterward, any dope dealer shot down because he'd left himself vulnerable on the street was referred to as being on the wrong side of the glass.

Navarro pointed toward Discount Liquors as they passed Seventy-ninth Avenue.

"He got it right there," Navarro said. "Turns out the drug dealers running East Oakland when he got out of the joint hadn't learned to respect their elders. The turf was theirs and they weren't about to give it back to an old man."

Drug dealers aged like professional athletes. Forty-five years old was ancient.

Navarro turned off International Boulevard onto the rutted Eighty-third Avenue, more of an alley than a street, then drove past ratty-clapboard and cracked-stucco houses for two blocks before pulling to a stop over an oil-slicked patch of pavement.

A generic, tattooed biker type was reclining in a ripped Barcalounger and drinking a beer on the porch of the gray bungalow where the murdered Ed Sanders had lived. An early 1970s Ford truck sat on blocks in the driveway next to a 1990s Chevy Camaro. A black Harley-Davidson stood on the hard-packed dirt yard.

The biker watched Donnally and Navarro walking across the street toward the house, and then reached back and rapped on the window. A woman appeared in the doorway as they climbed the steps.

Donnally expected her to be a biker chick with a meth-lined face, scraggly hair, skinny as an axel. Instead, she looked like a Home Depot checker, wearing jeans and a Pendleton work shirt.

"Can I help you?" she asked.

Navarro displayed his badge. "I'm trying to get in contact with Gloria Sanders."

"That's me, but why SFPD?"

"Can we talk inside?" Donnally said.

She glanced at the man on the porch, then said, "Okay."

The biker followed them in, but remained standing just inside the front door as they sat down, Donnally and Gloria on the couch, Navarro in a chair. Donnally had the feeling that while they'd be directing questions to her, they'd be getting answers, if any were forthcoming, from him.

"That's my brother," Gloria said, pointing at him. "People call him Tub, for Tubby." She smiled. "He used to be fat."

From the looks of his loose skin, Donnally figured he'd gone on a crystal meth diet and had shed the pounds fast. One of the risks of the drug trade was using your own product. The other one had been exemplified by the bullet-ridden body of Randy Freeman that had lain on a sidewalk a few blocks away.

"We're looking into some threats that were made against Mark Hamlin," Navarro said. "The attorney who was representing David Burger."

Gloria winced at the name as though Donnally had poked at a fresh wound, then said, "I didn't threaten anybody."

"Somebody did."

Gloria's eyes darted toward Tub, then back.

"Maybe because they think he tampered with the crime scene to make it look like self-defense," Donnally said.

Her eyes darted again.

Tub spoke. "We know Hamlin was in there. Knew it from day one. Couple of people we know in the East Bay Devils Motorcycle Club rode by and saw him going in a while before Burger called the cops."

"Who were they?" Donnally asked.

Tub shrugged. "It don't make no difference. They saw what they saw."

Donnally recognized he'd never get the names, at least from Tub, so he moved on.

"You threaten Hamlin?" Donnally asked.

Tub thought for a moment. "If I deny it and you can prove it, it'll look like I killed him. And I didn't." He looked down at his sister. "And nobody connected with us did him in either. If we had, you'd of never found his body. We just made some calls to him."

"Calls about what?"

"What Hamlin was doing in there. We wanted it back."

"Meth? He took meth out of the place before the cops showed up?"

"No, man." Tub looked back and forth between Donnally and Navarro like they were passengers who'd somehow gotten onto the wrong plane. "My brother-in-law's share of the forty grand him and Burger got for the meth they sold to the Norteños the day before."

CHAPTER 24

The son of a bitch went in there to collect his fee before they called the police."

Donnally had left it up to Navarro to tell the tale to District Attorney Hannah Goldhagen the next morning in her Hall of Justice office. His face was twisted with anger by the time he'd reached the punch line.

"The question," Donnally said, "is whether Galen knew about it and went after money that no one would miss or that no one could ever talk about. Burger couldn't complain without having to explain where the money came from. And Takiyah Jackson said she didn't know about it. She didn't even know Hamlin had a stash at home."

"Do you believe her?" Goldhagen asked.

Donnally nodded. "She's the one that sort of put us on this trail."

"And Sanders's wife and brother, are they still suspects?"

"Barely," Navarro said. "Killing Hamlin was the one sure way they'd never get the money back."

"Unless the homicide was just an interrogation gone wrong," Goldhagen said.

"Except that the autopsy doesn't support that,"

Navarro said. "No injuries consistent with having been hit or beaten. I looked at Tub's rap sheet. He's the kind of guy who'd have done lots of bone breaking if he was trying to get something. Why take the risk of strangling Hamlin to death when a couple of broken fingers or a slice across the chest would've gotten him the information he wanted?"

Goldhagen smirked. "Or maybe shocked him with a Harley-Davidson battery to get it?"

"Or shocked him with any kind of battery. He's the kind of guy who'd want to see blood."

She paused and tapped the desk, and then looked at Donnally.

"Then your recommendation is we draft some kind of cooperation agreement with Galen."

"'Some kind' are the operative words since the information he provides will be filtered through a third party, which is me. So the execution of the agreement wouldn't be directly between him and your office."

"And the next step would be that you start going through Hamlin's case files with Galen and see what he has to say about them."

"And with Jackson."

"Do we need a cooperation agreement with her?"

"That would only scare her off. She'd never want to see herself as a snitch."

Goldhagen smiled again. "And Galen would?"

"He'll find a way to justify it," Donnally said. "After all, he was the extortion victim, right?"

"But only because he chose to become an embezzler."

"And an embezzler only because he got caught. Bottom line is he's a snake. I called the court on the way over here. Galen notified the clerk's office

A Criminal Defense   137

within five hours after Hamlin's body was discovered that he was substituting in on the Burger case."

Goldhagen smirked. "That ain't gonna happen."

"Maybe it has to. Things have got to seem normal while he cooperates, otherwise people will start asking questions."

Goldhagen sighed and dropped her head.

"How will that look when the truth comes out? The DA's office has a hammer over the defense attorney and the defendant doesn't know it." She looked up. "How many constitutional violations is that? Let me count the ways." She paused and bit her lip. "Can't do it. You'll be heading back up to pine tree country when this is over to flip flapjacks and I'll be up for reelection. I can't win with the California Supreme Court tap-dancing on my head."

Donnally couldn't argue against her. She was right. It was only because of Galen they'd discovered facts about the case that could provide a motive for the homicide. The theory would be that Burger killed Sanders not in self-defense, or even in a heat of passion, but because he wanted both shares of the dope money. A self-defense, or at worst a manslaughter, would turn into a capital murder—just . . . like . . . that.

Navarro stirred in his chair.

Goldhagen cast Navarro a hard look. "Don't even think it. No cluing in Oakland homicide or the Alameda County DA's office about Hamlin going in there or about the money. Short-term, it would help their case, but long-term, whatever conviction comes out of it would be overturned."

"That's only if the defense ever finds out how we got the information," Navarro said. "OPD has got an anonymous tip line and there are a few pay phones still around."

"I'm not going to be blackmailed by Galen for the rest of my career. He'll be able to figure out what happened."

Navarro shrugged his consent to remain silent.

"I'll draft the cooperation agreement," Goldhagen said, "and run it by Judge McMullin. In the meantime, you two need to divide up the labor"—she nodded toward Navarro—"so Ramon doesn't end up in the middle of attorney-client issues again."

"I'll be working on Hamlin's cell phone records," Navarro said, "and trying to re-create his movements during the days before he was killed. I'll pass on what I find."

"And the gun?"

"That, too. I'm sure it wasn't there for self-defense. Otherwise it would've been within easy reach like the 9mm he was supposed to have had in his nightstand, instead of hidden under a floorboard."

None of them said the words, but all were wondering whether the gun, like the forty thousand dollars, had also been removed from a crime scene, not for direct profit, but to conceal evidence in order to help a client beat a case.

"Maybe you better let Harlan do that," Goldhagen said. "Or at least bail out if it starts heading in a hinky direction."

She looked at Donnally.

"I'll start going through his client files," Donnally said. "I can justify doing it now. With the Burger case and what Galen knows, it won't look like a fishing expedition when the defense bar finds out about it later."

CHAPTER 25

Donnally sat back in his chair in the conference room in Hamlin's office and examined Takiyah Jackson typing on her laptop. They'd spent the day matching Hamlin's calendar for the last two months with his files, determining which clients had hired him, what work he'd done on the cases, and what appearances he'd made—and Donnally had been astounded to see that Hamlin had done very little preparation on any of the cases.

The briefs Hamlin had filed were boilerplate, cut-and-paste motions for discovery, motions to disclose informants, motions to retest forensic evidence. There wasn't one that couldn't have been prepared by a paralegal. Just insert the defendant's name and a paragraph outlining the facts of the case and press "print."

Hamlin had hired private investigators, but only to do basic work like taking photos and measurements at crime scenes, performing court research on prosecution witnesses, serving subpoenas for records. Nothing that an intern couldn't have done.

Jackson printed out the list of private investigators Hamlin used and the cases they'd worked on.

Donnally skimmed down the list. He recognized a few names from the old days and blew out a breath, not liking what he saw.

She caught the meaning in the gesture and said, "None of the legit investigators would work for him, so he was limited to the desperate, and therefore flexible, and the already twisted."

Donnally noticed some of them were paired up and said, "I don't understand why Mark would use two different ones on the same case."

"Sometimes so that the left hand, so to speak, wouldn't know what the right hand is doing. Say Mark needed an investigator to get on the stand to testify about one thing, even if the DA got into other parts of the case, the investigator wouldn't know anything about them." She pointed to her right. "Like he sends one guy to take photos of the scene"—she pointed left with her other hand—"then sends another to try to talk to the victim. Victim later complains to the DA about being harassed, the first investigator doesn't know anything and the DA can't question him about it when he testifies about the photos he took. He wasn't there. And the DA isn't allowed to call a defense investigator as a witness all on his own."

Jackson nodded toward the list.

"Most of those investigators would probably have trouble finding their shoes in the morning. Mark just liked having a posse and would get the client to pay for it. Soon as the client agreed to Mark's fee for coming into a case, usually about twenty-five grand, he'd hit him up for five for investigation. Always.

Whether there was anything to investigate or not. Then he'd hire one of these guys to do gopher stuff. It built up loyalty. Lots and lots."

"Loyalty for what?"

"When he needed to . . . uh . . ."

"Push the limits?"

Jackson hesitated, then gave in and nodded. He took it as an opening to try to move her a little farther around the barricade of her resistance.

"How'd you feel about that?"

Another hesitation, and then, "Sometimes it seemed like a war."

"And all is fair in war?"

Jackson looked at him dead on. "You know what happened to me, right? I figure you took the time to check me out."

Donnally nodded.

"The cop who shot Bumper in the back while he was sleeping left SFPD and went to work for the Orange County Sheriff's Department. He ended his career down there twenty years later as a captain." Her voice hardened like a hammer. "A cold-blooded killer. A fucking executioner. He should've spent the rest of his life in prison, instead he's spending his retirement years getting a tan and playing golf in Palm Desert."

Jackson fell silent. Her eyes moved back and forth like she was watching an internal movie. It seemed to Donnally like she was looking for a scene to describe the cop, one that captured, or maybe justified, Hamlin's acts of war against law enforcement.

Finally, she spoke. "How many street dope cases

do you think are righteous? I've been around. I lived in the Pink Palace before we moved across the bay to Oakland. You been out there."

The Pink Palace was an eleven-story public housing project just a few blocks from City Hall, named for its paint color. It was also known as the Den of Thieves. The day came when it became so dangerous even the homeless refused to accept free apartments there and it was closed down.

"Those dropsy cases," Jackson continued. "Cop testifying that he was driving along and the drug dealer spotted him, then dropped the dope and ran." Jackson spread her hands and her voice rose. "Who but a fucking racist judge is gonna believe that shit? Drop the dope and *then* run away? Not run first? Not duck behind a car or a bush or the fattest guy on the block and dump the dope where the cop can't see?"

Donnally knew she was right, that's why he'd refused an assignment to the street drug task force and later to the vice detail. Either he would've had to lie to make enough cases to achieve the body count the chief wanted or lie to cover other officers so they could achieve theirs.

It just hadn't crossed his mind until now that the perjury of drug cops had become a recruiting mechanism for people like Jackson to sign on to the agenda of corrupt lawyers like Hamlin.

The truth—that Donnally knew, that she knew, that every cop in the city knew—was that the task force officers would just sweep into the projects and round people up and search them and the area. If the cop found dope on somebody, he'd falsely testify he'd seen the dealer drop it. If the cop found it in a wheel well or in a bush or in a fence board knothole, he'd look for the guy with the worst attitude or who was already on probation or parole, and lay it on him.

Donnally thought back on his conversation with Janie at the kitchen table and understood that while his father's lies had driven him toward a uniform and a badge in search of the truth, Jackson's past had driven her toward a life beyond truth and lies.

"You're right," Donnally said. "But I suspect the private investigators Hamlin hired weren't like you, hadn't had your experiences, weren't from the street. I'll bet they're all college grads who never stepped into a housing project until they got paid to."

Donnally pointed up at the courtroom sketch in the Demetrio Arellano case, the one showing Hamlin looking at his watch. It was the case in which the private investigator working for Hamlin had left a threatening message for the main prosecution witness, who then fled to El Salvador.

"Is that what you mean by pushing the limits?" Donnally said.

Jackson cringed and lowered her head.

Donnally pushed on. "I don't understand how your moral outrage at the stuff that happened to you, and at the things you've seen in your life, transformed into a way of looking at the world that allowed you to work for Hamlin."

Donnally watched her taking long breaths, not looking up. He wondered whether he'd jammed her too hard and too fast. After half a minute, she spoke.

"I don't know." She looked up. "It wasn't about

the money for me. Not like it was for his PIs. Money bought them. They pretended they were in it for the cause, but they were no more than lab rats, conditioned to do tricks for the pellets. For me . . ." Her voice faded. After a moment, she made another attempt. "For me, I guess, he was the only game in town."

"Where else did you try?"

"The police review commission. I worked there for two years." Her voice ratcheted up again. "What a bunch of incompetent assholes. They were all in it for the swagger. Didn't do shit. The same rotten cops kept coming through over and over, but nothing ever happened to them. They beat people. Lied about them. Never got fired. Hardly ever even got suspended."

Jackson paused and her vision clouded. Another trip back into the past.

"Then one day in a preliminary hearing in a dope case, I watched Mark nail one of the worst of those cops." She blinked and focused on Donnally. "Ripped him a new one. Did more in ten minutes than the commission did in a generation. The cop resigned that same day, afraid to ever testify in court again. I walked in here the next morning and asked Mark for a job."

"I'm not sure that answers my question."

"And I'm not sure I can answer it. All I know is everything looks different now that Mark is dead." Jackson pressed her lips together, then lowered her gaze. "For some reason I keep thinking about Jonestown. My uncle committed suicide with the rest of them down there." She looked again at Donnally, but her eyes seemed dulled by a terror that had turned inward. "People who stayed up here and survived told me after Jim Jones died it was like they all woke up and saw what insanity it had been all along."

"Got a lead for you," Navarro told Donnally over the telephone just after he'd returned to Hamlin's desk. "A court clerk just called me. A couple of months ago, one of the victims in a case confronted Hamlin outside of court after a not guilty verdict. Threatened to kill him. Wasn't the kind of thing she'd ever seen happen before. Victims break down and cry in their seats when the crook goes free, they don't run to the hallway to issue threats. It was *People v. Thule.* Got lots of local press coverage."

Donnally located the case on his list, found the closed file in a cabinet in the conference room, and brought it back into the office. According to the SFPD summary sheet, Thule was a mall owner who hired Gordon & Sons Construction to replace a steel pedestrian bridge from the second floor of a parking garage to the shopping area. The structure collapsed a year later, on the day before Easter, killing two shoppers, one of whom was pregnant, and injuring four others. The cause of the collapse was faulty Chinese steel used by the construction company.

John Gordon told the police and OSHA, and

testified at the grand jury, that Thule had directed him to purchase all the steel from a particular U.S. importer. He produced letters to support his claim. The defendant, Thule, refused all law enforcement interviews and pled the Fifth at the grand jury.

The DA charged Thule with three counts of manslaughter for the two adult victims and the fetus.

Donnally found two private investigators' invoices in the file. One did all but one interview. That one was done by Frank Lange, among the most well-known private investigators in the city. He was one of a very few that politicians, business leaders, and the wealthy hired when the truth was against them. Donnally had never seen him and had no reason to pay attention to him during his cop years since Lange had never been hired to work on the defense side of any of Donnally's cases.

According to news clippings in the file, Lange had testified in Thule's trial that he'd confronted Gordon with what Lange claimed were the true versions of the same letters, ones from Thule, not directing the contractor to buy the Chinese steel, but warning him against using it. Lange also testified that faced with this evidence, Gordon had admitted forging the ones that allegedly incriminated Thule.

Interviews of the jurors after the trial showed three of the jurors believed Lange, and those three convinced the rest that Lange's testimony provided sufficient reasonable doubt for a not guilty verdict.

Donnally placed the investigators' invoices side by side on the desk blotter.

The investigator who did most of the work charged a hundred dollars an hour and billed a total of twelve thousand dollars.

Lange billed at a flat rate of fifteen thousand dollars—for one interview and one hour of testimony.

Donnally called Jackson into the office to ask her about the connection between Lange and Hamlin.

"Mark and Lange go way back," Jackson said. "They started out at about the same time. I guess you could say that they grew up together in the business. Because of how much Frank charges, for the last ten years Mark only used him for the make-or-break interviews."

"Like the Thule case."

Jackson nodded. "He specializes in impeaching witnesses and victims, and jurors love him. Maybe because he seems like an ordinary guy, one of them. Somebody you'd go to have pizza with and complain to about your wife. I went to watch him a couple of times. Comes across kinda mousy. Yes-sirring and no-sirring the DA and the judge. The prosecutor gets aggressive with him and the jurors feel like they're under attack, too. But when he got back here after testifying in court, he wasn't that way at all. They'd come in swaggering and hoot it up like they'd bluffed their way to winning the World Series of Poker. High-fiving like juveniles."

"You ever see any proof he perjured himself?"

Jackson smiled and gazed at Donnally as though at a child who'd selected the correct square peg, but couldn't quite fit it into the hole.

"I can see you don't get it yet," Jackson said.

"Around here there was no such thing as proof, no such thing as facts. There were only differing opinions. That was the fundamental principle of life in this office. It could've been etched in wood and nailed above the door. 'Abandon Truth All Ye Who Enter Here.'"

"Which means you never checked."

"There was never anything to check. What was I going to check it against? I wasn't there when the crime was committed or when the witness or victim said what they said. No way for me to know what really happened."

To Donnally she sounded like too many of the cops he'd served with. Whenever internal affairs accused an officer of beating a suspect—even when the officer's baton was painted with blood and the suspect was lying in intensive care—nearly every officer in the department would go coward and say the same thing: "I don't know. I wasn't there."

But that didn't prevent those same officers from arresting burglars when they didn't witness the burglary, or murderers when they didn't witness the murder, or child molesters even when the molestation took place a generation earlier in a school classroom or in a priest's office of a church that had long since been torn down.

It reminded Donnally of a history professor he had at UCLA, an old guy who claimed that since history is just a form of memory and had to be expressed in words whose meanings change over time, there was no such thing as historical truth.

Donnally had liked the professor, had even been invited to his house for dinner, but was glad the man had decided to become a teacher rather than a doer—or a filmmaker like his father, a man who'd combined French cinematic theory with American war movies to create an Academy Award–winning career of mindless violence and historical mythology.

One idea Donnally took with him from college when he moved up to San Francisco was that an offense report was a kind of history that was either as true as the Holocaust or as false as one of his father's movies. And he swore his would always be the former, even if some of those around him specialized in the latter.

Donnally rose from his chair. "I'm going to do my best to find out what the truth is."

Jackson stared at him for a moment, then said, "Take your best shot."

Donnally recognized the sarcasm in her voice, but also heard an undertone of longing, suggesting she meant it.

He walked with Jackson to the outer office, then drove south toward the Gordon & Sons headquarters near the San Francisco International Airport.

The ride down Highway 101, called the Central Freeway where it wasn't central, the Bayshore Freeway long before it came close to the bay, and the James Lick when people weren't sure what to call it, was less like driving than being swept along. Maybe it was because the freeway was a gateway from the constraints of the city to the liberation of possibility. A hop over the hills, a skip along San Francisco Bay, and then a launch from the San Francisco Airport into the sky.

Donnally felt the surge of motion on takeoff like

everyone else, but didn't like the feeling of being wrenched from the earth. He'd fly places if he had to, but preferred having his tires on the ground and the steering wheel in his grip and the speedometer arrow fixed at a speed that kept him in control.

As he transitioned from the freeway to the frontage road just north of the airport, he knew the chances were small that John Gordon would talk to him. The judge had suspended the victims' civil suit against Gordon and Thule until the criminal trial was over since the defendants had Fifth Amendment rights. It was as though the judge had said to Gordon, *You have the right to remain silent and if you're smart, you'll use it.*

Even some of the witnesses who worked for Gordon and for Thule would also have refused to testify in the civil case until they were certain the DA wouldn't expand the indictment to include them in a broader conspiracy.

Donnally pulled into a guest parking space in front of the two-story administration building. Gordon's secretary directed him out to the football field–sized yard in the back where he found Gordon talking to a hard-hatted worker. Gordon sent the young man into the warehouse, then turned toward Donnally, who concluded from Gordon's ruddy and wind-beaten face and hard eyes that he'd built the business. He was Gordon himself, the father, not one of the sons.

Donnally told him about the threats to Hamlin and asked him whether any of the victims had also threatened him.

"My lawyer's gonna shit his pants when he finds

out I talked to you," Gordon said. "But what happened, happened. I never should've used that steel. Never did before that contract and never did afterwards."

"What about that PI, Lange?"

"Sure I talked to him." Gordon jerked his thumb over his shoulder toward his office, as if to say that was where he'd been interviewed. "He's a lying son of a bitch. I told him the same thing I told everyone else. The victims knew it. They had no beef with me about that. They blamed me for the steel, but not for torpedoing the case against Thule."

The concussive engine roar from a plane rising off the airport runway vibrated the metal roof and sides of the warehouse as it skimmed the bay. Donnally waited until it faded, then asked, "Why did Thule want to use steel from that particular importer?"

"My guess? And he can sue me for saying it if he wants to, but I think it must've been some kind of kickback scheme. I paid about five hundred thousand dollars for steel that would've cost seven-fifty if it had been manufactured over here. The wholesaler could kick back a hundred to Thule and still clean up. That kind of thing happens all the time, all across the country."

Donnally knew that if Gordon had made a tape of his interview with Lange, he would have given it to the DA, so he didn't ask.

"You have any proof of a kickback?" Donnally asked.

Gordon shook his head. "These guys are smart. Maybe they did it offshore. That way there wouldn't be a paper trail."

It was clear to Donnally that Gordon had thought about pursuing that theory, maybe had even suggested it to the district attorney, but there was no way a local DA's office could pursue an international financial investigation. And with Gordon's testimony, they probably didn't think they'd need it to get a conviction. But the DA hadn't counted on Frank Lange bending the jury away from the truth.

"Aren't you going to ask me if I killed Hamlin?"

"No. You strike me as a guy who takes responsibility for what he does and lets the world go its own way."

Gordon looked out toward the bay for a moment, then said, "I'm my father's son. That's the lesson he learned in World War II and the one I learned in Vietnam." He pointed toward the warehouse and the office building. "I built a good business, but I'm not sure I've been a very good citizen."

"Like maybe you should've at least punched Hamlin out?"

Gordon nodded. "I should've done it when one of the victims was yelling at him outside of court after the verdict."

"You think that victim later did it himself, or worse?"

"Not a chance. The guy was in a wheelchair. He was never gonna walk again. No way he could've lassoed Hamlin and hung him up out there."

Gordon paused in thought and he gazed out toward the bay.

"Anyway," he finally said, moving his gaze to Donnally, "if anybody was gonna get hit, it would've been that scumbag investigator."

Hamlin's reception area seemed hushed, even kind of funereal, when Donnally walked in. For the first time he noticed the thud of his shoes and the muted squeaks of the worn wood-planked floor.

Jackson rose from her desk chair. She'd already called to warn him Hamlin's family would be coming in. She intercepted him, pointed at the inner office, and said in a low voice, "Mark's parents and sister are in there already. Matthew and Sophie and Marian, but everyone calls her Lemmie."

Donnally took in a long breath and exhaled. He had nothing good to say about Hamlin, and therefore nothing to supplement the standard condolences that were due a grieving family.

The moment he reached the door he grasped that not all the family members were grieving.

Hamlin's parents sat in chairs facing the desk.

His sister stood next to the couch, looking out the window at the brick façade of the building across the street, poised like a tourist guessing at the type of architecture or an artist deciding whether a scene is worth painting.

They all turned toward him as he crossed the threshold.

Donnally introduced himself and expressed his sympathies. He didn't want to be seen as supplanting their son and brother by sitting behind Hamlin's desk, so he pulled a chair away from a wall and placed it so it formed a semicircle with the couch and the chairs in which the parents sat. He waited until Lemmie took a seat on the couch, then sat down.

On his second look he recognized Lemmie. He'd seen her photo on the backs of best sellers that had migrated on and then off Janie's nightstand over the years. She appeared to be at least ten years younger than her brother. He didn't find it surprising that he'd run into a writer during the investigation. Writers crowded San Francisco the way actors crowded LA and painters crowded New York. He just hadn't connected the Hamlin last name from her to her brother. Maybe because she was always referred to in conversation and in the press by her first name alone.

Under Janie's prodding, he'd tried to read one of Lemmie's novels, but got through only ten or twelve pages, put off by too many adjectives and adverbs and everything being said sweetly, or intriguingly, or bewilderingly.

As he put the book down for the final time, Janie said, "Too girlie, huh?"

Donnally figured he'd be safer by answering with a shrug.

After that, Janie came to accept that Donnally was a noun-and-verb kind of guy. And that had shown in his work. When he was a patrol sergeant, he'd made an officer remove the word "brutally" from a report of a stabbing in the Pink Palace, asking if a single stab wound was brutal, what was a dismemberment or a stabbing followed by a rape?

And sitting with the parents and sister of Mark Hamlin, he found it hard to imagine that any literary flourish or device could add to the knowledge they shared about his death.

Rope.

Tied.

Hung.

Strangled.

Dead.

And, worst of all:

Erection.

"We got into town from Boston this morning to help Marian with the funeral arrangements," Matthew Hamlin said.

The family's naming scheme hit Donnally when the father said the name Marian. Matthew, Mark, and Marian.

Donnally's own father, Donald Harlan, Sr. had also imposed a naming scheme on his children. Donald, Jr. and Donnally. And it had been part of Donnally's rebellion to reverse his name, from Donnally Harlan to Harlan Donnally, in order to disguise his connection to his father.

He wondered whether Marian's adoption of the name Lemmie was part of hers.

"And to find out where you stand in the investigation," Lemmie said, leaning forward on the couch.

Lemmie sounded more like a reporter asking a

question than a mourning sister. It was the sort of
tone that can turn a family member from source of
information into a suspect, like a husband seeming
too interested in the mechanics of how his wife died
or a son too anxious for the police to take the yellow
tape off his elderly parent's front door and release
the crime scene.

"I'm afraid I can't tell you any of the details of
the investigation," Donnally said. "The court appointed me special master so that means—"

"Do you have any leads?"

Matthew glared at her. "Let the man talk."

Lemmie pulled back as though evading a punch.

Donnally was surprised by the force of the old
man's personality. He had to be in his late eighties,
an age when most parents have long since begun
deferring to their children, sometimes even their
grandchildren.

His wife looked down and twisted a tissue in her
hands.

"It's all right," Donnally said, focusing on Matthew, and feeling Lemmie's role in his mind shift
from murder suspect to domestic victim. "I understand. What happened to Mark is bad enough, it's
far worse when you don't know why or who did it."
He looked at Lemmie. "We're pursuing some information we've received." Then back toward Matthew.
"This is a complicated situation since my work may
involve attorney-client matters in the sense that—"

Now Matthew cut in. "No need to explain. I
practiced law for over fifty years, young man."

Donnally felt his face warm. He expected, or
maybe hoped, Matthew's wife would reach over and

pat his hand and say, *Now, dear*. But she didn't stir and didn't raise her head. She seemed to withdraw inside herself, and it seemed like a practiced move. He suspected he had discovered a clue about why Mark Hamlin had authority problems, seemed to view all authority as an enemy to be subverted or overcome, but his focus at the moment wasn't to solve that mystery. It was to solve another one.

"Then you'll understand why I have to be even more careful in what I say, even to family members, than I might be in another investigation."

"What assurance do we have that you're capable of this kind of investigation at all?" Matthew tilted his head toward the reception area behind him. "My son never seemed to be able to surround himself with competent people, and the press keeps hinting about some mysterious link between you and Mark."

Lemmie made a movement as if she intended to interject herself on behalf of Donnally or apologize for her father's rudeness, but then sat back, the gesture orphaned in the silent office. Donnally suspected if it hadn't been her brother's death that had brought her into this room with her parents, she might've expressed what was on her mind.

Donnally recounted his background, his single contact with Hamlin after he left police work, and how it was that he came to be chosen by Judge McMullin. He was in the odd and uncomfortable position of having to minimize his connection with their son even more than it was in order to buttress his own credibility. Lemmie's downcast eyes told him she also understood and felt the sad irony.

Matthew seized the opportunity supplied by Donnally's offering of his thumbnail biography to offer his own. Once a name partner in Boston's largest civil firm, he had represented most major U.S. airlines and pharmaceutical companies, and had served as ambassador to Ireland under Ronald Reagan. After that, he worked as an informal adviser to George H. W. Bush, and then retired from politics after the election of, in his words, "that son of a bitch Bill Clinton."

Until that moment, Donnally had assumed Lemmie had picked her parents up at the airport and had driven them to the office. He now imagined there was a limousine double-parked around the corner, and he wished they were already in it and driving away.

"When is the funeral?" Donnally asked, trying to transition the conversation toward their exit.

"We'll have a service here in a few days," Lemmie said, "then they . . . we . . . will take his body back to Boston for the burial."

Lemmie said the word "we" in a way that suggested she'd already prepared her living will and it specified that there would be no Marian next to Matthew and Mark in the family plot.

"I assume you'll have someone there to videotape the attendees," Matthew said.

Her hand shot out. "Please stop, Father. He knows how to do his job."

"I had intended to," Donnally said, "and expect to be there myself."

Donnally and Lemmie rose, and after a moment's hesitation, the parents did also.

As he walked them to the elevator, he overheard Lemmie tell her parents she had an appointment and would meet them at their hotel. From the incline of her head and the lean in her body, Donnally felt a kind of tension being broadcast toward him.

After shaking their hands, Donnally waited as the doors closed. He then stepped back and leaned against the wall. Two minutes later, the doors opened again and Lemmie stepped out.

CHAPTER 28

"Mark turned into our father," Lemmie said as they sat facing each other in a booth in the Backroom Bar on the first floor of a gray colonnaded former bank building around the corner from Hamlin's office. "Or at least his mirror image, and I hated him for it."

Lemmie took a sip from her neat double bourbon, then tilted the tumbler and rotated the bottom edge on the oak table. She worked the liquid up the side near the top, then back down again, as if tempting it to overflow. She stared at the revolving glass, upper teeth working against her lower lip.

Donnally didn't think she stopped speaking in order to elicit a response from him. It was more that she seemed to be saying that the way things stood between her and her brother were what they were, now fixed in space and time like a name etched on a marble headstone. His agreement or disagreement, approval or disapproval, was irrelevant.

"It was once both of us against Father, then sometime in the last fifteen years it became each of us in our own way against him. Mark set out to fight him on his own turf, the law, and I set out to fight him on the page."

Lemmie fell silent again, staring at her rotating glass, then furrowed her brows and looked at Donnally as though she just realized that they hadn't started the conversation at the same place and with the same knowledge.

"You know who my father is, right?"

"Only what he told me."

"How about I'll start with a prologue?"

Donnally nodded.

"He was a staff lawyer for the Senate Subcommittee on Investigations in the 1950s. Senator Joseph McCarthy's communist witch hunt. He was hired at the same time as Bobby Kennedy, but stayed on after Bobby wised up to what was going on and left."

Now Donnally recognized the name. Matt Hamlin, known in the press at the time and now in history books as Mad Matt. He'd read about him in a political science class at UCLA.

"After that blew up, my father stopped using the name Matt and only used Matthew, and always stuck in his middle name, Hutchinson, to help in the disguise. Matthew Hutchinson Hamlin."

"But your father was young in the Red Scare days, and young people get in over their heads."

"He was no younger than Bobby and Bobby knew when to get out. My father stayed and enjoyed every minute of it." Lemmie smirked. "You know why he asked you whether you'd be videotaping the memorial service?"

"I assume it's because experience suggests that

killers sometimes appear at the funerals of their victims, just like some arsonists join the crowd to watch the fires they set."

"What experience suggests has nothing to do with it. He only thought of it because if he'd been the killer, he would've shown up to enjoy his work. That's what he did in the old days. Look at the photos from when people who'd refused to testify before McCarthy's committee got arrested and perp-walked down the steps. He's always there, in the crowd watching, wearing his G-man fedora, glorying in their humiliation."

Donnally now understood why all of Lemmie's novels were about dysfunctional families and psychologically abused children, most from the perspective of bewildered little girls or alienated women. He imagined that in one or more of those books was a scene of a mother cowering under her husband's stare.

For the first time since he stood gazing at Hamlin's body, he was beginning to get a sense of what had made Mark Hamlin, Mark Hamlin.

"And you and Mark grew up identifying with the victims."

Lemmie nodded. "I think that's how Mark got into the mind-set that the cops were the real crooks." She let go of her glass and spread her hands. "Think of the people McCarthy and my father went after. Dashiell Hammett. Langston Hughes. Arthur Miller. Lee Grant. Garson Kanin. Martin Ritt. Joseph Losey. Orson Welles."

It wasn't lost on Donnally that the last four were movie directors, like his father.

Before he had a chance to comment, she flattened her palms on the table and said, "I know who you really are."

Donnally felt his body tense, not because she'd somehow figured out who his father was, but because her voice had the are-you-now-or-have-you-ever-been tone about it.

What he was, and had always been, was the son of Don Harlan. And because of his name change, she must've put some work into tracking him.

But who he was inside and separate from his role as an ex-cop and the special master in her brother's murder, she was never going to find out.

He decided to punch back. "Nothing turns a person more quickly from a witness into a suspect than them taking the time to investigate the investigator."

Lemmie smiled. "Then it looks like I've been a suspect for twenty-five years."

"How do you figure?"

"I've always been interested in what happens to the children of famous people. You've been on my radar since I saw your father's first Vietnam movie in film class in college, *Shooting the Dawn*, and found out your older brother had been killed in the war."

Donnally cringed, flashing back to himself staggering out of the movie's premiere as a young boy, as bewildered and horrified as one of Lemmie's fictional little girls.

"And I learned in the Pentagon Papers that your father himself made up the lie that had led to your brother's death."

Donnally had made the same discovery in high school. That's what prompted him to move out of the house at sixteen and to change his name at eighteen.

"Your father portrayed the Vietcong as pure evil, and the Vietnamese villagers as if they'd brought the My Lai and Korean massacres on themselves, and he portrayed every American soldier as a maniac driven to wanton violence by the enemy. If that's how he viewed your brother, I wondered how badly he twisted up his surviving kid."

Donnally didn't respond. She was right about his father, but she was only partly right about him. He'd moved up to San Francisco and became a cop as a way of untwisting himself.

"And as bent as your father was," she continued, "I couldn't figure out how you came out so straight, until today."

Donnally had no interest in heading down the road of amateur psychoanalysis; he had a professional back at his house.

"Except his last film," Lemmie said. "It was like a confession to all his past sins. I saw it in one of the art houses downtown." She smiled. "It didn't get much in the way of distribution. I doubt it played up in Mount Shasta."

When Donnally didn't engage the issue by offering a smile back, hers faded and she said, "Is that how he communicates with you, through movies?"

Donnally pursed his lips and shook his head. His father's recent movie represented more than just an attempt to communicate with the public, it was also—in a fitful, stumbling sort of way—an attempt to communicate truthfully and honestly with his wife and son.

But opening this door further into his and his father's lives wouldn't get Donnally closer to understanding who might have wanted to kill Mark Hamlin, so he tried to slam it shut.

"Is this a hobby of yours?" Donnally asked. "Or a form of self-defense?"

Lemmie drew back. "Touché. I guess I was getting a little intrusive." She paused, her face displaying the uncertainties and anxieties within, her hand now gripping her unmoving glass. "The truth is I do it to try to figure out whether I'm normal or not. To try to gain some perspective. Otherwise I'd just have my brother to compare myself to."

"And how twisted was he?"

"I think he had no more respect for the truth than your father did. He fictionalized everything." Lemmie's upper teeth worked against her lower lip again, then stopped. "Is there such a word as 'theatracized'? If so, that's what he did. Truth wasn't real. Victims' suffering wasn't real. Everything was an act in a play."

Lemmie's eyes went wide and her mouth fell open.

Donnally could tell she was seeing something in her mind that wasn't visible to him.

Tears formed and squeezed out onto her cheeks as she blinked.

"I'm afraid . . . I'm afraid even death didn't seem real to him until the moment he faced it himself."

She swallowed hard. "Do you . . . do you think he knew he was dying?"

Donnally knew the truth. There was no reason to think Hamlin was unconscious when he was strangled. But that wasn't the answer he chose to give.

"I don't know," Donnally said. "There's no way of knowing."

He never viewed himself as a human polygraph, but Lemmie's last sentences had taken her off the suspects list.

Lemmie reached into her purse, withdrew a tissue, and wiped her eyes. Her voice hardened again as she asked, "Doesn't the condition of his body mean . . ."

Donnally understood she was referring to her brother's erection and answered, "Not necessarily, that happens sometimes when a victim has been strangled. We still haven't gotten the toxicology report, so we don't know whether it was induced medically."

"And you don't know about other drugs yet, either?"

"You know something?"

"Will my parents find out?"

"That depends on where it leads. If it leads to the killer, then it will eventually come out in court. If it fades, it'll stay with me."

Lemmie took in a long breath and exhaled. "Mark chased the dragon."

"Opium?"

Lemmie nodded. "Didn't you find a long clay pipe in his apartment?"

Donnally thought for a moment. "There was a collection of them on a bookcase in his living room. Old ones, maybe even antiques."

"Hiding in plain sight can be the best camouflage."

"How long was he doing it?"

"Off and on for about ten years."

"Where did he get it?"

Lemmie shrugged. "Somebody in Chinatown, I guess. Or maybe Little Saigon down in San Jose."

Donnally pulled out his phone and called Navarro. "Did you get the tox report yet?"

"Just came in. Looks like Hamlin may have had a heroin problem. The preliminary results showed opiate metabolites in his blood. I checked the autopsy report. No track marks, so he must've been smoking it."

"I think it may be opium." He looked up at Lemmie, but said to Navarro, "Do me a favor. Hustle over to Judge McMullin and get a court order sealing the report."

"Will do. I already told the medical examiner to hold it close because some media people have been lying in wait for it."

"Anything else show up?"

"Alcohol. It was at .04. The blood was otherwise clean—and there's one more thing. Dr. Haddad says it was a heart attack that actually killed him. Strangling, panic, death."

Donnally disconnected. He decided to keep Lemmie on the drug path and not risk diverting her into speculations about the murder and to painful imaginings of her brother's last moments.

"Did he do it alone or with other people?"

"Recently, I don't know. When he started, it was with a private investigator he hung out with, Frank Lange. They tried it for the first time on a trip to Thailand on a case. Their client hooked them up."

"How'd you find out about it?"

"The ICE beagle at SFO sniffed out a pipe they brought back and agents questioned them for a couple of hours. I know because I was in the arrivals hall waiting. The supervisor came out and told me what the holdup was. Their story was that they bought the pipe at a souvenir shop in Bangkok. It was a lie. My brother and Frank were laughing about the whole thing as I was driving them home. It could've cost both of them their licenses, but they thought it was a laugh."

"Do you know where he hid his opium?"

"I'm not sure, but he hinted once that he had a secret compartment somewhere in his bedroom."

CHAPTER 29

Except for the motion and whoosh of cars and trucks, there was little change from the shadow and neon of the Backroom Bar and the night and neon of the sidewalk onto which Donnally and Lemmie stepped. It reminded Donnally of what a deceased friend used to say. *Walking from a dark bar into sunlight reflecting up off concrete was like descending into hell.*

The distress still showing on Lemmie's face suggested she was stuck in purgatory, and Donnally knew he could do nothing for her. He wasn't sure that even solving her brother's murder would provide an escape. He thought he'd at least try to break the mood by asking her how she got her nickname.

"When we were kids, I was the adventurous one. Whenever we went someplace new, like the circus, when there was a ride to try or a high dive at the pool, I would always scream, 'Let me, let me, let me.' Over time, that became Lemmie."

She paused and gazed at the oncoming traffic, seemingly oblivious to the headlights jittering on the uneven pavement and the rumble of tires. Finally, she said, "As it turned out, Mark was the aggressive one as an adult, and I've spent my life holed up in front of a computer monitor living the lives of imaginary people." She half smiled. "My nickname now should be Leemee, as in leave . . . me . . . alone."

"Does that include me?" Donnally asked.

She shook her head. "I'll do everything I can to help you."

Donnally nodded. "Have any reporters made the connection between you and your brother?"

"Not yet. My parents are refusing to talk to the press and I haven't placed an obituary in the *San Francisco Chronicle*. After time passes and things have died down, maybe I'll step out of the closet on that one."

Donnally hailed her a cab, watched it take her down toward Market Street, then turned and started back toward Hamlin's office. He stopped with an after-work crowd at the crosswalk and waited for the switch from "Wait" to "Walk." Most of those around him already wore their bovine BART faces, preparation for the see-nothing, hear-nothing, think-nothing, no-eye-contact commute from urban work to suburban home. Even the eyes of those texting on their cell phones seemed vacant.

He sensed people crunching up behind him, followed by jostling, then someone crowding him from behind. He felt something hard dig into the middle of his back, then a male voice with a light Vietnamese accent whispered into his ear, "Don't move."

A hand locked onto his left bicep.

"And don't look around."

Donnally pressed his right arm tight against

his side so the man couldn't too easily get to his gun, then looked down, trying to catch a glimpse of the man's shoes and pants. Neither was what he expected. He spotted creased wool suit slacks and black alligator penny loafers, unblemished.

"Let the people pass around you."

The signal changed.

What Donnally understood to be a gun barrel jabbed hard against his spine. He also understood that even a small caliber slug would paralyze him from that spot down to his toes. And spinning and grabbing for the gun would likely cause it to discharge into one of the pedestrians, shocking them awake from their after-work slumber just in time to watch one of them die.

He decided to do what the man said until they were in a spot that would be safer for him to make a move.

Those to the front of him stepped off the curb and into the street. The ones behind him worked their way past.

"You look at me and I might as well shoot," the man said, once the area around them had almost cleared. "I may shoot anyway, but there's no need to force the issue."

As the last of the pedestrians ran to beat the light, the man said, "Keep your eyes facing the direction you're going and turn right and head down the sidewalk. There's a parking garage a half block up. We're going in there."

It was the same eighty-year-old structure where Donnally had parked his truck. He wished both that he'd paid more attention to the layout and that he'd chosen one to park in with better lighting. Walking toward it now, he imagined the third floor where he'd left the truck was more shadow than light. But, at the same time, it might not be too isolated since office workers would be coming to collect their cars for the ride home.

After they made the turn onto the ramp rising to the first floor, the man prodded him toward the stairs. Now Donnally was certain that they were heading toward his truck.

He was wrong.

As they approached the second floor door, the man said, "This is where we get off. Step through and hang a left along the wall."

Donnally followed his orders and saw that the gunman had planned well. All of the spaces were taken up by vehicles used by a medical delivery service, their workday done, the engines cooling, ticking in the silence. The man had either cased the area searching for the perfect place for what he had in mind or worked in a nearby office building and already knew the layout.

Fifty feet farther, Donnally found himself boxed in by the soot-caked corner of the building and a gray panel van. The shoulder-width space was too tight for him either to make a go for his gun or spin and take a swing.

That was also smart planning on the crook's part.

"Don't you think you should tell me what this is about?" Donnally said. "Maybe you've got the wrong guy."

The gun jabbed him in the back again.

"Raise your arms."

Donnally followed the order and felt the tug and rip of Velcro and the yanking of his semiautomatic from its holster. He then felt two barrels against his back.

"I know exactly who you are," the man said, "and I'll tell you exactly what this is about. First, I want to know where my money is, and second, what was the deal you had with Hamlin."

"What money?"

"Don't fuck with me."

"I found some money, but it's been seized by SFPD. I couldn't get it for you now even if I wanted to. And with that gun at my back, trust me, I want to."

"I don't believe you. The only reason you're involved in this is because you and Hamlin had to be partners and you're protecting your interest. Last thing you'd do is let the police grab a quarter of a million dollars."

"I didn't find two-fifty. I found about one-forty in cash, that's it. There are witnesses who watched me count it and hand it over. A homicide detective and Hamlin's assistant."

The man didn't respond. Donnally felt the gun barrels move against his back, the man's outward movement reflecting inward uncertainty.

Finally, the man said, "What do you mean seized? Like forfeited?"

Using the word "forfeited" sounded to Donnally like an inadvertent admission that the funds were the proceeds of crime.

"No, just booked into evidence."

The man mumbled to himself. Donnally could

only make out the words "none" and "cash" and "*đụ má*," a Vietnamese swearword that Janie's father had taught him: motherfucker.

"I take it that it wasn't supposed to be in cash," Donnally said.

"That son of a bitch."

"Maybe you should've checked into that before you killed him."

"If I killed him, we wouldn't be standing here. I would've gotten what I wanted first."

"Sometimes accidents happen."

"Keep playing the fool and an accident may happen to you."

He's wrong about that, Donnally thought. Nothing would happen to him as long as the slick-shoed gunslinger believed Donnally controlled Hamlin's money.

"You have to give me a hint," Donnally said, "How will I go about finding it if I don't know who it's from, or what it's from, or why you gave it to him, or how you gave it to him."

The man didn't respond.

"Or were you expecting me to write a two-hundred-and-fifty-thousand-dollar check made out to To Whom It May Concern?"

The man still didn't respond.

"There was no inside deal that brought me into this," Donnally said. "And I didn't want to do it. Other than when Hamlin cross-examined me in homicide trials, I only talked to him once. And that was a year ago and on the phone."

The man mumbled again. Donnally could only make out the swearwords, and they seemed directed at himself, rather than at Donnally or Hamlin. There must've been something the man had been good at, or at least good enough to afford the clothes he was wearing, but it wasn't kidnapping. As if to confirm Donnally's opinion, what the man said next just sounded stupid.

"If he had the cash you found," the man said, "maybe there's more. In fact, I'm thinking that there has to be. Lots." Another jab with a barrel. "And you're going to find it and hand it over."

"You got a business card or something?" Donnally said. "We'll need to keep in touch."

"Don't worry. You'll hear from me."

"Maybe we can do lunch."

"Fuck you."

Donnally heard the shoe scrapes of the man backing away, and asked, "What about my gun?"

"I'll . . ." The man hesitated. He hadn't thought this part through. Donnally guessed he had to decide whether he was a crooked businessman trying to recover money or a just a mugger. "I'll leave it in the wheel well of the car nearest the stairs." He forced a laugh. "I suspect you'll need it. Mark Hamlin kept a lot tougher company than me and I need you alive."

"That's something we can agree on," Donnally said. "I need me alive, too."

CHAPTER 30

As Donnally slid his semiautomatic back in its holster and descended the ramp to the sidewalk, he was less concerned about a second visit from the flustered Vietnamese gunman than about what Hamlin was doing with the quarter-million dollars. There was no question in Donnally's mind that it was crime proceeds, but what crime and by what device had Hamlin received it, and what had the crook expected him to do with the money?

The easy answer, maybe too easy, was that Hamlin was laundering it.

The man expected the money to still be in cash, while the problem for drug traffickers was to find ways to convert it into untraceable assets. That suggested Hamlin would've received it just before his death and hadn't had time to launder it.

After again stepping into the flow of pedestrians and heading in the direction of Hamlin's office, Donnally thought of his conversation with Lemmie. Maybe it wasn't about money laundering, at least not directly. Maybe Hamlin had chased the dragon all the way into the drug trade and he was supposed to have used the money to purchase opium from his connection in Thailand.

What better cut-out for a drug trafficking organization than a white lawyer with a confidential trust account to move money to Asia to purchase narcotics?

But again, the man expected Hamlin still had the cash, which implied that the deal—if it really was a drug deal—hadn't been done yet.

In either case, where was the money?

Donnally suspected the man felt a little foolish as he'd left. He'd come with a gun only because he fantasized that Donnally and Hamlin were partners and that Donnally was a crook like him who could be intimidated because he couldn't run to the police for protection. But there was no basis for that belief other than a wish that it be true.

Now, standing in the same spot at the same intersection, Donnally felt an itch between his shoulder blades, wondering who would be next to press a gun barrel against his spine.

By accepting the role as the special master to investigate Hamlin's murder, Donnally realized that he had become a proxy for the man, the living dead, and he didn't want to become the dead dead.

Donnally took a few steps up around the corner to separate himself from the crowd, then called Navarro and asked him to find out whether the garage had a videotape surveillance system and to get a copy of the recording for the last two hours. That would be enough time to spot the gunman casing the garage, if he did, and him and Donnally walking inside, and then exiting.

As he turned toward the corner, he noticed patrons lined up in front of Café La Maison across the street, queued up men and women dressed in suits and long coats, confined by woven stanchion ropes. Stepping forward, then pausing. Stepping forward, then pausing. Sure that when they arrived inside the wine would be exquisite, the dinners would be satisfying, and the desserts would be just.

Maybe that's what he needed, Donnally told himself. A series of lines, or perhaps chutes, to organize all those who had unresolved issues with Hamlin—and perhaps even for the one who had resolved his issue through murder.

One for the tricked.

One for the cheated.

One for disappointed crime partners.

One for those denied justice.

And one line labeled "Other."

He suspected that the last would be the longest.

"Wait" changed to "Walk" and he continued on, arriving at Hamlin's office five minutes later.

The door lock made the kind of hollow click that sounds when a room is empty, and this was.

And dark. Lit only by the diffused light from the street below and the windows of after-hours workers in the opposite building.

Donnally felt a little foolish doing it, but he pulled the Velcro strap on his holster free and gripped his gun as he flipped on the reception area light switch. The fluorescent flicker and burst of light illuminated nothing but office furniture. He passed through and into Hamlin's inner office. Nothing there but dead wood. The only thing new was a manila envelope lying in the center of the desk blotter. He secured his gun, then dropped into Hamlin's chair and slid the contents out. A DVD. He spun it around to read the label.

Frank Lange Investigations
People v. Thule
Interview of John Gordon
Confidential Attorney/Client Material

Donnally knew what the secret recording would show even before he listened to it. John Gordon had not confessed to Lange that it was his idea to use the defective Chinese steel in the mall walkway.

And he suspected it was Jackson who'd left it for him.

Perhaps because of the fresh recollection of the gun at his back, the kind of incident whose lingering memory can transform fear into paranoia, he found himself wondering whether the recording was a bread crumb that would lead him to the reason for the murder or whether it was a form of misdirection to take him down a false trail away from something that might implicate her directly.

At some point, Hamlin's crimes and professional misconduct would slop back on Jackson and she had to start protecting herself, one way or another, maybe just by diverting his attention to someone else.

Hamlin's misdeeds were certainly about to slop back on Frank Lange. In his cross-examination, the prosecutor would've asked Lange whether he'd taped the interview of Gordon, and Lange would've lied. And the proof of his perjury was lying on the blotter and would end Lange's career.

It was just the kind of leverage Donnally was looking for to get backdoor access to parts of Hamlin's work that were either hidden from Jackson or that she was afraid to talk about for fear of self-incrimination.

Donnally called Hannah Goldhagen on her cell phone. He could hear background restaurant noises of rumbling conversations and rattling dishes. He then suffered what he knew was an irrational thought, based on an irrational connection, that she was sitting in Café La Maison down the block. He suppressed it and asked:

"Hypothetically, if you could prove the defense used forged or fraudulent evidence to get a not guilty verdict in a state court case, could you somehow avoid the double jeopardy problem and get it moved into federal court and retried?"

Goldhagen laughed. "I don't think you mean hypothetically. You're just not willing to tell me who did it and what case they did it in."

"And the answer?"

"No, we couldn't get it into federal court unless it could be construed as a civil rights case."

"It can't. But, hypothetically, you could keep it in state court and pursue obstruction of justice against the defendant if you could prove he was involved."

She laughed again. "Not hypothetically, actually, and we can ask for penalties as heavy as for the original crime. Hold on." The restaurant sounds were eclipsed for a few moments, then she asked, "And when am I going to find out which case it is?"

"It may not even be in San Francisco. You may have to find out about it in the newspaper."

"I think not." Her voice stiffened. "Be careful, Donnally, I know you're doing a lot of poking around and have been playing things close, but pretty soon push is going to come to shove and some of this stuff has to come out."

He threw it back at her. "And the sooner you get Sheldon Galen signed on, the sooner you can get to pushing and shoving."

"It'll be done tomorrow. He lawyered up as though he wanted to fight, but then caved. He's supposed to be in at high noon. I'll send him your way right afterwards."

CHAPTER 31

Donnally looked up Frank Lange's address on the Internet, located his photo in the *San Francisco Chronicle* archives, and then headed out. A half hour later he slowed his truck near a three-story Victorian where Castro, Divisadero, and Waller came together, just three blocks east of Buena Vista Park. Mark Hamlin's apartment was on its opposite side. He verified the address, then drove on until he located a parking spot a couple of streets away, and walked back.

Any thought of confronting Lange with the tape got drowned out by party noises emanating from the house. From the recessed doorway of an apartment building across Divisadero, Donnally watched too many people in a dining room under a too bright chandelier jostle for places near the buffet table.

He didn't recognize anyone and didn't see Lange.

Donnally took a couple of photos with his cell phone, then worked his way around the perimeter of the Y intersection until he obtained a view of the Waller side of the house. He spotted Lange stand-

ing in the living room looking like a politician surrounded by reporters. The head shot Donnally had
found on the Internet disguised Lange's girth. That,
combined with his red sports jacket, made him look
like a child's party balloon. It seemed to Donnally
to be the perfect match of ego and physique.

Lange wasn't an investigator who relied on
stealth. And if Jackson was right about the kind of
work he did for Hamlin and for other attorneys like
him, he didn't need to be furtive. It didn't make any
difference whether witnesses or victims could see
him coming, for he'd either just make up what he
wanted victims or witnesses to have said, or try to
intimidate them into saying it or into silence.

Lights were off on the upper floors. Donnally
imagined Lange's bedroom and office were on the
second story and that he used the angle-roofed
third floor as storage. The ceiling seemed too low
for regular use.

Donnally watched Lange and a skinny woman at
least twenty-five years younger than Lange's early
fifties turn together and walk toward the interior
of the house. A minute later a light burst on in a
second floor room. The angle of view was such that
he couldn't tell what it was used for.

They faced each other.

She was glaring at him, her thin arms folded
across her chest.

He stood with his hands extended.

Soon they were both jabbing fingers and waving
hands.

From the violence of her gestures, Donnally
guessed she could be angry enough at Lange to dis-

close some of his secrets, if she was in a position to know any.

Donnally snapped a photo, thinking that Jackson or Navarro might be able to identify her.

Lange reached for her shoulders. She stepped back. He reached again. She slapped him, then spun away. He stood there for a few seconds rubbing his cheek, then followed her out of Donnally's sight and the light went off.

Donnally took more photos of the people in the living room, then slipped his phone into his pocket and surveyed the third floor windows.

Assuming Judge McMullin would accept the argument that Lange kept his own copy of the Gordon interview recording in storage, Donnally didn't think it would be long before push did come to shove, and Navarro would be kicking in Lange's door to serve a search warrant.

Donnally leaned against the brick wall behind him. He'd expected his discovery of the perjury would give him a feeling of solidity, of having found a foothold; instead it was one of vertigo, of losing focus on what he'd been asked to do: figure out who killed Mark Hamlin—and not go on what McMullin had called a fishing expedition, even though Donnally guessed that he could pull some monsters from the deep—for who knew how many similar tapes might be discovered in Lange's storage room.

Forget the search warrant fantasy, he told himself. It wasn't going to happen, or it would come too late. He needed the recording as leverage to find out whether Lange knew, or even suspected, who the killer was—even at the risk of incriminating himself in other crimes.

But the danger of confronting Lange was—no, the consequence would be—that he would move anything incriminating out of his house.

Donnally pushed off from the wall. The chess game in his head continued while he walked back to his truck. He leans on Lange, then has Navarro spot on the investigator's house to see if he tries to sneak any boxes of records out, then follows Lange to where he stashes them.

Nope. Not worth the risk. What if Navarro gets caught? The defense bar goes haywire, the department gets embarrassed, and both Donnally and Judge McMullin get ripped in the press, Donnally for playing cop when he was supposed to be acting as a special master and McMullin for appointing him.

A guy like Lange, who does what he does and has so much to hide, always has to be looking over his shoulder.

Always.

Nobody will be sneaking up on Frank Lange.

I went to a conference today over at the USF Medical Center," Janie said when Donnally walked into their bedroom. She was propped up in bed, drinking tea, and reading Lemmie Hamlin's latest book. "I asked around about whether anyone had ever worked on any cases for Mark Hamlin."

Donnally kissed her on the forehead. "I suspect no one would admit it now."

Janie smiled. "You wouldn't make a very good shrink. The urge to confess relationships with victims seems to follow like a vulture in death's wake."

"Very literary." He pointed at the book. "Is that where you got that line?"

"No. It just stirred my creative juices."

Donnally grinned and raised his eyebrows. "Any other juices get stirred?"

"There was a great sex scene in chapter seven, but I didn't need the stirring." She grinned back. "You know me."

"Let me take a shower and I'll see what I can do."

"Don't you want to know the gossip?"

Donnally nodded and sat down on the edge of the bed.

"Those who do forensic psychology in criminal cases are trapped in a weird conflict. They're proud to be known for their expertise, but they're embarrassed to have been chosen for their pliability. It hit me while I was listening to them how it really works. It's kind of like the way people adopt whatever religion they're born into, embrace it as though they'd chosen it themselves, and then become willing to kill and die for it."

"And these shrinks adopt the point of view of whoever calls them first," Donnally said, "and are willing to scheme and lie for it."

"That's the implication." She smiled. "And very poetic."

Donnally had watched dozens of those hacks in homicide cases, especially capital cases in which psychologists and psychiatrists were called by the defense for what the law calls mitigation, to testify about how a murderer's unhappy childhood caused him to plan and execute a robbery murder, or even a series of them.

It angered him, even though he was no fan of the death penalty and would never vote for it himself either on a referendum ballot or as a member of a jury. And the advantage of working in San Francisco was that the DA rarely charged special circumstances and paid attention to a detective who argued against seeking death in a case.

At the same time, he hated the self-deceptions of the cottage industry that built up around capital cases. It was made up of attorneys, private investigators, mitigation specialists, psychologists, and social workers who always found a way to convince themselves that their particular crook's life was worth saving.

And it was absolute bullshit.

Murders have nothing to do with unhappy childhoods and everything to do with power.

Individually, none of the guilty defendants was worth saving. They were disgusting human beings who knew what they were doing, knew that it was wrong, and got a thrill out of doing it.

"I've never understood how people could do that kind of work," Donnally said. "They delude themselves and deceive juries about what these guys really are."

What made their lives worth saving was simply that they were human beings; that and the fact that errors were built into the system and it was wrong to exact absolute punishment without absolute certainty.

There wasn't such a thing.

Nobody with a half a brain needed an Innocence Project to teach them that lesson.

And by the time a capital case got to court, it wasn't about truth anymore, but about winning.

"It's not just the defense," Janie said. "These people also work for the prosecution."

"And that pisses me off, too. The DA's playing the same self-deluding game."

Prosecutors would match defense attorneys in lying to themselves and to juries, arguing this defendant, more than the defendants doing first-degree murder sentences or life-without-parole sentences, deserved death—even when the worst of the worst never got it.

Son of Sam. Charles Manson. Jeffrey Dahmer.

Kill two. Get death.

Kill ten. Get rewarded with life for just telling the cops where all the bodies are buried.

In Donnally's experience, the more maniacal the crime, the more likely the jury would be looking for reasons why the defendant got so twisted. And once the jurors started down the psych road, it was hard for them to think of the killer as a willing, thinking, choosing human being, and that prevented them from seeing him as the murdering son of a bitch he was.

"Hamlin knew how to play these people and do a little psychological dance with them," Janie said. "He'd drop by their office and present the case hypothetically—"

"I tried that today with Goldhagen. She wouldn't go for it."

"All the people he hired did. He would describe the murder, straight police report kind of stuff. The blood and guts and the premeditation and planning. The psychologist would lean back in his chair and stroke his pasty chin and say, 'I don't see anything there. That seems awfully cold-blooded. Not much chance of finding any mitigation. I'm not sure I'm in a position to assist you.'

"Then Hamlin would tell him that the defendant's mother was a dope addict, that he was abused as a kid, that his father ran off when he was two, that he got beat on the head when he was six, that he was molested by this uncle when he was ten—that kind of thing. Then the psychologist would lean forward again, furrow his brow, and say, 'I think I was mistaken. Clearly, this is not the sort of defendant the death penalty was enacted for.'"

"I thought shrinks were supposed to see through those kinds of games," Donnally said, "not get self-justifications out of them."

"All three I spoke to who'd worked for Hamlin described having to be convinced to get involved in the case, and none of them realized they were all telling the same story and confessing to the same rationalization."

Jamie stuck a bookmark in her place and folded Lemmie's novel closed. Donnally took this as a sign she was about to hit the punch line.

"Hamlin hired one of them in a rape-murder case down in San Jose. It happened about two years ago. The defendant stalked the victim for months. At her home, at her office, even at the grocery store. She got a restraining order and the police arrested him twice for violating it. The defendant's parents were Silicon Valley, new-money types. They retained Hamlin with only one instruction. It was okay to lose in the guilt phase, they didn't care whether he got convicted of the crime, but it was a must-win at penalty phase. They weren't going to have a kid of theirs on death row and have the case coming up and coming up in the press over the next twenty years."

"I take it that it wasn't just the victim's family who wanted what people all call closure, but the defendant's."

Donnally hated to say the word. Closure was the

concept of choice for death penalty supporters. It seemed to him minds were more like windows than doors, and a victim's family watching the execution of her murderer through the green room glass couldn't thereafter shut in, or shut out, the past.

Janie nodded. "Exactly. The case finally got to trial about four months ago. Hamlin used the guilt phase as a long sentencing hearing. He didn't argue about the facts of the crime, only used it to set up the penalty phase. He didn't object to anything the DA wanted to use in evidence; even made himself look incompetent by seeming to stumble into letting the DA's own witnesses bring in crazy stuff the defendant did that the DA hadn't known about."

"And the DA didn't see it coming."

"Nope. By the time the jury was done finding him guilty, they were primed for the psychologist's testimony and he wove together everything into the story Hamlin wanted to tell."

"And the jury bought it."

"Back in an hour with a life-without-parole sentence. The psychologist told me he foolishly showed up to hear the verdict and needed the bailiffs to escort him to his car afterwards. The victim's father and brother tried to fight their way through the phalanx of officers in order to get to him."

"Did they bother him later?"

"A few calls and threatening notes. He got a restraining order, but he got one last call a month afterwards. A woman's voice saying that it wasn't over and he better watch his back."

"What about—"

"And that Hamlin better watch his, too."

Reaching for the ringing cell phone by the bedside, Donnally felt like he was fighting his way to the surface of a murky lake under a moonlit sky, except the moon was his screen. He looked at the time: 5 A.M.

"What were you doing outside of Frank Lange's house last night?"

It was Ramon Navarro and he hadn't waited for Donnally to say hello.

Donnally walked into the hallway and closed the door behind him.

"Making a dry run, it turns out. I was hoping to talk to him, but he had a party going on."

"Talk to him about what?"

"Perjury he committed in a case."

"That may have led someone to kill Hamlin?"

"I don't know."

"Then what got you started—"

Donnally cut him off. "What's going on?" He didn't like getting jammed. It was time to find out why Navarro was grilling him about Lange.

"A patrol cop who's been around a long time spotted you walking across Divisadero near his house."

"Who was that?"

"Doesn't make a difference who."

"Then tell me."

Donnally heard Navarro sigh. "Deondre Williams. He still has good eyes for an old guy. The only reason he recognized you is because of talk—a helluva lot of talk—in the squad room about you being the special master in the Hamlin case. There are mixed feelings about it."

"Despite the mixed feelings, tell him to keep what he saw to himself."

"Then tell me what you were doing there."

Donnally headed down the stairs to the kitchen to make coffee. He was now too alert to return to sleep.

"I have dead-bang proof of Lange's perjury in a case and I'm going to use it as leverage to get him to give me information about Hamlin and the dirty stuff that might've gotten him murdered."

"*Were* going to use it. He's toast. Roasted last night in a fire that burned down his house. He never even made it out of bed."

Donnally stopped between steps. He thought of Lange and the woman arguing upstairs.

"Arson?"

The words must have come out more like a statement rather than a question, for Navarro asked, "Why do you say that?"

"I saw him arguing with a woman. I didn't recognize her, but I've got a photo. I'll send it to you along with the rest of the ones I took. They're from across the street and through windows so they're a little fuzzy, but maybe you can do something with them."

"No question but it was arson," Navarro said. "So far we've found five main points of ignition. Looks like somebody used a gas can to soak a spot on each outside wall of the house, then ran lines of fluid from one to the other. They made certain he had no way out. Everyplace he looked down, he'd see flame coming up at him."

"That's four points."

"The fifth was on the top floor. In his storage area. His safe and the file drawers were open and the can was lying in the middle of the floor. At least that's what the guys on the ladders are saying. We haven't been cleared to go in there yet."

Unless Lange had left the safe open by mistake, something he wouldn't do while he was having a party, the arsonist must have been well-known enough to Lange that he would trust him—or her—with the combination.

"Looks like somebody was trying to destroy both him and his records."

"And they did a helluva job. Victorians like Lange's are nothing but painted kindling nailed together."

Donnally walked into the kitchen and turned on the television. A local news reporter stood across the intersection from Lange's house. Originally painted tan, the sides now were mostly black from flame and soot. All the windows visible to the camera were blown. Firefighters carrying a yellow body bag strapped to a stretcher were walking down the stairs and past Navarro, standing on the wet sidewalk among snaking fire hoses and framed by a ladder truck on one side and the medical examiner's wagon on the other.

"Is that Lange in the bag?" Donnally asked, "Or were there more victims?"

Navarro surveyed the crowd as though expecting to see Donnally among the spectators lining the far sidewalks. His eyes locked on the news camera.

"You watching on TV?"

"Yeah."

"Just Lange. Or at least we think it's Lange. Body's burned pretty bad, but it's the right shape."

"What about neighbors?"

Navarro pointed at the house next door. The near corner, visible in the camera frame, was blackened. "The place is being remodeled. Nobody is living there."

Donnally watched Navarro turn toward the medical examiner's wagon as it pulled away with the body inside.

"Got to go," Navarro said. "I'll have a look-see at the ME's office while the fire inspector does his work, then come back and go through the house if he's sure the place won't collapse on me."

"Mind if I come along?"

"A fishing expedition?"

"Let's not call it that."

CHAPTER 34 ══════════════════════

Donnally telephoned John Gordon at his construction company after he got into his truck. He had no doubt that Gordon would be there before anyone else, sitting at his desk, drinking the Folgers or Maxwell House coffee he brewed himself and checking the day's work schedule.

Donnally understood the difference in burdens of proof between criminal and civil cases—beyond a reasonable doubt versus preponderance of the evidence—but he wasn't sure how chains of evidence worked in civil matters. In a criminal case, the recording of Lange's interview of Gordon wouldn't even get in front of a jury without Lange alive to authenticate it. In a civil case, he didn't know. If the standard of proof was lower, maybe the evidentiary rules were different, or there was some kind of gimmick that would make it admissible. Even if it couldn't be used anymore to get Lange, or not even to get the mall owner convicted of obstruction, he hoped that it would at least save the contractor some money and help restore his reputation. Maybe his lawyer could scare the other side just by waving it around during a deposition.

"Are you in settlement talks with the plaintiffs in the walkway collapse?" Donnally asked Gordon, as he headed south through the foggy neighborhood on his way to Lange's house.

"I'd really like to settle this thing," Gordon said. "I don't want to make those people go through a trial. That only lines the pockets of the lawyers."

"I take it Thule is aiming to use his not guilty verdict in the criminal trial to shift all of the blame onto you."

"That's the problem. His lawyers are trying to split liability ninety-ten, with ninety percent me. Nine million on my end, one million on his. That would take the settlement way, way past our insurance limits and it would break the company."

Donnally turned onto the commercial Geary Street and merged with the commuter traffic coming from the Golden Gate Bridge and working its way toward downtown. He broke through the fog and lowered his visor against the rising sun.

"I ran into something that should help you," Donnally said. "It's key to a thing I'm working on and I need to sit on it awhile."

"But if—"

"You'll get it. I promise. Just don't settle the case until you hear from me."

"I'll tell my lawyer you have something that—"

"Let's keep this between us. I don't want him to go rabid and try to hit me with a subpoena. It'll really screw me up."

Gordon didn't respond for a moment, then said,

"Just don't take too long. Living with my life's work just a half inch from falling off a cliff is tearing me apart."

"You just got to hang on a little longer," Donnally said, then disconnected.

Although he couldn't use the recording to pressure Lange anymore, Donnally didn't want to deal with the free-for-all of subpoenas and court orders provoked by news of the perjury. Everyone with an ax to grind would try to sharpen it against Hamlin's and Lange's files, whether justified or not.

And he needed to protect Jackson. Since she was part of the chain of evidence, her role would have to be disclosed. He suspected Hamlin's crime partners, like Galen and their crew of private investigators, would assume she hadn't been cooperating with him. After all, she had the best credentials of any in that crowd. She was the only one among them who'd looked up the barrel of a raid-jacketed cop's gun and heard gunshots that killed a sleeping man. If anyone would stand firm, he imagined they would expect it to be her. And he didn't want them to find out too soon that they were wrong, at least where it concerned Hamlin's private investigators.

Donnally's cell phone rang when he was turning down the six-lane Van Ness Avenue toward Hamlin's office. It was Navarro telling him that the arson investigator was standing by to give them a walkthrough of Lange's house.

He stayed on the wide commercial boulevard past City Hall and down to Market Street, then swung through the Castro District and up to Buena

Vista Heights. He and Navarro pulled up in front of the house at the same time.

Arson investigator Arthur Lu was waiting at the bottom of the front steps. Before the seven-foot, six-inch Yao Ming came from China to play in the NBA, Lu had been known in the police and fire departments as 3T–BC, Too Tall To Be Chinese, and he didn't like it.

In the years since Donnally had worked a case with Lu, the man still hadn't learned to shake hands and smile. Walking up to him now, Donnally wondered whether the truth was the opposite. He imagined that Lu had taught himself not to shake hands and smile because everyone he met on the job wanted something from him before he was in a position to give it: the what, where, and how of fires he'd just started to investigate. Too friendly a greeting could be seen as an invitation he wasn't prepared to offer.

Lu turned at their approach and led them inside. He stopped in the charred and water-soaked dining room, halfway between the front door and the kitchen in back, with both in view.

The detritus of the previous night's party lay strewn around. Dishes, glasses, wine bottles had either been blown about by the firestorm's shuddering heat or had been slammed into walls and shattered by fire hose spray blasting them from the tables on which they'd been abandoned the night before.

"There was no forced entry down here," Lu said, raising his forefinger and waving it to encompass the three visible rooms. His hand stopped, centered in the middle of the invisible circle he'd drawn. "Upstairs, we're not sure."

Donnally recalled three stories of decking at the back of the house that could've been an arsonist's way up and down.

"The windows on the first two floors exploded outward," Lu said. "There were two on the top floor that went inward, but I don't know whether either one was caused by a burglar, or whether one or both were caused by spray from the fire hose."

Navarro glanced at Donnally. "Someone could've hidden in the house after the party, then let themselves out to get a gasoline can and came back inside again to spread the gas around."

"Or someone who had a key," Donnally said. "An employee or ex-employee."

Lu pointed at the melted remains of an alarm pad next to the kitchen door. "They would've needed the code, if Lange had set it."

"On the other hand," Navarro said, "Lange could've been too drunk to do that or even to hear a window breaking."

Lu turned toward the charred stairway.

"Stay away from the banister," Lu said, as he led the way again. "It's weak."

They followed him up a flight and into Lange's bedroom. The remains of the red sports jacket Lange had been wearing the previous night lay on the floor next to the bed. Donnally gave it a nudge and exposed the toe of a thin-soled red shoe.

Donnally looked at Navarro and asked, "He didn't wear those out in public, did he?"

"I saw him having lunch with a member of

the board of supervisors once. He was wearing those shoes, or ones like them. And Lange wasn't even gay"—Navarro smiled—"or Italian, for that matter."

"It would be like wearing patrol car overhead lights on his feet," Donnally said. "I don't get what kind of an idiot investigator would do that."

Navarro's smile died. "You know exactly what kind, and that's the reason why you're here."

It was Donnally's turn to smile, as a confession, then he glanced at Lu. "You find his wallet and personal stuff?"

"Wallet in his pants, with money in it, and"—Lu turned to lead them out of the door—"his watch and rings were on his desk."

They trailed Lu into Lange's office down the hallway.

"We found another point of ignition in here," Lu said, gesturing at the remains of the carpet. "Whoever did it soaked this thing and opened all of his desk drawers."

Navarro surveyed the room. "Looks like somebody was trying to destroy something they knew was in here, but couldn't find it so they torched everything. Or couldn't find it in the time they thought they had."

Lu glanced up. "They had enough time to dump all of the files out of the cabinets and boxes in the third floor storage before they spread the gasoline over them."

Donnally tried to think through the arsonist's steps, then asked, "Does that mean they staged everything, then started the fire on the top floor, moved down here, and finally lit the spots outside?"

"I'm not sure. Neighbors heard two explosions that could have come from gasoline on the top two floors being ignited by the flames coming from below."

Donnally gazed at the blown windows. "Lange must've been really dead to the world to have not woken up to that."

Navarro looked at his watch.

"Maybe by now the medical examiner has figured out how dead."

Donnally's experience working with informants and cooperating defendants like Sheldon Galen was that they told the truth at the beginning because they were shaken at having been caught and gave themselves confidence by acting childishly earnest.

Later, they would angle off course into lying out of fear or shame or the need to protect others and the need to protect themselves from accusations, and self-accusations, of snitching.

By then, the mental balance had shifted and the nightmare of public humiliation seemed less terrifying than spending a few years in jail.

In the end, they all had to be straightened out by threats and promises.

One look at Galen's pale face and his overactive tongue and lips as he walked into Hamlin's office confirmed for Donnally he was at stage one.

Because of Lange's death, Donnally hadn't been sure he would be. Although Lu hadn't released his arson theory to the press, Donnally suspected Galen felt like a metal duck at a carnival arcade, the two ahead of him, Hamlin and Lange, having already been flattened and him moving into the shooter's crosshairs, with a lot more at stake than an oversized teddy bear.

Donnally decided to hit Galen hard and in rapid fire to get what he could before this already twisted and squirming man slithered into stage two. The most important thing was to keep from fuzzying the focus by letting Galen drift into speculations about what had happened to Lange, and why, until he'd gotten what he needed about Hamlin.

Galen reached into his inside suit jacket pocket and withdrew a packet of tri-folded papers. He slid it across the desk and said, "Goldhagen said I should give you this."

Donnally knew what it was, but he unfolded it and read it anyway to make sure there was nothing that contradicted what he thought had been their understanding. After finding nothing troubling, he slid it into a folder.

"Will she . . ." Galen said, glancing behind him toward the closed door leading to the outer office.

"Jackson won't see it and she won't know about it. To her it'll just look like you're Hamlin's friend trying to help find out who killed him."

"You sure she'll believe that?"

"She know something you're worried about?"

As soon as he said the words and watched Galen's face assume a gazing-into-the-abyss expression, he knew he'd asked the wrong question.

"Don't answer that," Donnally said. "Let's get down to business."

Donnally slid a legal pad onto the blotter. The first page was blank. Concealed underneath was a list of questions he intended to start with.

He read down it, then asked, "Were you involved in the *People v. Thule* case, the walkway collapse?"

Galen swallowed. "I helped out on a lot of cases. Mark was brilliant in trial, but not so good in preparation. He'd let things slide and slide and it would get him into jams that were tough to get out of, so I did a lot of the pretrial work."

"I'll take that as a yes."

Galen nodded.

"And you knew about Hamlin turning in the federal judge who lied about watching his sister get killed?"

Galen nodded again.

Donnally looped back. "And you brought in Frank Lange to do the John Gordon interview."

A flicker of Galen's eyelids told Donnally he'd got it right.

"Are you telling me it was the surviving victims in the case who murdered Frank?"

"I don't know that anyone murdered him. We haven't excluded any possibilities."

Donnally reached into the middle desk drawer and pulled out the DVD of Lange's interview of Gordon, laid it on the blotter, and turned it toward Galen.

"I never listened to it," Galen said. "And I didn't prepare Lange for his testimony. He knew what he was supposed to do and he did it."

"And you knew he committed perjury."

"That was between him and Mark."

Donnally let his hand settle on the folder containing the cooperation agreement.

Galen's gaze followed. He took in a long breath and said, "Shit . . . son of a bitch . . . Yes. I knew he committed perjury."

"Did any of the victims threaten you?"

"They had no way of knowing I was involved in the trial. I was just a face in the gallery when the verdict was read. And frankly, they weren't the type to kill anyone. The only kind of threats that Easter shoppers like those people make are threats to sue. It wouldn't cross their minds to hurt someone. And if it did, they would've taken out Thule, not me or Mark."

Donnally flipped to the second page of his pad and, while making a checkmark, said in a casual way that didn't reveal he was assuming and asserting facts that would never be in evidence in any court, "Were you supposed to get a cut of the money Mark took out of David Burger's motorcycle repair shop in Oakland?"

Galen didn't hesitate in responding. One reminder of the cooperation agreement had been enough. "I did some of the trial prep, but he kept my share for working on the case as what he called 'interest' on the hundred grand he loaned me to cover what I took from my trust account."

Now Donnally looked up. "Like you were an indentured servant?"

"Let's just call it pro bono." Galen didn't smile.

"Did the victim's people come after Hamlin? Maybe Tub or Sanders's wife."

"That Tub is an asshole. He was big in the Oakland Hell's Angels chapter until he got caught skimming dope money and they stripped off his patches and kicked him out. Have you seen him?"

Donnally nodded.

"Meth cost him his house and about a hundred pounds of fat and muscle. You bet he wants the money, all of it, both shares. He knows Burger killed his brother-in-law in self-defense—even Sanders's wife believes that. Sanders had gotten all paranoid and crazy and had taken to pounding her, too. Burger killing Sanders probably saved her life. If Tub wasn't always chasing meth and desperate for cash, he'd say Burger deserved the money so he could hire Hamlin to help him beat the case."

"Did you ever witness Tub—"

Galen nodded. "Out there on Harrison Street, behind the Hall of Justice, under the freeway. We were walking up to Mark's car after court. Tub must've scouted out the place and hidden down the block. He comes riding up with a couple of guys from the East Bay Devils, leathered up like they were heading for the Fourth of July outlaw rally in Hollister. They all pull guns—right behind the police department. I looked over my shoulder and could see cops getting in and out of their patrol cars. Tub says, 'Look over there one more time and it'll be the last thing you see.' Then Hamlin told him he'd get the money, just needed some time, a week. One of the bikers climbs off his motorcycle and punches Mark in the gut. He doubles over, but doesn't go down to the pavement. Nothing else said. And they're back on their bikes and gone."

"Did Mark pay them?"

"I don't know. He was supposed to. I collected some cash from clients who owed me and gave him ten thousand."

Donnally thought of the currency with Galen's fingerprints on it and the other stash they found under Hamlin's bed. It struck him that Galen's relationship with Hamlin was like a sick marriage, the kind in which they go after each other with knives, then turn together against the cops or the relatives or the neighbors who arrive to intervene.

"Isn't that a little peculiar?" Donnally asked. "Mark extorts money out of you and you try to save him from Tub."

"I've got a big mortgage, and forty percent of my income came from Mark. I needed to keep him in business. I knew he was under financial pressure, too. He always spent every nickel he made. That was part of what was driving him, and he would've made it up to me in the end."

"Is that why he went to the old guys in The Crew to cover what he loaned you?"

Galen nodded, chewing on his lower lip. Finally, he said, "I know about Mark taking the money out of Burger's garage and the perjury in the Thule case—"

"And snitching off the judge and extorting money out of that homicide victim's husband, Rudy—"

"Rusch. I know. All of that and more. But he wasn't a complete scumbag. He did some good in the world."

It was news to Donnally and it also seemed like a

non sequitur, unless Galen knew something about the reason Hamlin had collected all the cash.

Or maybe Galen had already arrived at the point in the program when he started lying.

If Hamlin wasn't so bad, after all, maybe he wasn't either.

"Like what?"

"The kids. The gymnasts."

"The what?"

The puzzlement Donnally felt must have shown on his face.

"You know, in Southeast Asia. I don't know the details, but I know a lot of money went that direction."

CHAPTER 36

"Here's an overview of Mark's calendar for the last six months," Jackson said, as she walked into his office. She laid it on the blotter in front of Donnally, then leaned over, turned the pages, and ran her finger down each one. "You can see by the blank weeks when he was in Asia."

Galen had left to meet with a longtime client in the jail to help him choose a new lawyer. He and Donnally had decided Galen's cover story for resigning would be that he had a life-threatening medical problem that he had disclosed in private to Presiding Judge Ray McMullin. Donnally had called Goldhagen and gotten her consent, and then McMullin agreed to ask the judges hearing Galen's cases to allow a new lawyer to substitute in. Donnally had no doubt that Galen's pale face and uncharacteristic agitation would convince everyone in the court system the illness was real.

"Mark never talked about it," Jackson said. "But I checked once or twice, and his trips coincided with gymnastic competitions in Thailand and Vietnam. They're kind of a big deal over there. National pride involved. Got a lot of press coverage because the program was a ticket out of poverty for lots of village kids. There are even some videos on the Internet."

"How come he was so secretive?" Donnally asked.

Donnally felt Jackson's breast rub against his shoulder. He leaned to his right to break the contact. She bent down a little further and made contact again.

"I have no idea."

He thought back to what Navarro had told him about her background and her sexually abusive father and the kinds of things Janie had told him over the years about the abused women she'd treated. He suspected fear and panic about what he might discover about Hamlin and her had led her to revert to the use of a teenage weapon of self-defense: Buy off Daddy with sex. He also wondered whether she'd run that routine on Hamlin and whether he'd exploited it. He imagined her standing in Hamlin's shower on a morning after, cursing herself for sleeping with him and bewildered about why she'd done it.

But this wasn't the time to confront her about the facts of her current behavior or to try to test his speculations about her relationship with Hamlin.

Donnally rolled back his chair and stood. Jackson straightened up and put on her most suggestive Tina Turner face. He could feel the sexual tension coming from her and sensed her filtering everything he was saying and doing, and measuring it against her subconscious intent. And the fact that her eyes displayed a certain kind of vacancy, a vacuum of unthinking, told him it was motivated in a way she didn't herself understand.

But it was real. Blood-and-flesh real.

"How about gathering together all you can on what Mark was doing over there."

He suspected she already had some of the answers he was looking for, but he needed to use his question as a way to force them both beyond what could've become an impasse.

Jackson nodded and her shoulders settled. He felt the connection break and her emotionally backing away.

She licked her lips and her brows furrowed as though she'd just become aware of her desire and was wondering why it arose just then.

He decided to push her past the awkwardness of the moment.

"See if you can find out who else was involved," Donnally said. "Where they're located over there. How he paid for it. Anything else on the Internet."

She nodded again, then turned and headed to her desk. He watched her and recognized by the slight wobble in her step that she knew he was watching her. It was like she was aware that she was being captured on film for the first time and felt her everyday gestures turn into self-conscious performances.

Donnally waited until she passed out of his view, then sat down and scanned the calendar. Even if Hamlin's work in Asia was a kind of charity, that didn't mean the money funding it was clean. Using dirty money to do good and to buy legitimacy was the San Francisco way. All the tong and triad leaders made a show of contributing to the benevolent societies and funding the Chinese New Year parade, the Italian gangsters shoveled money to the churches, even the Hell's Angels bought turkeys for the poor at Thanksgiving and ran toy drives for Christmas.

Thinking of the cash in the safe and in Hamlin's bedroom hiding place, Donnally wondered whether Hamlin was engaged in transferring the money to someone in the old country on behalf of the man with the Vietnamese accent who'd held a gun at Donnally's back.

Donnally resisted the temptation to reduce the coincidence of the Vietnamese gunman's intervention and Galen's disclosure of Hamlin's Southeast Asian charity into effect and cause or even into links in a chain.

He also realized he had another temptation to resist.

No one had mentioned women in Hamlin's life. No wife or ex-wife. No girlfriend or ex-girlfriend. No boyfriend or ex-boyfriend.

Maybe the charity was a pretext for sex tourism, for hitting the brothels of Bangkok and Hanoi. Maybe Hamlin had a girlfriend over there. Maybe—he felt a shudder of disgust pass through him—maybe the half-naked kids who were supposed to be the beneficiaries of his charity were actually his targets.

CHAPTER 37

Money.

More and more Donnally was convinced the route to whoever killed Mark Hamlin would follow a money trail—

And he hated money trail cases.

As a cop, he hadn't lied to himself. He knew he didn't have the talent, he didn't have the mind for it. He couldn't see patterns in numbers and abstract the character of human actions from deposits and withdrawals and balance sheets.

He had a hard time just keeping track of the pluses and minuses of his café's money flow.

And now he found himself sitting at Hamlin's conference table surveying stacks of bank statements. Eight bank accounts, personal and business. All with connected ATM or credit cards.

Donnally felt straitjacketed. Paralyzed. Hamlin could've laundered money just by moving it among these accounts and Donnally knew he wouldn't be able to figure it out.

Sensing motion in the doorway, he looked up to see Jackson walking in. She'd undone the top two buttons of her blouse. He felt a surge of annoyance.

He wasn't in the mood for the manipulation. He was interested in the truth she was in a position to expose, not the cleavage she was intending to reveal.

Jackson stopped at the opposite side of the table, leaned over at the waist, and tapped one of the piles of bank statements with her fingernail. "There's an easier way to get the answers you're looking for."

Donnally fixed his eyes on hers, resisting the temptation to let his gaze fall where she wanted it to. Her maneuver made him recall a female suspect who'd cozied up next to him in the bar where he'd sought her out, and had asked, "Is there any *physical* way we can resolve this?"

"How do you figure?" Donnally asked.

"We have a sophisticated accounting program, not your in-a-box, buy-it-off-the-shelf kind. We bought it to make it easy to export the financial data to Mark's accountant so he could calculate his quarterly tax payments and prepare his returns."

"How complicated is it?"

"Not too. I can show you how to search it and to create reports."

Donnally wished Janie was around to sit Jackson down and take her back to the critical moments in her childhood and then return her to the present so she could understand what she was doing.

As he looked at her, he wondered whether her behavior was just an expression of grief and dislocation after the loss of a father figure, for Hamlin might have been the most important person in her life.

At the same time, maybe she'd begun to fear

A Criminal Defense 217

Hamlin, as she feared her own molesting father, even before Hamlin's death, perhaps as though he was her own Peoples Temple Jim Jones.

"Maybe you can give me the manual to look at," Donnally said.

Jackson straightened up, but lowered her gaze, her lips pursed into a little girl's pout. She folded her arms below her breasts, forcing them up into the opening in her blouse, her skin reflecting the fluorescent light shining from above.

Donnally thought he had better give her some encouragement until he could figure out how to deal with her.

"After I get familiar with the program, maybe you can show me some of its tricks."

Jackson smiled and headed back toward her desk, nearly on her toes, almost like she was skipping.

Donnally followed her and waited while she located the manual on her bookcase. He turned away after she handed it to him, but before she could offer any more help, and then took it into Hamlin's office.

But it was hard to concentrate.

He felt like Jackson was looking over his shoulder, breathing against his ear and neck. It made him feel like she'd won a round, gotten into his head, but he wasn't going to show it.

He found the application icon on the screen and activated the program—

And she won another round.

Jackson knew he'd need to come to her to get the password.

In order not to have to do it in person, he called

her on the intercom. She insisted on coming into the office to give it to him.

Donnally rose and stood by the wall behind the desk. She slipped by him, leaned over, entered the password, and then clicked a box on the screen to make it visible: "showmethemoney."

He didn't need to write it down.

Jackson straightened, gave him a we've-got-a-secret smile, and then returned to her desk. He wasn't sure whether the secret was the password itself or the fact that the phrase "show me the money" was at least a subliminal confession on Hamlin's part that he'd left the greater good behind him in his race to the bank.

Or maybe the word Donnally wanted was subconscious, not subliminal, a manifestation of a professional schizophrenia.

Except that Hamlin had to have been aware of his metamorphosis from a soldier of justice into a soldier of fortune. For, eventually, even for people like Hamlin, the self-justifications have to run out.

CHAPTER 38

Donnally closed the office door and then sat down and called Janie. He described what he called Jackson's "symptoms."

"I'm thinking it's some kind of defense mechanism," Donnally said. "Like she's acting out."

Janie laughed. "Who appointed you shrink for a day? A defense mechanism, Dr. Freud?"

He knew she'd caught him. He'd felt a little awkward saying the words, like he'd been paddling into her professional pond on a makeshift raft.

"You have a better idea?"

"Transference."

"You mean like she and Hamlin were sexually involved and she's switched to me?"

"Maybe. Or maybe she had some kind of psychological dependence on him, like a father figure."

"I guessed at that one. At least give me a gold star for that."

"Let's make it a cigar, it's more Freudian. That kind of thing happens all the time between patients and their therapists. The therapist becomes a substitute for the parent or for the abusive boyfriend and the feelings get redirected from one to the other, or from the past to the present."

"What do you make of her acting like a sexualized little girl? Who am I supposed to be in that fantasy?"

"I wouldn't make too much of the sexual part. It's a weapon of the weak." Janie paused for a moment, then said, "If you can understand the nature of the transference, what she's trying to communicate, you'll better understand her relationship with Hamlin."

"And whether she's now trying to protect him or herself?"

"Very good, Sigmund. Insights like that will make you famous someday—got to go. I have some paid shrinking to do."

Donnally hung up, realizing that he had now crossed borders into two territories he wasn't good at. Finance and psychology.

After gazing at the door and imagining Jackson on the other side, he decided numbers were more manageable and looked again at the monitor. He spotted a command button titled "Reports" and clicked on it. The drop-down list showed one named "Current Year–Combined." He accessed it and discovered Hamlin didn't have much in the way of fortune, at least in his bank accounts. The bottom-line figures for money in and money out were almost equal. Unless he owned his duplex free and clear or had investments or a retirement account, most of his assets were composed of the cash Donnally had discovered.

He opened a browser and checked San Francisco County Recorder's and Assessor's Office records. They showed that Hamlin had paid off the duplex he lived in six months earlier and then had transferred it into the Mark Hamlin irrevocable trust. He knew from his parents' tax planning that making a trust irrevocable meant it couldn't be changed without the beneficiary's permission. Hamlin had thereby given up all control over the assets in the trust to the beneficiary. But the answer to the question of who that was didn't show up in the online records.

Donnally wondered whether Hamlin had made the trust irrevocable because he didn't trust himself, maybe because of his opium problem.

He checked his watch. There was enough time to make it to City Hall before it closed to try to find out who Hamlin did trust.

Later, after he'd discovered who killed Hamlin, he figured he'd also discover whether that trust was well-placed.

If his guess about the value of Hamlin's duplex was anywhere close, whoever the beneficiary was had cleared an easy couple of million dollars the instant Hamlin's heart seized up.

CHAPTER 39

When Donnally stepped out of the elevator and into the marble-floored lobby, he spotted Navarro coming in through the double front doors.

Donnally flashed a palm, holding him in place, as he approached.

"What do you have?" Donnally asked, looking down at the four-inch-thick accordion file in Navarro's hand.

"More phone records."

"How about walk with me over to City Hall?" Donnally pointed at the clock above the elevator doors. It showed 4:40. "I need to check something quick."

Navarro nodded and followed Donnally out.

Donnally glanced down at the file. "Anything interesting?"

"A problem Judge McMullin may have to resolve. After getting court orders for the subscriber information for all of the phones Hamlin called and the ones that called him for the last month, I started to flowchart the calls. But I had to stop."

"Because they were telling you too much?"

"Exactly. I may be drifting into attorney-client areas."

They turned down Larkin Street and could see the grassy east end of Civic Center Plaza and the west end of the farmers' market.

"Give me an example," Donnally said.

"Calls with Reggie Hancock."

Donnally's stomach tensed and his fist clenched, even though he wasn't surprised there might have been phone traffic between Hamlin and Hancock. It was the mere thought of Hancock.

Reginald Leotis Hancock had started out as LA's Mark Hamlin in the seventies, drifted into handling big drug cases in the eighties, and then into high-profile homicide cases at the end of the nineties. Some of those he was hired on to from the start. Others he injected himself into. Countless times he'd worked his way from the sidewalk where he commented on cases for cable news networks to a spot behind the defense table. His audience, when he was speaking into the mikes, wasn't the long distance voyeurs sitting in their living rooms, but defendants sitting in their nearby cells, desperate for a defense strategy that might win for them.

"Calls between guys like that wouldn't be unexpected," Donnally said. "I'm sure they worked together on north-south cases. And I'm not sure the fact of the calls themselves can tell you what the content was."

"It's the surrounding calls," Navarro said, holding up the accordion folder like he was showing off evidence. "Hamlin calls Hancock, then calls the DEA, then calls the U.S. Attorney, then calls a cell number belonging to an old-time drug trafficker named Hector Camacho, and then calls Hancock back."

Donnally stopped and turned toward Navarro. "How'd you know it was Camacho? Those guys don't have phones in their own names."

Navarro swallowed before answering. "I . . . uh . . . checked with our intelligence unit."

The move reminded Donnally of Navarro's preemptive search of Hamlin's apartment.

Donnally let it go. Jamming him wouldn't change what he'd done, and his face showed he knew he'd done wrong.

"You think Hamlin was planning on surrendering Camacho on a still secret indictment?"

"I don't think that's it. More likely Camacho is trying to cut a deal to roll on somebody. That had to have been the reason the DEA was in the loop. Hancock represented Camacho in the late 1980s in LA. He pled out and did seventeen years in the federal pen."

"That was a big sentence back then."

"And he was a big guy, and tough, too. He left a few murders in his wake the local DA couldn't prove, so the U.S. Attorney hit him as hard as he could. And my guess is that Camacho is not up for doing another seventeen."

"How old is Camacho?"

"Early sixties. Given life expectancy in the joint, another seventeen years would be a death sentence."

"He's back in the trade?"

"Intelligence says he's moving a hundred kilos of cocaine a month. That puts him at the top of the federal sentencing guidelines."

Donnally pointed ahead to indicate he still needed to get to City Hall, and they walked on.

"I think there are two ways to look at it," Donnally said. "It isn't all that privileged if the DEA and the U.S. Attorney are in on it. And if the telephone company can look at the phone records, they're not all that confidential." He looked over at Navarro. "Except they wouldn't know that Camacho was using that particular phone."

Navarro cleared his throat. "Sorry about that one. My finger is always close to the trigger."

Donnally reached out his hand for the file. "How about I take it from here?"

Navarro passed it over.

"I'll call this one a no harm, no foul," Donnally said. "I don't think it will go anywhere. If somebody was going to get hit, it would've been Camacho, not Hamlin. He's the snitch, he did the damage, or is going to, so he's the dangerous one."

CHAPTER 40

"He didn't ask me if I wanted to inherit his duplex," Lemmie Hamlin told Donnally, sitting across the table in her kitchen an hour and a half later. "He just did it."

Lemmie pointed through her atrium window toward Golden Gate Park and beyond it at the sun flaming out in the Pacific Ocean. It was what the real estate brokers called a million-dollar view, but this one was out of a multimillion-dollar town house.

"It's not like I need the money."

"Wanting and needing are different things."

Her brows furrowed. "Did you ever read any of my books?"

Donnally smiled. "You mean, all the way through?"

Lemmie nodded.

He shook his head.

"Then you'll have to trust me on this one. I know the difference." Lemmie's face seemed to wince, then she said, "I guess you could say that I'm compelled to write, not to hunt and gather and acquire money. And I can write what I want, because people buy whatever I put on the page. I don't have to write for the market, or try to time it."

"No compromises."

Lemmie nodded again. "I know it's a luxury others don't have."

Donnally took a sip of the coffee Lemmie had poured for him.

"Then why did he impose his duplex on you?"

"Maybe guilt. Maybe to make me a coconspirator in his compromises."

"I'm starting to think his problem was far worse than mere compromising."

"You're probably right. I'm not even sure he could've articulated what position he was compromising from. And I'm not sure any of the people he worked with, and who acted like he acted, could either."

"Like Reggie Hancock?"

Lemmie drew back. "Why do you mention Reggie?"

Donnally was surprised by her reaction. "Why, why?"

"Mark once set us up on a date. Reggie made my skin crawl. He's beyond arrogant. He has no values at all, believes in nothing. He bragged about things other people would be embarrassed even to admit."

Lemmie glanced toward her laptop on a table in the corner, overlooking her garden. Her writing desk.

"He's a character in my new book, except I made him a medical researcher who falsifies his clinical trial test results instead of a lawyer and I made him East Indian instead of black. He figures that since thirty percent of people have a placebo effect anyway, he can claim a thirty percent success rate. For some drugs on the market that's not so bad. Where he goes wrong—where he deceives himself—is that it's a cancer drug he's developing. There is no placebo effect on cancer, and people will die."

"Did Reggie ask you out again?"

"Yeah, when he came into town to meet with Mark or appear in court up here. And I went. For research."

Lemmie leaned back in her chair. She closed her eyes and took in a long breath and then exhaled as though steeling herself for an assault of memory.

"Reggie was a petri dish of corruption." She opened her eyes again. "I watched it grow over the years like a virus that escapes from the lab and infects others."

"Like Mark?"

"Like Mark. He turned my brother's rebellion against my father from a fight for justice into a kind of nihilism. Into a justification for substituting his own judgment for the law's. It's like . . . like . . ." She winced again. "Shoot. I can't think of the word. It's when a jury sets aside the law."

"Nullification."

"That's it. Nullification. The jury finds someone not guilty who everybody knows is guilty because they think the law is bad or the defendant's motives were good, or at least not evil. The problem was that for Reggie his aim became nullification in every case and by any means necessary."

"Except it wasn't in the interest of some notion of justice."

"At the beginning, it may have been. At the end, no. I think Reggie was opposed to drug laws on principle. He felt virtuous fighting those kinds of cases, and he was good at it, and got rich doing them."

Donnally watched the sides of her mouth turn up as a thought came to her.

"I guess you could say virtue is easy when there's money to be made, then it somehow transforms into the virtue of easy money."

Donnally smiled. "You should write that down and use it in a book."

"I did." Lemmie smiled back. "That's what you get for not reading my novels all the way through. It's a continuing theme."

"And you got on that road because of people like Reggie?"

Lemmie's smile faded. "No, my father. None of the people he persecuted were guilty of anything, they simply refused to snitch on people like themselves who did nothing but exercise their constitutional rights. For my father, the law was merely an instrument, sometimes a scalpel, sometimes a hammer, sometimes an ax."

"And you think Reggie had a role in leading your brother down that same path."

She shrugged. "Maybe it was Mark running to catch up. I'm not saying Mark wasn't ambitious all on his own, didn't want the money and the notoriety. He did. It's just that how he chose to do it changed. And that was his own responsibility. He couldn't blame that on our father or Reggie."

Lemmie gazed toward the window as though the

view would provide some kind of mental escape, but night had fallen and the glass mirrored the inside of the kitchen. Donnally watched her eyes settle on a spot, his reflection, but he wasn't sure she was actually seeing him.

Finally, she looked over and asked, "How did Reggie's name happen to come up now?"

"He and Mark were trading lots of calls during the last month. I checked previous years and it seems to be part of a pattern. One month a year. Lots of calls."

"Maybe they went on vacations together."

The words came out of her mouth fast, then she reddened as though she'd opened a door to something obscene, or set him up to open it. And he did.

"Like little jaunts to Southeast Asia to look at muscled kids?"

Lemmie clenched her fists on the table. "I don't know what they did over there. Anyway, it was something Reggie got him involved with."

Donnally reached down to the floor and picked up a manila envelope containing printouts about Hamlin and his alleged charity that Jackson had left for him at the office. He opened it and slid the contents onto the table.

Lemmie reached for a photo showing her brother receiving an award from the Southeast Asia Youth Gymnastics Association. Hamlin looked awkward, uncomfortable, standing in a row of middle-aged Asian and Australian men under the stage lights.

"You ever work the prostitution detail?" Lemmie asked, as she stared at the pages. "Especially ones that targeted child predators."

"Only as part of the arrest team."

She pointed at the man standing to the right of her brother. A heavy-set Thai, with his belt drawn tight across his stomach, just below his rib cage, Humpty Dumpty–like, sweat glistening on his forehead and darkening his dress shirt collar.

"Look at the eyes on this guy," Lemmie said. "Look at the eyes on all of them. I've gone down to the Tenderloin, watched men cruising, looking for teenage boys and girls. They're the same eyes these guys have. Somehow both dead and calculating."

"But not on your brother."

"He just looks embarrassed."

Donnally spread the papers on the table. Some of them showed other photos from the same association meeting.

"I don't see Reggie in any of these," Donnally said.

"As I said, I don't know what they did over there."

Other photographs showed teenagers posing in tiny outfits. The thin girls encased in spandex and the boys with arms and leg muscles like bodybuilders, so lean and defined they looked like they'd been skinned.

Donnally looked again at Hamlin standing with the certificate in his hands.

"You think this was a pretext to travel over there to buy opium?" Donnally asked.

"It would be a weird one and wouldn't make a very good cover story. Everybody who knows he made regular trips over there would think—or at least entertain the idea—he was a child molester." She glanced up at Donnally. "Just like you do."

Lemmie slid the photos back, saying, "Another weird thing. Reggie and Mark used to smoke pot together and drink Black Label and sing along with that old Creedence Clearwater song 'Proud Mary.'" Crank it up and pound the table. *And we're rollin'*"—she tapped the tabletop in time with the tune—*"rollin' on the ri-ver."*

Donnally was just a child when the song came out. When he was growing up all the kids assumed that "Proud Mary" was code for marijuana and "rolling" meant rolling joints. Grown men like Hancock and Hamlin getting high and singing it just seemed childish.

But sitting there listening to Lemmie he realized there was something sophomoric about everything Hamlin did, absolutely everything, maybe even fatally so.

CHAPTER 41

Sheldon Galen didn't show up on time for his 8 A.M. debriefing with Donnally. He didn't answer his cell phone and he hadn't gone to his office.

Donnally wasn't surprised Galen had chosen to arrive late, like a six-year-old testing his parents' limits, so he figured he wouldn't lean on him too hard, yet.

Donnally spent an hour searching Hamlin's computer for Web sites he'd visited, expecting that if Hamlin had a sexual interest in children, it would show up on his hard drive. Navarro had referred him to a child exploitation specialist in SFPD who'd walked him through the steps to check Hamlin's Internet search history, Web sites visited, temporary files, and other trails. He didn't find anything. This either meant it wasn't there or that Hamlin was good at concealment.

Other than saying hello when she arrived at the office, Jackson had avoided him. She'd arrived buttoned up. Overcoat belted tight around her waist, lapels overlapping, all three suit buttons snug, blouse closed up to the neck. She had tied her hair back like a 1950s librarian, and her usual array of gold rings and bracelets was missing.

Donnally was relieved not to have to deal again with yesterday's erotic assault, but was troubled he didn't understand Jackson's latest incarnation. It was starting to feel like a game of tag, except that every time Jackson popped up from behind a bush, she was someone else.

The clock on Hamlin's computer told Donnally that it was 9:15. Time to go on the hunt for Galen.

He wasn't angry because he'd expected it, and while Galen might be feeling unique and might be telling himself what he thought were unique excuses for not showing up, Donnally knew that every informant had the same feelings and made the same excuses.

Hamlin's contact list gave Donnally Galen's home address in Berkeley. He called Navarro as he drove across the Bay Bridge, but Navarro didn't answer. Donnally left a message asking whether he'd identified the woman who had argued with private investigator Frank Lange on the evening before he died, and whether he knew how to find Hector Camacho, whose number had shown up in the middle of Hamlin and Hancock's telephone traffic.

Navarro still hadn't called back by the time Donnally arrived on Galen's block. It was off a tree-divided, commercial avenue in the north end of town in an area known as Gourmet Gulch.

Donnally had driven by Alice Waters's Chez Panisse Restaurant on his way up from University Avenue. Passing it, he remembered when Janie had taken him there for his birthday. It was at a time when the place was just getting focused on slow food. He hadn't realized going in that four courses over three hours was what they'd had in mind.

That had annoyed him more than Galen not showing up.

Donnally glanced at Galen's hedge-bordered house as he drove past looking for a parking place on the crowded street. He spotted an SUV that took up most of Galen's driveway. There was no room for him to park behind it without blocking the sidewalk, but at least it suggested that Galen was home.

As he drove on, he noticed that some of the vehicles on the street hadn't been moved in months. Dusty windshields, oak leaves and pine needles had collected on the pavement and surrounded the tires, rain-spotted handouts were stuck under wiper blades. With parking places so hard to find, he wondered whether the residents had decided they would walk or take the bus rather than give them up.

Creeping along, he wished he was still a cop and all he had to do was slide into a red or yellow zone and hang his mike over the rearview mirror to show he was official. But civilians got tickets and he was now a civilian and he didn't want to pay the fine. It was costing him enough money paying his cooks and waitresses overtime up at the café to make up for his absence.

And all this was costing him time. He was supposed to be in town just long enough to replace Janie's rain gutters, but he'd now spent days in a legal sewer.

After ten minutes, he found a spot three blocks from Galen's bungalow, down the hill and near

Chez Panisse. He walked past a homeless guy zipping his pants as he stepped out of the bushes along the side of a student apartment building and then by two Indian-looking Hispanic laborers who angled their faces away as he approached. He took a right onto Galen's street and got a stomach-turning reminder of one thing he hated about detective work: the queasy feeling the guy you were trying to run down had walked away two minutes before you'd arrived.

Donnally's stomach flipped back when he spotted Galen's *San Francisco Chronicle* still on his porch and through the open front curtains saw a light on in the kitchen.

As he climbed the steps, he steeled himself for the "Yeah, I was just on my way" or the "I'm waiting for AAA to jump-start my car" or the "I thought you meant tomorrow."

But he'd learned over the years that informants and cooperating defendants are like baby chicks and puppies; they needed to be cradled, not confronted, at least at first. He knocked on the door and listened for footfalls. He heard none. He stepped to the living room window and peered in. No movement.

"Can I help you?" It was a woman's voice coming from a neighboring porch. Her tone announced she was the captain of the neighborhood watch, or aspired to be. She wore a pink robe, her hand clutching the lapels together under her chin.

Donnally pointed down the hill. "I was supposed to meet Sheldon at Peet's Coffee an hour ago, but he didn't show up." He walked toward her, then bent over the railing and looked along the side of the house toward the backyard. "I'll check back there. Maybe he's working in his garden."

"I'd prefer you didn't."

Welcome to Berkeley.

Donnally's cell phone rang. He glanced at the screen and recognized Navarro's number. He then looked back at the woman and answered, "Detective Donnally."

The woman's face went hot red and her jaw clenched as though Donnally had ripped off her block captain's insignia in front of all her neighbors.

"You're starting to take this all too seriously," Navarro said. "You signing up again to wear a badge?"

"I'll explain later," Donnally said, then continued on for the neighbor's benefit. "Galen didn't show up for our meeting this morning. I'm at his house."

The woman turned and huffed her way back through her front door.

"I didn't know he was supposed to."

"I'll explain that later, too."

"You think he skipped out?" Navarro asked. "If they're gonna run, this is about the time they start thinking about it, before they've done any real damage to anybody."

"I don't know. Hold on a sec." Donnally walked down the steps and around to the side of the house, and then toward the back. He peeked into the living room and dining room windows as he went. Everything neat. Coffee table books fanned out. Asian-themed tables, credenzas, and hutches clean and slick. "What's going on at your end?"

"Two things," Navarro said. "The first is that Frank Lange had a massive dose of Rohypnol in his blood, and I don't think it was because somebody intended to sexually assault him while he was out."

"They just didn't want him waking up as his house heated around him."

"Exactly. And second is we've ID'd the woman who you photographed fighting with him. A former employee recognized her. She worked for him for a while, ending a few months ago. Her first name sounds like river—spelled with a Y and two V's—R-Y-V-V-E-R. Middle name Moon, normal spelling. Last name Scoville, normal spelling."

Donnally squinted through the kitchen window as he repeated the name to himself. The light he'd spotted when he'd walked up the front steps fell on a remodeled kitchen. Gray marble counters, matching stainless steel stovetop, oven, and refrigerator.

"Ryvver Moon sounds like the love child of some hippie kids," Donnally said, "and she looked to be about the right age for it."

Donnally knocked on the back door.

"Bingo. I found out she's the daughter of a lesbian couple Lange was friends with in the late seventies. He called them his Lost Years because he was stoned all the time. Hamlin and Lange both. Or at least Lange told it that way."

Hearing neither footsteps nor Galen's voice, Donnally worked his way around toward a rear-facing window.

"The woman we talked to couldn't figure out why Lange hired her. She was a little loony. Maybe even clinical, with ups and downs like she was on her meds only half the time. And not all that competent, even for shuffling papers in the office. Hiring her must've been a favor to her mothers."

Through a slit between the curtains Donnally could see a made bed in what appeared to be the master bedroom. He imagined Galen really had gone down to Peet's to get his morning latte or whatever was now the fad in Gourmet Gulch.

"Have you caught up with her?" Donnally asked.

"No. Her last real address, or at least the last one she paid rent on, was in Santa Monica. We had local officers go by. The person she sublet to says she hasn't shown up there. She crashed with some friends a few blocks away from Lange's place when she worked for him, but the apartment is empty now."

"What about her mother and mother?"

"Running a bookstore in Guerneville along the Russian River. She's had no contact with them for over two months."

"Or that's what they say when the cops come calling," Donnally said. "They may be frozen in seventies paranoia like bugs in amber."

"Very literary. Who you been hanging out with?"

Donnally decided to accede to Lemmie's wishes not to disclose that Mark Hamlin was her brother.

"A writer."

"You on your way back to this side?"

"This place is empty. I'll be out of here in a couple of minutes, but I think I'll head up to Guerneville to talk to Ryvver's folks. Maybe they'll have an idea what Lange and her were arguing about. I'll call Goldhagen on the way and tell her Galen has skipped and ask her to get Judge McMullin to issue a warrant for embezzling from his trust account. No bail so we won't lose track of him."

"I can't say I'm all that surprised. I just hope I'm the one who gets to slap the cuffs on him. It's every cop's dream to haul in a criminal defense attorney."

Donnally stepped around a collection of rakes and shovels leaning against the side of the house, and headed toward the front gate. The double-hung bathroom window was raised an inch.

He peeked in.

He took in a quick breath.

"What's going on?" Navarro asked.

Galen's body lay sprawled on the floor in front of the toilet. Vomit splattered the seat and the surrounding tile. He was wearing the same clothes as the day before.

"I found him," Donnally said, as he turned toward the rear of the house. "Call an ambulance and the Berkeley police. Let them know I'm kicking in Galen's back door."

CHAPTER 42

I'm not sure how long I can hold out on these guys," Navarro whispered to Donnally in the hallway outside the intensive care unit of Berkeley's Alta Bates Hospital. He motioned with his chin toward two BPD homicide detectives who had just gotten off the distant elevator and were walking toward them.

"You don't need to tell them about the cooperation agreement," Donnally said, "just that he was helping us find out who killed Mark Hamlin." He glanced toward the window into Galen's room. "We don't know yet whether this was an attempted suicide—"

"Or maybe one that will still be successful."

"Or an attempted murder. But the agreement couldn't have been a motive for someone to kill him because no one knew about it."

"Unless there was a leak from the DA's office," Navarro said. "Galen's not a popular guy."

One of the detectives stopped at the nurses' station, while the other continued toward them.

"I almost dropped my cell phone when dispatch said a Harlan Donnally had kicked in the door,"

Detective Dan Edwards said, as he shook Donnally's hand.

Edwards and Donnally had hit it off at a California Homicide Investigators Association meeting fifteen years earlier and they had fished for steelhead together on the Klamath River a few times after that.

Donnally introduced Navarro, then said, "You're probably wondering how I happened to be at Galen's house."

"It crossed my mind," Edwards said, looking through the window at Galen. "Then I remembered reading about the special master business in the Hamlin case."

"Galen was helping me figure out who Hamlin's latest enemies were."

Edwards pointed over his shoulder at his partner. "You can put both of us down as suspects." He wasn't smiling. "I don't mind a lawyer attacking the evidence. I don't even mind him attacking me, trying to make me out to be incompetent. I can defend myself. But that asshole had a way of trivializing victims and how much they suffered. There's no excuse for that."

One of the things Donnally appreciated about Edwards was that he never did that himself. No defensive sarcasm. No sick humor at crime scenes. No minimizing the value of a life, no matter how its owner had wasted it with drugs or devoted it to crime.

Edwards's partner walked up and nodded at Donnally and Navarro. "The doctor will be out in a minute. They don't have a tox result yet, but"—he looked at Donnally—"they think it's more than just sleeping pills from the bottle you found."

"That's probably right. The prescription was for thirty and there were still twenty-five left." Donnally tilted his head toward Galen, lying fifteen feet away, comatose and hooked up to a ventilator, with IVs spreading upward from both forearms to infusion pumps. "I don't think five would've done that."

"I don't know what it would be," Edwards said. "I had a patrol officer who used to be a paramedic go through the house. He found lots of medications, which means lots of interactions. He's on his way over here with a list so the doc can run them through the pharmacy database to see if it might be a combination of drugs that did put him out."

Donnally looked at Edwards's partner. "The doctor think Galen will wake up?"

"He didn't say."

They turned at the squeak of rubber soles on the linoleum floor and widened their circle to give the doctor a place. He didn't introduce himself, letting the name "S. Sugarman, M.D.," stitched on his lab coat, do it for him.

"It's watch and wait," Sugarman said. "We were too late to pump anything out of his stomach. Whatever it was had already been absorbed."

Edwards asked, "Any idea what—"

"His mother called saying that he'd started taking an antidepressant a day or two ago. She thinks it was an MAO inhibitor." He shook his head. "It can work like a blasting cap if he was using any of a hundred other things. Legal or illegal." He looked back and forth between Navarro and Donnally.

"People in Berkeley take all kinds of idiotic concoctions without telling their doctors. Take enough St. John's wort, and an MAO will kill you."

Donnally felt Navarro's eyes on him and knew they were thinking the same thing. That Galen had run from his collapsing legal practice to a psychiatrist's office in order to find himself a chemical place to hide.

"Did you find an MAO card on him?" Donnally asked.

He knew, from Janie's expression of worry about prescribing the drug to veterans for whom nothing else worked, that some users carried special ID cards because of those interactions.

"No," Sugarman said. "Nothing."

"You find any bruising or other injuries that would suggest he was forcibly given whatever it was?" Edwards asked.

"Just the normal kind of redness on his arms and legs that's associated with the EMTs lifting him onto a gurney and the orderlies moving him to a bed. But feel free to check yourself. I could've missed something."

The tone of Sugarman's last words was not that of an admission, but an exit line. He turned and walked away.

"You want to do it?" Edwards asked Donnally.

Donnally extended his open palm toward Galen. "It's your case."

CHAPTER 43

Hector Ignacio Camacho-Fernandez, aka Nacho—
and if Ramon Navarro had come to the right
conclusion from his analysis of Mark Hamlin's cell
phone traffic—aka *Raton*. A rat. A snitch.

And Navarro was right. The file lay on Hamlin's
kitchen table in front of Donnally. He and Jackson had searched Hamlin's office cabinets, desk,
and storage room, but hadn't been able to locate it.
Donnally had then driven to Hamlin's house and
pawed through the mass of papers on his living
room floor and dining table, until he found what
he hoped was all of it. But he couldn't be certain.
Hamlin's filing system seemed geographical, with
related pages sharing a general area of the house,
rather than specific, with everything fitted into a
particular folder.

Scribblings on a page torn from a legal pad told
most of the tale.

At the top were Hamlin's notes of meeting with
Camacho.

*Camacho knows he's under surveillance. Thinks his calls
are being tapped. A fifty-kilo load of cocaine from Mexico*

*was seized from a shed in Salinas. The spot had been men-
tioned only in a single call from his Mission Street taqueria to Juarez.*

That was followed by notes of a call to Hamlin
from an Assistant U.S. Attorney for the Northern
District of California.

*DEA is agreeable to considering a cooperation agreement
with Camacho as long as he doesn't get a complete walk on
the case.*
*Conditions: He names his sources in Michoacan and in
Long Beach, identifies everyone in his organization, agrees
to a full debriefing, surrenders drug profits including the
house in Daly City and his cars. Can keep his taqueria.
Will consider a reward of up to $250,000, based on assets
seized from targets he IDs.*

Then notes of a call between Hamlin and Reggie
Hancock.

Deal possible. Camacho willing to roll on Rafa.
*Split 40/60 from Guillermo, 60/40 from Nacho, and
40/60 from Rafa.*

The flurry of calls ended with notes from Hamlin's meeting with Camacho.

Agreed. Debriefing in a week. Lange will sit in.

Even as he searched for other notes, a phrase
kept repeating itself in Donnally's mind like a tune
he couldn't get out of his head.

Can keep his taqueria.

The last time Donnally walked toward a taqueria on Mission Street to meet an informant was also his last day on the job as a police officer.

Can keep his taqueria.

Donnally pushed the notes aside and thought back on that day, then winced at the clash of past and future in his present memory, and closed his eyes. He saw himself getting out of his car on the west side of Mission Street, looking over his hood toward the restaurant door.

A laugh from his left. A young couple, maybe Salvadorean or Guatemalan, compact bodies, Mayan faces, sitting at a wrought-iron table in front of a coffee shop. Magazines spread on top. A woman posing in a wedding dress smiling from the cover of one.

He had taken a step toward the front of his car, then—

Bam-bam-bam.

Gunshots from behind him, but not at him, from a Norteño gangster up the sidewalk, ten yards away, maybe fifteen, shooting at a Sureño down the other way.

He'd ducked behind his hood, reaching for his gun and yelling to the couple, "Down! Down! Down!"

Too late. The male slumped over. The female screaming.

Bam-bam from Donnally's left. He caught the motion of the Sureño's black, silver-toed boot and pressed Levi's pant leg disappearing behind a trash can.

Donnally's gun had followed his eyes. Barrel steadied by a double-handed grip braced against his car. So focused on each other, neither the Norteño nor the Sureño had spotted him yet.

Bam-bam . . . bam-bam-bam. The Norteño firing. But Donnally had lost sight of him. He was using the cars behind Donnally's as cover.

The Sureño tumbled forward and over the curb, then raised his semiautomatic, but Donnally fired first.

Bam-bam from his right.

The Sureño slumped onto the oil-slicked pavement.

Then again from his right. Bam-bam . . . bam-bam.

Donnally felt a thud against his hip and his leg gave way. He reached up, locking the fingers of his left hand into the gap between his hood and the windshield. Pain from shattered bone lit up the wound, then vibrated down his leg and up his side.

Thunking leather. Boot heels on concrete getting louder, running toward him.

Metal scraped against metal as the Norteño jammed in a new clip.

Bam.

Glass fragments burst from holes in the back window and windshield.

The footsteps stopped.

Bam-bam-bam.

The clunk of punched metal and the tink, tink of fractured glass.

He pulled himself up and fired at the Norteño through his own car windows.

Bam-bam-bam-bam-click-click-click.

The Norteño reached for his chest and staggered into the street.

Screeching tires. No thud.

The Norteño dropped to his knees, balanced for a moment, then pitched forward. A head-thunk against a bumper.

The smoke of burned rubber swirled and attacked Donnally's eyes. He looked toward the woman, now splayed over the table, dead arms reaching in a final gesture toward her fiancé.

Distant sirens, then silence.

Coming to consciousness again.

An EMT putting pressure on his hip. A paramedic leaning over him, speaking into his radio.

Officer down. Four dead.

Donnally opened his eyes. The legal pad a bright, painful yellow on the desk in front of him. He thought of Hector Camacho sitting in his office at the back of his restaurant. *El Raton*. Norteño gangsters at one end of the block. Sureños at the other . . .

I don't want to do this again.

CHAPTER 44

Donnally left the city just before noon by way of the Golden Gate Bridge, heading north through Marin County on the Redwood Highway toward the Russian River. With "Proud Mary" playing in his head, he realized that what Lemmie had seen as merely juvenile—Hamlin and Hancock getting stoned and singing and pounding the table—was worse, it was corrupt and cynical. In their minds, "rolling" referred not only to smoking pot, but to snitching one client on another. It was nothing less than a celebration of betrayal.

He knew he'd be going back to Mission Street. He knew that soon enough he'd pull up in front of Camacho's taqueria, get out of his car, look up and down the sidewalk, and head toward the entrance—

Just . . . not . . . yet.

The Sir Francis Drake Boulevard exit to coastal Highway 1 rose up like a suppressed temptation, and not just because a longer trip up along the ocean to the mouth of the river then inland to Guerneville would delay his return to Mission Street. But because he hated the outlet malls and car dealerships that were filling in the land between San Rafael and

Novato, and between Novato and Petaluma, and between Petaluma and Rohnert Park, and between Rohnert Park and Santa Rosa. Driving past them was like walking down the aisle of an Eddie Bauer outlet store filled with people buying clothes they didn't need and pretending to themselves they'd go places where they'd never go. Or maybe it was like a dollar store, the oppression of too much stuff overwhelming the necessities of life.

A minute later, the urge to cut off the highway had faded and he was shooting north past where redwoods used to be. And a few minutes after that, the Marin County Civic Center appeared on his right. He remembered driving there soon after he completed the police academy to pick up a suspect, wondering where else but in Marin did people hire an architect like Frank Lloyd Wright to design a jail. But then San Francisco built one that looked like a European art museum, undulating like a wave that seemed to wash the jail out of jailed.

An hour later, Donnally slipped off the freeway onto the Old Redwood Highway, turned west on River Road, and headed toward the bookstore owned by Ryvver's mothers.

Donnally felt a tingle in his fingers and a bump up in his heart rate when he got his first glimpse of the Russian River, wide like a lake and blue like a lagoon except where sunlight painted yellow and gold on the moving surface. He knew that people fishing for steelhead were working the riffles and holes downriver, maybe one now stood waist-deep in waders near the sand and gravel spit where he'd caught his first one, each turn and run by the fish, each pump of the rod shooting adrenaline through his body. It was that moment, more than any other, that fated him to someday move north to Mount Shasta where redwoods still grew and close to where steelhead and salmon still ran. That someday had come a lot sooner than he'd expected, but he'd made it nonetheless.

River Road turned into Guerneville's Main Street, a few mostly one-story commercial blocks north of the river that was just inside the far border of quaint and that had become too gay even for Ramon Navarro. He'd once told Donnally that any-place referred to as a playground wasn't for him.

As Donnally stepped down from his truck in front of Mothers' Books & Café, a blue-façade Tudor storefront, he wished he wasn't wearing cowboy boots. He should've checked with Navarro about local politics, whether the leather-soles-in-cow-shit locals from the dairy farms in the foothills were still at war with the Vibram-never-leave-the-sidewalk outsiders.

At least in Guerneville, unlike San Francisco's Mission District, he didn't have to worry about finding himself in anything worse than a verbal crossfire as he stepped onto the sidewalk.

A tinkling bell announced his arrival as he pushed open the door.

He'd checked the bookstore Web site before he left Hamlin's office, so he recognized Scoville Mother Number One behind the drinks counter in the café half of the store. She was a little shorter and a little wider than her picture, but was wearing the same wire-rimmed glasses and a similar tan work shirt with the business name stenciled in brown on the front. He walked up, ordered a decaf coffee, and asked if he could talk to her.

"About what?"

Only loud enough for her to hear, Donnally said, "Ryvver," and then tilted his head toward the end of the counter, ten feet beyond the tattooed teenage boy working the espresso machine.

Mother One bit her lip, anxious and uncertain, then came around and walked with him to a corner table at the back of the café. She folded up a local newspaper and slid it aside as they sat down.

"Aren't you supposed to show me a badge or something," Mother One said, then flicked her thumb toward the entrance. "And aren't there supposed to be two of you?"

"I'm an ex-cop, so my badge wouldn't mean anything," Donnally said. "And I was never very good at pairing up."

She glanced at his left hand. "No ring."

Donnally got the feeling that she was in no hurry to talk about her daughter.

"Never married."

She smiled. "I never would've guessed."

Donnally smiled back. "You?"

"That's kind of hard to say at the moment." Her smile faded. "I've got a ring and a certificate, but there's three levels of appeals courts between us and the promised land. Once they tell me what the law is, I'll know whether I'm married or—"

"Or just civilly united?"

Mother One shrugged. "I guess you could say it's mostly civil."

Donnally saw an inadvertent opening.

"Does the uncivil part have anything to do with Ryvver?"

Her eyes widened as she saw herself being pushed into the gap.

"How come you want to know?"

"I was appointed special master in the murder of a lawyer in San Francisco."

"Mark Hamlin. I read about it."

Donnally nodded. "I've been trying to get in contact with people—"

"Suspects?"

"Ryvver isn't a suspect," Donnally said, and finished the sentence in his mind: *At least in the murder of Mark Hamlin.*

"Then why . . ."

"She had an argument with Frank Lange the night before he died and I think Hamlin and Lange were in the middle of something together."

"They were in the middle of something together for decades. They shared what they called the Lost Years." Mother One paused, then the tinkling bell drew her attention to the door. She watched an old couple walk hand-in-hand up to the counter. He thought he saw envy in her fixed gaze. She blinked and looked back at Donnally, then leaned forward and folded her arms on the table.

"Let's cut to the chase," Mother One said. "Ryvver didn't kill Frank Lange."

"I didn't accuse her of—"

"Close enough. It would be called patricide."

Donnally drew back. "Lange was her father?"

Mother One nodded. "From the days before

artificial insemination, or at least before lesbians got access to it."

She gave a shudder from which Donnally understood that he was supposed to assume her act of intercourse with Frank Lange in order to conceive Ryvver was the most distasteful thing she'd ever done.

Donnally decided to display that he did, and said, "I hope she appreciated your sacrifice."

Mother One took in a long breath, then exhaled, "Not always. But it wasn't exactly my sacrifice, it was my partner's."

Donnally understood that Mother One's sacrifice was pacing a living room floor while Mother Two had sex with Lange. He wondered how they decided who'd be the one to spread her legs under him. Maybe they picked straws or maybe they just measured their levels of revulsion on some kind of scale, like a noise meter. Or maybe they just got high and flipped a coin, each praying to the Her Who Art in Heaven as it spun in the air.

Donnally also wondered how Ryvver's life could ever have seemed normal when it began with what the mothers considered to have been an original sin against their nature.

"How'd you pick Frank?" Donnally asked.

"He was the best of a narrow range of options and he wasn't yet the fat asshole he turned into."

Mother One sighed as though saying, *If I only knew then what I know now.*

"Do you know why Ryvver was upset with Frank?"

"In general or in particular?"

"Start with the particular."

"There are too many possibilities. Mostly father-daughter possibilities, or maybe I should say the sort-of-father-sort-of-daughter possibilities."

"Then how about start with the general, non-sort-of-father-daughter type."

Mother One gazed around the restaurant with a how-did-I-get-here expression, then said, "She didn't have a whole lot of contact with Frank growing up. Just a week or two during the summers. That changed after college, what she did of it. It was only after she started working for him that she got a good look, and she didn't like what she saw."

"What had she expected to find?"

"You ever see Frank on television or read in the newspaper the kinds of things he said?"

"I don't remember seeing him at all or reading any quotes from him."

"You'd think he was the guarantor of the U.S. Constitution, sounding like Earl Warren. Equal justice and all that shit." A bitter laugh burst from her mouth. "He used to call himself The Equalizer. Almost sued the production company when that TV show came on in the late 1980s using that same name. But the fact was he was a louse. A fucking louse. He was a dirty-dealing, money grubbing Un-Equalizer. We kept our mouths shut and never poisoned her thinking about him, but that's what he turned into."

"Turned into from what?"

She thought for a moment. "I'm not sure. We might've been wrong about him right from the beginning, and just didn't see it."

"And do you think there's a connection between the general and the particular that got her fighting with him?"

"All I know is that a friend of hers committed suicide in prison. She went racing down to see Frank right after she found out about it. I got the feeling she'd tried to get Frank to help him just after he got arrested and while she was working for Frank, but he refused."

"Who's the guy?"

"We called him Little Bud." She waved her hand in a high arc behind her, as though beyond the confines of the café. "He had a marijuana grow up in the hills. For decades. Lived like a sharecropper in a shack above it. Helluva view of the river from up there. No electricity. No television. No radio. Just a wood stove for cooking and a gas lamp for reading. Ryvver used to spend hours up there with him."

She paused and her eyes and face took on a kind of longing.

"Little Bud was like an older brother to her and she loved him in that way. I mean really loved him. He did for her what the meds could never do, what we could never do. Calm the racing thoughts and anchor her back into the world—then he got busted. Thirty fucking years in prison."

She glanced toward the book section of the store, and a hard edge entered her voice. "From *Call of the Wild* to *The Count of Monte Cristo*."

"He must've had a hillside of plants to get that much time."

Mother One spread her hands like she was making a plea at a sentencing. "It was just pot, and he gave almost all of it away to medical marijuana clubs he thought were legit. And him being five-two and a hundred and twenty pounds and stuck in the federal pen with real crooks and heavy-duty gangsters . . ." Her voice trailed off.

"And he couldn't take looking at the rest of his life caged up."

"Hung himself after two months."

"Why didn't he cooperate? Give them someone else. Isn't that how the game is played in federal court?"

"Somebody had to be the last domino, and he decided it would be him. The DEA wanted everyone he sold to or gave away stuff to and everyone he knew who had grows going and everything about what they did with their money. Especially that." She looked through the front window. Donnally followed her eyes toward a real estate office across the street. "They really, really wanted the real estate brokers who structured deals so the growers could turn their cash into land and houses. But he refused to do it."

"I'm not sure what Frank could've done to help him," Donnally said. "Some cases can't be beat. And if Little Bud was living right on the property he grew the pot on, I don't see what kind of defense he could've cooked up."

Donnally then had a thought. Maybe Mother One was looking at this thing backward. Maybe Ryvver was angry because Lange hadn't been willing to play the Un-Equalizer and play dirty on Little Bud's behalf. Maybe pull a John Gordon routine on whoever the government's witness was or maybe find somebody to take the fall in exchange for money like the formerly brain-tumored Bennie Madison had claimed. A guy like Lange could come up with lots of angles.

But Donnally didn't transform that thought

into speech. Instead, he asked, "And you think she blamed Frank?"

"I don't know. This is all theory, anyway. She hasn't been back up here to tell us about it."

"You have any idea where she went?"

"Nope. And she hasn't been answering her cell phone since two days before Frank died." She shuddered again. "I can imagine what she's going through. She was devastated by Little Bud's death, and she was a fragile person to begin with." She half smiled. "How two dykes like us ended up with a daughter who wouldn't pick flowers as a kid for fear of causing the plant pain, I'll never know."

Donnally reached into his pants pocket for a pen and tore off a piece of paper from his notepad. He wrote down his cell number and handed it to her.

The bell tinkled again. Mother One looked over. "Shit."

Mother Two moved like a subatomic particle. One instant she was standing at the door, the next she was leaning over the table.

"I can tell a fucking cop when I see one."

Her face burned with outrage and her fists were hard by her sides.

Mother Two glared down at Mother One. "Why are you talking to this guy?"

It wasn't a question.

Then to Donnally, "What do you want from us?"

This one was a question, and he answered it.

"I'm trying to get in contact with Ryvver."

Mother Two's palm shot out toward him in a straight arm that stopped inches from his face.

"Not through us, you won't."

CHAPTER 45 ════════

Donnally stopped by the sheriff's substation in Guerneville and obtained Little Bud's true name and identifiers and the name of the San Francisco–based DEA agent who'd supervised the joint narcotics task force that had targeted him. He then drove east toward the Redwood Highway, thinking a mother bear couldn't have protected her cub with more aggression than Scoville Mother Number Two had shielded Ryvver. Donnally had the feeling even while he was stepping back out onto the sidewalk from Mothers' Books & Café to the sound of the tinkling bell, that she'd been doing it all her daughter's life.

The odds were as low as the Russian River in a drought year that Ryvver had drugged and murdered her father in the planned and calculated manner in which Lange had been killed. Donnally had learned in homicide training, and his experience never contradicted it, that patricides were usually Lizzie Borden crimes of passion, not premeditated murders.

As he squared the block to get turned around to head back to San Francisco, he tried to remember the first-degree murders of parents in California. The only one he could think of was the Menendez brothers in Beverly Hills in the late 1980s. It was a case that involved a dummied-up defense, too. It rested on false allegations the father had sexually abused the boys and had emotionally abused their mother, and on a bizarre claim that the boys killed her to put her out of her misery. It also involved a defense attorney who leaned on the psychiatrist to alter his report, a move that later left her taking the Fifth twice during questioning by the judge.

Hamlin in Northern California and Reggie Hancock in Southern California didn't have a monopoly on manipulating psych evidence—they'd just never been examined under oath.

Donnally slowed while driving over the River Road bridge. He watched a truck shoot past him, then looked down toward the sandbar that narrowed the wide water flow into a roiled chute a hundred and fifty yards downstream. It was right there more than two decades earlier, standing waist-deep, drifting salmon roe, sweeping it across the current at the end of long riffle, that his first steelhead had struck.

And in that instant, the mystery of whether there were any fish moving through that part of the river ended with a bucking rod and a pounding heart.

As he looked again at the road in front of him and accelerated, he realized his trip hadn't served as a sandbar to narrow his case and now he wasn't sure he was even fishing in the right river to catch the killer of Mark Hamlin, or even of Frank Lange.

He reached for his phone. Ramon Navarro answered on the second ring.

"I was just about to call you," Navarro said.

"That mean Galen has returned to the world of the conscious?"

"No. He's still out and we've got no ETA. But that's not today's topic. I got Judge McMullin to issue an order for a pen register and trap and trace on Ryvver's cell phone and for cell site and GPS info so we can track her and her calls."

"Her mother, or at least one of her mothers, said it was turned off."

"I think she has at least two. It looks like she bought a new pay-as-you-go phone and is using it to check messages on her old one. If so, she's still in San Francisco. All of the calls are from a cell site out in the avenues near Golden Gate Park."

"All?"

"All."

"That means she's not moving around," Donnally said. "She's probably holed up somewhere."

"Or maybe only going as far as the corner store."

"Or maybe is using a phone we haven't ID'd yet."

Donnally noticed a service station coming up, then glanced at his fuel gauge and saw it was low. He pulled in next to the island.

"Hold on a second. I need to get some gas."

As he was getting out, he spotted the truck that had passed him on the bridge. It had pulled off to the side of the road fifty yards away, the driver's side mostly shielded by a freestanding metal sign in front of a café.

"I think somebody is following me," Donnally said. "Hold on again. Let me try to get the plate."

Donnally raised his phone like he was checking for a telephone number or a text message, and took a photo of the truck. He then zoomed in, targeting the front plate, and read it off to Navarro.

"Can you check that quick?"

"No problem."

Donnally heard keystrokes in the background as he removed the gas cap, fed the nozzle into the neck of the tank, and started pumping.

"Scoville, Leslie," Navarro said. "Goes to a 2006 Ford pickup."

"That's it. Mother Number Two."

"What do you think she's up to?"

"Maybe she thinks I have a better chance of finding her daughter than she does and wants to piggyback off me."

"I wouldn't be so sure," Navarro said. "I asked some guys in the department who hang out around Guerneville on weekends in the summer. They say she's a pretty tough cookie who gets what she wants. I'm thinking she wants to stay close to you in case you get close to Ryvver. That way she can forearm you to give Ryvver time to get away."

"From what? Chances are slim she killed Lange. She's his daughter."

"No shit?"

"None at all." Donnally thought for a moment, then said, "I wonder if Ryvver is hiding because she knows something and doesn't want to be questioned about it. Maybe something Lange did. The thing they argued about. Mother One told me about a guy named Little Bud who committed suicide in federal prison after he got thirty years on a marijuana beef. Robert Earl Bowling."

Donnally watched the numbers rise on the gas pump as he listened to more of Navarro's typing in the background—

Then a laugh.

"Guess who his lawyer was?" Navarro asked.

The laugh had already given Donnally the answer: "Mark Hamlin."

CHAPTER 46

I never saw the Little Bud file," Takiyah Jackson told Donnally when he got back to the office.

They were standing on the rug in front of Hamlin's desk. He suspected from her outfit, a V-neck sweater and a push-up bra, that he would have a problem with her again. He felt himself in the middle of a sort of crossfire with Jackson poised next to him and a mother bear parked in her truck down the block.

It had made no sense to try to lose Mother Number Two since she could catch up with him whenever she wanted, at Hamlin's office or at Janie's house, which was still in his name. He also didn't want to clue her in that he knew she was following him by making any quick moves.

"I'm not sure there even was a file," Jackson continued, "or at least much of one. It was a bang-bang thing. I think Mark only made three appearances. When Little Bud was arraigned, when he pled guilty, and when he was sentenced."

"Didn't he even file a motion to find out the name of the informant who snitched him off? Or to suppress the evidence in the case? I thought that was routine."

"It is, but he didn't. And not out of laziness. It didn't make any difference who the informant was and there's no way to suppress evidence that's in plain view. The DEA flew a helicopter over the site. Even hidden among the ferns and tomato plants, the pot glowed in the infrared camera like landing lights." She pointed upward and made a circling motion, then curved her hand down toward the floor and leveled it off like a landing airplane. "And they swooped in."

"And I take it he didn't try to negotiate for a better deal."

"The U.S. Attorney played hardball. She threatened thirty years, figuring Little Bud would cave and cooperate. She put it to him as an ultimatum. First, last, and best offer. Snitch or do the time. She couldn't back down. He couldn't back down. Because of the length of his sentence, they sent him to a level four prison. Hard-core."

"Did Frank Lange have anything to do with the case?"

Jackson's eyebrows narrowed like it had never crossed her mind Lange had a role in it, then she shrugged and said, "I don't think so."

"What about his daughter?"

Her brows went deeper and the skin folds between her eyes seem to crevasse. "How'd you know about her?"

It was Donnally's turn to shrug.

"Frank didn't talk about it much," Jackson said. "He wasn't the fatherly type. But I knew."

"You know her?"

Jackson looked away. "Ryvver didn't spend much time in San Francisco."

"That wasn't my question."

She looked back. "It's complicated."

"Then uncomplicate it for me."

"I'd see her once in a while at Frank's when she was a kid and she stayed with me for a couple of months after she got out of . . . of . . ."

For some reason, Jackson couldn't get the words out. It made Donnally want to hear them all the more.

"After she got out of what?"

"She . . . uh . . . lived in Mann House."

Donnally hadn't heard the name for more than a decade. It had been a home for mentally disturbed kids.

"You know what the diagnosis was?"

Jackson shrugged again. Donnally knew she knew, but didn't press her for fear she would feel he was trapping her into attacking Ryvver, or perhaps reducing her identity to a mental illness, by saying it aloud.

"I didn't want her to go back to Guerneville and into the mess with her mothers. She was a lost soul and I didn't think she could find herself up there. And I couldn't bear her living with Frank. He couldn't even take care of a dog, much less someone as troubled as her. She finally got herself together and went home after a few months, but then came back to San Francisco to work for Frank."

"You know who she stayed with down here?"

"She shared an apartment with a couple of guys

out near Golden Gate Park. But they're gone. Moved overseas somewhere, Thailand or Vietnam or someplace, but not the same thing."

"The same thing as what?"

She didn't answer, only smiled at the implication. She reached out and gripped his upper arm.

"As far as I know they had no interest in teenage kids. They were straight up do-gooders, like in the Peace Corps."

Donnally glanced at the computer monitor and used that to set up an excuse to turn away and break her grip.

"Maybe I can find some notes in his computer," Donnally said, then pulled his arm free and walked around to the other side of the desk. He didn't sit down, waiting for her to return to her desk.

"I didn't mean anything by that," Jackson said.

"I think you did."

She forced a smile. "I'm just a touchy-type person. Black people are like that, you know."

"Don't try that cultural bullshit," Donnally said. "I think you're afraid of something."

"You?"

"Some*thing*. Not some*one*."

She tilted her head toward the couch along the wall below the window. "You want me to lay myself down so you can play therapist?"

"No. I want your help, and I don't like these games getting in the way of my getting it."

Jackson straightened herself and folded her arms above her breasts. "Is that better?"

"It'll do for now."

Donnally spotted a parking place in front of Hector Camacho's Taqueria Michoacan at Twenty-fourth and Mission. He also spotted a lookout leaning against the wall of the liquor store at the end of the block. He took the next corner, drove down the street until he found a space just beyond a machine shop driveway, and slid in. He figured he'd only be gone from the office for an hour, so he'd slipped out and left the parking garage by the rear exit, leaving Mother Number Two in her surveillance position. He also instructed Jackson to leave the lights on after she left for the day to suggest he was still working inside.

His cell phone rang. It was Janie. "I was near Hamlin's building so I stopped in. Looks like I just missed you."

"I'm out trying to get ahold of a guy." Donnally didn't want to tell her it was in the Mission. His worries were her worries, and hers were his. No reason to put her through it again.

"Takiyah was just closing up when I got there. It was interesting."

"Personally or clinically?"

"Both. You have a run-in with her today?"

"She started the sexualized little girl thing again and I had to shut her down."

"Whatever you said left her teary-eyed and bewildered. I had the feeling she's starting to see what she's been doing and she didn't like what she saw. I think she wanted to apologize to me for trying to move in on you or wanted to explain herself to me or maybe wanted me to explain her to herself. She called me Dr. Nguyen, so I think she knows I'm a psychiatrist. Did you mention it to her?"

"No. But she could've asked around, checking me out. How'd it end?"

"She stammered and then froze up and ran out of the office. She was in the elevator and going down before I could catch up."

"I'll keep that in mind when I see her tomorrow. Maybe it means she's getting close to opening up to me."

Donnally looked up. Fog was crawling over the western hills and darkening the city, graying the pastel apartment buildings in the next block and chilling the air. His gaze lowered to street level. A couple of mid-twenties Norteños wearing red plaid shirts stared at him from where they leaned against a bus bench in front of a body shop. His hand went to his holster and he checked the strap.

"Mind locking up for me? Just make sure the desk lamp in Hamlin's office is still on. I'll see you at home."

Reaching for the door handle after he disconnected, thinking of Jackson and of himself, a phrase came to him.

Being of two minds.

He'd heard people use the expression over the years, even used it himself, but he hadn't really thought about what it meant for a long time. But he did now as he got out of his truck and felt the stab of pain in his hip as his foot hit the pavement. And, on second thought, he wasn't sure he understood it right even then. He just knew that in walking back around the corner, he'd have to push through the resistance of the past, force his way into the present—and not blow the brains out of the lookout, thereby making him the victim of a memory not fully understood or overcome.

A minute later, heading down the shadowed Mission Street sidewalk, watching the lookout's head swivel toward him, he knew all he really grasped of the shooting was the mechanics of it, not the meaning.

How did it happen that the Norteño and the Sureño had been stationed on opposite ends of the block?

Who had been the target?

Him?

Or the informant waiting in the booth inside?

The only thing the detectives in the gang task force would say was that dead men tell no tales. And by the time Donnally had gotten through rehabbing his hip, whatever trail there might have been had been overgrown by a jungle of other crimes.

Little girls in Catholic school plaid skirts stepped out of a pandaria, giggling and biting into sugar-covered empanaditas. Donnally felt his legs tense and his knee bend for a run toward them, his mind racing ahead to thoughts of a crossfire. He forced himself to stop and turned toward a clothing store window and took a breath, listening to the girls' laughter as they walked behind him.

When his eyes refocused, he realized he was staring at rows of women's spike-heeled pumps like he was a fetishist from South of Market. He imagined the lookout watching him, laughing to himself, dismissing him as a threat. The crook coming to the right conclusion for the wrong reason.

Hector Camacho was sitting in a rear booth, his fingers working an electric adding machine, the gears grinding out the paper against the background of banda music drifting down from dusty loudspeakers wedged into the upper corners of the dining room.

Donnally wondered whether he was counting up the money he'd have left after the government was done seizing his house and cars.

As Donnally zigzagged through the three rows of empty Formica tables, through the smells of roasted chilies and grilled meats and fresh tortillas, he heard a whistle from behind the counter and saw Camacho's right hand slide from the table down to his lap.

Donnally raised his hands, slowed, but kept walking. Only now did he wish it was still the old days when he had his we're-the-good-guys detective's shield clipped two inches to the right of his belt buckle.

Ten feet away, Donnally said, "*Quedate tranquilo.*" Stay cool. "*Yo tengo identificación.*" I have ID.

Camacho raised his left palm.

"*Muestrame de donde es usted.*" Show me from where you are.

Donnally stopped, reached into his back pocket and pulled out his retirement badge, and turned it toward Camacho.

"My name is Harlan Donnally."

Camacho pointed at Donnally's left side, then slid his finger over until it pointed at his right.

Donnally pulled back his jacket and showed the gun on his hip.

Camacho nodded and covered his paperwork. He signaled Donnally to come forward and said in English, "Sit down and keep your hands on the table."

Donnally slid in across from Camacho and laid his palms flat in front of him. Close up, the man looked weary, wearing a face like those of the World War II and Korean War vets his father employed as extras in his first combat movies. The sort who lived in the ghosts of dead comrades and revisited the battlefield each night in their dreams. Donnally had the feeling that while Camacho had the will to fight, he preferred to be done with fighting.

"I want to talk to you about Mark Hamlin," Donnally said. "I was appointed by the court to look into his death."

"I saw something about that on the news." Camacho smiled. "Special master made it sound like you'd be some old white-haired guy." His smile left his face. "You talking to all his clients, or just me?"

"I can't answer that."

"And you're darkening my door because . . ."

Donnally caught motion of a cook walking from the kitchen toward the counter with a takeout order.

"Is it safe to talk in here?"

Camacho waited until the cook finished his return trip and disappeared from view, then said, "Good as anywhere."

Donnally leaned forward and lowered his voice. "My understanding is that you cut a deal."

Camacho didn't respond.

"Somebody rolled on you and you rolled on someone else, and Frank Lange was with you during the debriefing."

Camacho's face hardened. His hand came up from under the table. Donnally tensed, ready to dive and roll and come up shooting. Camacho's hand was empty.

"You been talking to that flaky throwback hippie chick?"

"Which?"

"Moon River or River Moon or some bullshit name like that. A couple of months ago she was poking around about who snitched on who. A hundred pounds of crazy, and pathetic as hell."

"I can't tell you whether I talked to her or not, but I can tell you I saw some paperwork in Hamlin's files. All of his records are still privileged, but the judge is letting me look at anything I need to."

Camacho spread his hands in a kind of defeat. "What happened, happened. Somebody was gonna snitch me off someday. I shouldn't have gone back into the trade. Sure I was pissed it was one of Hamlin's other clients, but—"

"What?"

"Just what I said. One of his other clients rolled on me. Since Hamlin could see it coming, he was able to work something out for me before they kicked in my door." Camacho flashed a grin. "Gave me time to clean things up a little."

Donnally thought of the line in Hamlin's notes.

Split 40/60 from Guillermo, 60/40 from Nacho, and 40/60 from Rafa.

"Who rolled on you?"

"Didn't she tell you that already?"

"Was it Guillermo?"

Camacho nodded. "Guillermo Gutierrez." His lips pressed together as though he was a disappointed parent thinking about an ungrateful child. "And I gave the motherfucker his start, gave him my connection when I went to the federal pen."

"And you gave up Rafa."

"Is that a question?"

"No. I saw his name in Hamlin's file. Was he one of Hamlin's clients?"

"No. Reggie Hancock's. In LA. Rafa was big down there"—Camacho grinned again—"until last month."

Donnally now understood the splits. Hamlin and Hancock split sixty-forty or forty-sixty depending on whose client was rolling. And he wondered how far back the scheme went, since, according to Navarro, Hancock had been Camacho's attorney in the case he was convicted on decades earlier.

"And how would you know the details of his operation, or at least enough to roll on him?"

Camacho smiled. "The flake didn't go running to you, did she?"

And Donnally had the answer. It was Lange. Lange fed Camacho the information he needed to set up Hancock's client, which meant that Hancock fed the information to Lange first. And Ryvver must have figured it all out and was looking for a way to use it to help Little Bud.

"I told you," Donnally said. "I can't say who I've talked to."

"Have it your way."

"What about the money?"

"You mean Hamlin's fee?"

Donnally nodded.

"He was gonna take it out of the reward, from my cut of whatever the government forfeited from Rafa. They found almost half a million in his house. I got fifty thousand out of that. The DEA said I could get up to two hundred and fifty altogether, depending on how much they find."

Donnally thought of the Vietnamese gunman who kidnapped him off the street and took him into the garage. He wondered whether the quarter-million-dollar figure was a coincidence.

"I take it the DEA would send a check to Hamlin," Donnally said, "and he'd deduct his cut and forward you the rest."

Camacho nodded. "In cash. I didn't want no kind of trail between the government and me."

Listening to Camacho, it was clear to Donnally he was no genius. But he didn't have to be to succeed in the drug trade. He just needed to be able to count the money and protect his link in the distribution chain.

Was it possible Camacho hadn't yet figured out that if Guillermo got a cut of his property, and he got a cut of Rafa's, and Hancock and Hamlin got a cut of everybody's, the whole thing must have been a setup from the start?

CHAPTER 48

"I'm in pretty deep in the attorney-client end of the pool and can't feel the bottom," Donnally said to Judge McMullin in his oak-paneled study a couple of hours later.

The furniture had that old-money feel, not museumlike, but used in a respectful way. Donnally imagined somewhere in the mansion, which the judge had referred to as "my place" when he had asked Donnally to meet him there, were stacked four or five sets of antique translucent china and silver service for dozens and enough glassware for an opera gala. Not that the judge used any of it anymore. He was too modest a man and the last of his line.

"If I understand you," McMullin said, "you suspect Camacho went after Mark Hamlin after he figured out the rolling scheme."

Donnally nodded. "I don't believe Camacho is as stupid as he wanted to sound today. The only reason he talked to me was because he thought he'd look guilty of the homicide if he didn't. He's a tough guy. He'd never want to be taken advantage of, and Hamlin's stunt cost him everything he owns except his restaurant, and may cost him his life when Rafa figures out that Camacho set him up."

The judge leaned forward in his wing chair and rested his forearms on his thighs. "How many bodies has Camacho left behind him in his life?"

"Before he went to the pen? Four, maybe five."

"And now two more?"

"He puts a rope around Hamlin's neck, gets him to confirm what he suspects about how the dominoes fell, then he goes after Lange. Camacho had a lookout on the corner and was armed when I went into his restaurant, as though he was waiting for Rafa to reach out from jail and send someone to blow his brains out."

The judge sat back with kind of a body sigh, like he'd struggled over a crossword puzzle and had given up. "The problem is I don't see enough probable cause for an arrest, or even a search warrant for Camacho's house and business."

"We also need biological evidence. We found two hairs in Hamlin's bathroom that the forensic people say weren't his."

Judge McMullin paused and his brows furrowed. He repeated the word "dominoes," and then asked, "How long do you think Hamlin was doing this, setting up one client to roll on another?"

"I don't know." Donnally looked the judge straight in the eye. He recognized the impact his next words would have. "But I know who does. The Assistant U.S. Attorney who handled these cases and negotiated the deals with Hamlin."

The judge looked down shaking his head, and

then exhaled. "Jeez." He looked up. "Bet you wish you were up in Mount Shasta flipping burgers." He didn't wait for a response. "I know I wish I was. You think the cable news channels made a big deal about Hamlin's death? Wait until they get ahold of this one. I'm not sure there's any worse kind of violation of a defense attorney's oath than to betray a client or any more outrageous governmental misconduct than a prosecutor conspiring with the defense attorney doing it."

Donnally knew the judge's choice of the words "outrageous governmental misconduct" wasn't just chance. The phrase was etched into the law. And it was a sign that marked one of those gaps between the ideal of justice from its practice that the judge had viewed as his duty to mend from the moment he was appointed to the bench.

Dismissals and reversals were the prescribed remedies for this kind of wrongdoing, and there was no flourish of legal language in which to disguise it.

Just the opposite. In the idiom of the law trade, it was a bell that couldn't be un-rung.

Donnally knew both he and the judge were wondering the same things. How many clients had been set up by Hamlin and Hancock with the complicity of the U.S. Attorney's office and how many dismissals and reversals there would be.

"The longer I delay acting on this," the judge said, "the greater the risk it will look like I'm a co-conspirator, getting the last ounce of flesh from the defendants before their cases get tossed. Even worse, defendants are deciding right now whether to cooperate and to risk getting their brains blown out or to plead guilty and do their time, and some are already serving prison sentences."

Donnally thought of Little Bud hanging in his cell. Even if he could prove Hamlin had used another client to roll on him, it was way too late for a reversal to do Little Bud any good.

There's no coming back from dead.

"You need to wrap this up," Judge McMullin said. "I'm not sure how long I can sit on this kind of thing."

Ryvver. *That flake.* That's what Camacho had called her. But without her, Donnally couldn't reach probable cause to go after him.

She'd gone running to Camacho after she figured out the rolling scheme, having put together stories she'd heard from Lange and things she'd seen in his files about how Little Bud and Camacho and all the others had been set up.

That flaky throwback hippie chick.

Donnally imagined Ryvver had hid out in an apartment in the avenues, pacing the floor, twisting her hands and biting her nails, imagining Camacho and his guys tying Hamlin to a chair, slapping him around—it never crossed her don't-pick-a-flower-for-fear-of-hurting-a-plant mind they'd actually kill him.

And now she was hiding out again, pacing and twisting and biting, an unwitting coconspirator in a murder, facing a choice of going down on a homicide conspiracy or rolling on Camacho and running for the rest of her life.

Donnally thought of Mother Number Two sitting outside, parked along the tree-lined street, watching the judge's door and Donnally's truck. So far, he didn't think there was any harm in her following him. The newspapers had said he'd be reporting to the judge. His visit wouldn't mean anything special to her now. But eventually it would and he'd be facing a mama bear again.

"I need to bring Navarro in on this," Donnally said. "It's no longer a one-man job. We need to figure out where Ryvver is. We need to lean on some of Camacho's people to get them to roll on him, at least enough so we can get a search warrant. We need to go to LA and talk to Reggie Hancock. For all we know there are other crooks out there besides Camacho who figured out what happened and wanted to put a noose around Hamlin's neck." He took a breath. "And there are other leads we need to follow. Some Vietnamese guy stuck a gun in my back wanting money he said Hamlin had, and a biker was threatening Hamlin because of cash he took out of a crime scene, and the family of a homicide victim and the victims of a walkway collapse also wanted a piece of him."

McMullin looked down, shaking his head. "Hamlin had enough enemies to make up a firing squad." He looked up again and nodded. "I'll clue in Goldhagen that the investigation is both moving deeply into attorney-client matters and that law enforcement involvement in every area is unavoidable." He tapped his chest. "Have Navarro call me. We need to make sure everyone involved in the investigation understands there will be no leaks to the press. None."

CHAPTER 49

Donnally checked his watch as he left the judge's house. He had an hour before Janie was supposed to meet him at Hamlin's office to go for dinner and talk about what he should do about Jackson. He decided to use the time to examine the accounting records, to see if he could figure out the scope of the rolling scheme from deposits into Hamlin's trust account and payments made out of it. He was certain Camacho wasn't the only gangster with a motive and found himself worrying about how many potential suspects might turn up in his search.

Leading Mother Number Two through San Francisco seemed to him like an inverted child's game. He wondered what was the opposite of hide-and-seek.

Night had made it hard to keep sight of the headlights of her truck in his mirrors, and the fog seemed to round her square headlights. He had to make a couple of early stops on yellow lights so she could stay with him, and she seemed to figure out what he was doing. He decided to make it clear to her that he was going downtown and then let her roll the dice that he was heading for Hamlin's building and catch up on her own.

The door to the conference room was closed when he walked in. He could make out women's voices inside. He wondered whether Ryvver had decided to come to him, better to seek him out than to wait for him to knock on her door.

Donnally eased the latch closed so that if his opening of the door hadn't already given him away, the closing of it wouldn't. He crept over and listened. The voice now speaking was Jackson's. There were pauses and sniffling. She was talking about the night Bumper was murdered in his bed and about feeling later that Hamlin had rescued her. Then Hamlin going wrong. And her anger and her feeling trapped by him and her past. The tale coming in a rush. It sounded like she was climbing a mountain of hurt and shame, ready to roll down the other side, maybe all the way to a confession to having killed Hamlin in a rage.

Finally, Jackson, now full-on weeping, saying, "He didn't deserve to die."

The other voice, even, professional. Janie's. "You sound like you feel guilty about it."

Fists pounding the table, like a little kid kicking at something in frustration.

Donnally wondered why Janie was in there, or even at the office. It was still a half hour until their dinner date. Had she come early hoping Jackson would tell her what she had wanted to say before she ran away last time? Knowing Janie, her gentleness and sincerity, it wasn't hard to imagine a conversation flowing into a therapy session.

It had happened enough to him.

"Ryvver wouldn't have known about Camacho

if I hadn't told her," Jackson said, "and if he hadn't found out what happened to him, he wouldn't have killed Mark."

"Why did you tell her?"

"I was angry. Angry as she was over Little Bud killing himself. He was such a sweet, harmless man. And so kind to Ryvver even at her worst, when she was the most lost and out of control, when there was nothing I could do for her. It just slipped out. And she . . ."

"She what?"

"She knew from when she worked for her father what Frank and Mark and Reggie Hancock were up to. Or least guessed at it."

"And you gave her confirmation."

"I had just figured it out myself. Harlan thinks I knew everything that Mark was doing all along, but I didn't."

"Did you confront Mark about it?"

Jackson didn't respond, at least aloud. Maybe she shook her head. Maybe she nodded. Donnally had no way of knowing.

Janie changed the subject, so the answer must have been no. "Were you going to tell Harlan?"

"I told him about Little Bud."

"Everything?"

Silence. A long silence.

Donnally heard wood scraping wood, maybe chair legs on the floor. He crept toward Hamlin's inner office, wincing at the faint squeaks of the old parquet flooring. Then the click of heels, but not getting closer like she was walking toward the door. Pacing. Had to be Jackson. Janie always wore flats.

He decided he didn't want to take the chance of getting caught eavesdropping, so he continued into Hamlin's office and sat down behind his desk.

A tap on the keyboard revealed the desktop under the screensaver. He clicked on the accounting program icon and entered the "showmethemoney" password.

Looking past the monitor as the program loaded, at the chairs in front of the desk and the couch under the window, he felt the history of the last few days.

Lemmie and her parents playing out the family drama against the background of a real tragedy.

Jackson imagining herself a Jonestown victim, first guilt-ridden for having survived and now for having broken free.

Galen cutting a deal, with Navarro watching him like a visible conscience.

Galen.

Donnally still didn't know whether the man had intended to kill himself or whether his collapse into a coma was an accident of misunderstood medication. He would've heard from Edwards by now if the Berkeley detective had found anything suggesting it had been an attempted murder.

Donnally pushed the mouse up to the top of the screen, and clicked on the "Reports" tab. He ran the same one as last time, "Current Year–Combined," and looked for categories that might cover informant payments, checks coming in from the government, and then cash or checks going out to Hancock and the informing clients. He was certain it wouldn't be called by a recognizable name. And it wasn't. He tried "Fees," "Retainers," "Services,"

"Consulting," "Salaries," "Bonuses," "Royalties," even "Other" on the income side and "Commissions," "Professional Services," and "Wages" on the outgoing side. Nothing. Not a hint.

He stilled the keys, listening for sounds from the conference room. After waiting a full thirty seconds, but hearing none, he reached for the accounting program manual and checked the table of contents and the index, looking for a gimmick that would guide him to where he needed to go.

But then a thought interjected itself between his eyes and the page.

Soon as they come out, they'll guess I heard them in there.

His mind drifted from the book on the desk in front of him to an image of the two women talking together in the conference room. But there was nothing he could do but try to catch a cue from Janie about how he should act when they came out, if there was a way. He suspected that for Jackson exiting the conference room would feel like leaving a shadowed confessional in which one admits, one repents, and one is forgiven, and then steps back out into the glare of an unforgiving world that judges anew and penalizes, and in which the past is never past.

Another picture replaced that one. Jackson standing in the office in her low-cut sweater, reaching for his arm. He wondered whether Janie had found a way to confront Jackson about her attempt at sexualized manipulation and find an explanation in her childhood. But maybe she didn't need to. Guilt and shame for inadvertently setting up Mark Hamlin would have been impetus enough.

The conference room door opened. Donnally watched Jackson walk out of his view and toward her desk, heels clicking on the floor like a metronome, her neck rigid, face forward, knowing he was watching her. He heard her desk drawer open and close, then the office door open and close.

Janie appeared in the doorway and came toward him.

"How much did you hear?" Janie asked.

"Did she know I was listening?"

"I don't know. She knew you were in the office, but over her crying I'm not sure she could tell when you arrived."

"So it all could've been a performance?"

"I don't think so. What you heard was the second time through, a more chronological account. She'd already done a scattershot of bits and pieces."

She dropped onto the couch.

"I didn't expect it. At least not this way. Not after she ran away last time. It was like she couldn't help herself. Needed just to let it out. It blew me away." She released a breath. "She felt all this pressure building up from you being here all the time. I think I was partly a proxy for you. She won't ever admit it, but I think she wanted you to hear what she was saying."

Janie leaned back and closed her eyes for a few moments, then opened them and said, "She'd come to hate Hamlin. Really hate him. I got the feeling that what her father had done to her sexually, Hamlin had done to her intellectually and emotionally, and she didn't recognize it as abuse until way, way, way too late."

CHAPTER 50

I just got a heads-up the feds have a wiretap on Camacho and all his people," Navarro told Donnally in a late night call. "Our narcotics task force is staffing the wire room and doing some of the surveillances."

Donnally covered the speaker and whispered, "Navarro" to Janie across the kitchen table. She set her spoon and chopsticks down alongside her takeout beef noodle soup.

"You mean the DEA thinks Camacho is double dealing?"

"No. The cooperation deal requires that he roll down on everybody in his own organization. He handed over the names, cell numbers, drop spots, and where they lay their heads. The intercepts and surveillances are to develop enough other evidence so the government doesn't need to use him as a witness—that's the good news."

"And I take it the bad news is that if he thinks his calls with these guys are being intercepted, there won't be anything on the tapes about doing Hamlin in."

Donnally heard brakes squeal in the background and then Navarro mumbling.

"It's pretty late," Donnally said. "Must be ten o'clock. You driving home?"

"No. Your place. There's other good news. A deal is going down late tonight and they hope to snag both Camacho's guy—Chino—and the buyer."

"Will they give us the first shot at him?"

Navarro laughed. "I told them if they did, they might be able to take down some criminal defense lawyers. Chino's all ours."

Donnally thought about Ryvver's mother and whether she was still parked on the street in front watching the house.

"How about circle the block before you land here," Donnally said. "Check to see if Leslie Scoville is out there or whether she's given up for the night."

"Hold on, I'm just turning off Geary. If she's there, do you want me to have a patrol officer chase her off? People out here are always worried about their kids being kidnapped. We can tell her we got a call about somebody loitering."

Donnally thought for a moment. Mother Two would know she didn't fit the profile, so she'd figure it was a pretext to ID her or to allow Donnally to break free.

"No," Donnally said. "If she's there, I'll go over the back fence and meet you on the other side of the block."

As it turned out, Donnally didn't need to. She was gone. But then he realized he'd missed an opportunity. He should've had her followed. Maybe she'd find Ryvver on her own and lead him to her.

As he slid into Navarro's car, Donnally heard a

voice announce over the two-way radio, "He's on Mission, turning right on Ninth Street, toward Market."

Navarro flicked on his overheads and shot through intersections until he reached Balboa, then hung a left toward downtown. Donnally knew why he picked the street. There were few stop signs and fewer lights.

"What's Chino driving?" Donnally asked.

"A silver Escalade."

The voice again. "He's crossed Market Street."

Navarro slowed at the next intersection, backed off a driver who tried to shoot across in front of him, and punched the accelerator.

"Left on Hayes."

Another intersection. Navarro blew past the stop sign.

"He's pulled over, checking for surveillance. We'll pass him by. Chuck and Freddie take over. We'll drop down and parallel him on Fell Street."

Pole-lit intersections and neon-blasting store-fronts passed them by like they were tumbling down a kaleidoscope.

A different voice. "He's moving again. Right on Webster . . . left on Fell. Watch out. He may spot you."

Navarro turned right on the steep Masonic Avenue, nose down toward where Fell bordered the north side of the Golden Gate Park Panhandle.

The original voice. "He's about sixty yards ahead of us . . . Shit. He's pulling over again. We're trapped. No place to stop. He's gonna make us."

Donnally pointed at the Chevron station on the

opposite side of Masonic. Navarro cut across two lanes of traffic, pulled in, and turned off his lights.

The second voice. "Forget the deal and the money. Let's just grab him and the dope."

A jumble of voices and sirens blared from the radio.

"Fell at Broderick . . . Fell at Baker . . . Fell at Lyon . . . Fell at Central."

Navarro flipped on his lights and siren and eased into the intersection. Donnally could see patrol overheads coming toward them on the one-way street; leading the pack was the silver Escalade, jerking and swerving into the lanes to his left and right. Donnally imagined Chino both trying to watch the road and trying to reach for the cocaine and throw it out the window. And moments later Donnally saw flashes of light on plastic as kilos arced from the truck and bounced along the pavement and then puffs of white as they exploded and fogged the street.

Navarro angled his car, forcing the Escalade into the far lane, but he didn't leave enough room for the SUV to get by. Just before it would've hit, Navarro shifted into reverse and backed out of the way, but too late for Chino to react. He scraped door-to-door with vehicles parked along the curb until his front bumper caught the rear deck of a delivery van, spun tail first, then slid to a stop.

Chino pushed off from the driver's side like a football lineman, head down into a sprint toward the Panhandle. Donnally had his door open by the time Chino had cut between two cars and was crossing the sidewalk, trying to get beyond the reach of the streetlight and into the darkness of bushes and trees.

Donnally heard Navarro broadcasting the route. Siren wails enclosed him like a tornado of sound as he started after Chino. Cutting between the same cars, voices yelling behind him, surveillance cars accelerating again to cut through the park and intercept Chino on the other side.

The slap and squish of boots on wet grass led Donnally into the shadow between the trees. His front foot hit a lump and his leg went out from under him. A shock of pain tore into his hip. He fell onto his back, his breath blown out of him. He rolled over and onto the leather jacket he'd slipped on. He guessed it was Chino's and that he'd tossed it aside to change his appearance for when he emerged from the park. Donnally grabbed it and pushed himself to his feet and ran toward the sound of distant sirens—then a thunk and a yell twenty yards ahead. He spotted Chino on his knees reaching up toward a low oak branch to pull himself up. Donnally accelerated and dived, driving a forearm into Chino's side, ramming him into the trunk. Then footsteps from behind him and hands grabbing and cops yelling, "Got 'em, got 'em, got 'em."

I t wasn't me, man. I was just taking a piss in the park and I heard sirens and people running and I had some weed in my jacket so I ran."

Sitting across from Chino at the gray metal table bolted to the concrete floor, Donnally could see why he had the nickname. He looked Chinese. Square-jawed. Black-haired. Mongolian-eyed.

Donnally and Navarro's agreement with the DEA and the narcotics task force was that they wouldn't say anything to Chino that might disclose the wiretap and how they knew he'd be making a delivery that night.

Navarro pointed over his shoulder toward the door leading from the SFPD interview room, and said, "Look, Chino—"

"My name ain't Chino."

"Don't play that game," Donnally said. "Your face is practically a confession."

"In ten minutes we'll have latents lifted off of the kilos you threw from your Escalade," Navarro said, "and from the steering wheel and the door handle and the rearview mirror and the console."

Chino stared ahead, not responding.

"All we want from you is a good faith gesture," Navarro said. "Something I can take to the agents waiting out there that'll encourage them to cut a deal with you."

Chino swallowed hard. "Like what?"

"First, who you're working for."

"And second?"

"Let's see if we can get past first."

Donnally cut in. "You got kids?"

Chino nodded.

"They're saying they recovered ten kilos. Sentencing guidelines say that's twenty years in the federal pen. Credit for good time, you'll be out in eighteen years. That'll make you . . ."

Donnally wanted him to fill in the data, make him give up something.

"Fifty-three." Chino looked down at his folded hands, then up. "Why you asking me, you have to already know. If it was the buyer who snitched me off, you would've been waiting at the spot for me to show up, not following me there because you wouldn't know where I was starting from. That means I got set up from my end."

"So, say the name of the guy. But don't lie. Lying means you won't get anything out of this."

"Hector Camacho."

Donnally and Navarro knew it was a lie, or at best a half-truth, since he and Camacho could still have some unfinished business, but it was the name they wanted to hear. Chino had decided to talk about somebody who was now out of the business and couldn't be hurt, rather than give up the name of the distributor he was working with now.

The DEA would squeeze the true name out of him later.

"That's a start," Navarro said, then opened his folder and took out a legal pad. He drew a square at the top, and then ten more below it, and drew connecting lines to make an organizational chart. "Let's fill in the boxes."

Donnally imagined the DEA and narcotics task force agents comparing the names Chino then gave with the names that Camacho had given them and that they had used to target the wiretaps. They'd shown Donnally and Navarro the list when they had arrived at the station.

Chino told them a name that wasn't on Camacho's list.

Navarro asked about a couple of others to disguise his approach. Finally, he got to it.

"Tell me about, uh . . ." Navarro scanned the boxes as though he'd forgotten the man's name. "This guy . . . Calaca."

"Skinny old man. Been close to Camacho since high school in Mexico. Not really part of the operation. More like a silent partner, somebody Camacho talks to, gets advice from. A godfather to his kids. Story is that he was with one of the first cartels."

"A guy he'd call if he needed help with something that really worried him?" Navarro asked. Like a murder.

Chino nodded, almost smiling. "Camacho had sort of a bat phone to call him. Two, three times a day. Didn't use it for nothing else."

And Donnally was certain Camacho hadn't told the DEA about it when he agreed to cooperate.

"You know anybody who's got the number?" Donnally asked.

Chino shook his head. "I don't even know whose name it's in."

Navarro asked about a few more on his chart, then returned the legal pad to the folder. He and Donnally stood up.

"We're gonna run this by the guys outside," Navarro said, "and see how much it bought you."

CHAPTER 52

After four hours' sleep, Navarro arrived grim and red-eyed at Donnally's front door at 8 A.M., and thirty minutes later they were sitting in a surveillance van across the street from Camacho's house. A canine officer was stationed around the corner along the route to Camacho's restaurant.

Camacho backed out of his driveway into the on-coming lane, then Hollywood-stopped at a red light and took a right turn out of Donnally's view.

A patrol unit siren blared for a second.

Navarro circled the block and stopped across the street from where the officer had pulled Camacho over. The officer glanced over his shoulder at them, then opened Camacho's door and signaled for him to get out. The officer grabbed Camacho's arm just above the elbow. Camacho pulled away. The officer pretended to lose his balance, then reached for Camacho's wrist, twisted it behind him, and walked him to the front of the patrol car and bent him over the trunk.

"The idiot fell for it," Navarro said. "We've got him on resisting."

They needed Camacho to commit at least a misdemeanor in order to search him more thoroughly than just a pat down. The traffic infraction wasn't enough.

The officer kicked at Camacho's ankles, forcing him to spread his legs, then handcuffed and searched him, setting Camacho's cell phones and wallet onto the hood. He then eased Camacho into the backseat of the patrol car. He slid into the driver's seat of Camacho's car so he could examine the phones out of Camacho's line of sight, then called in a warrant check.

Ten minutes later, Camacho was again on his way. Twenty-minutes later, Judge McMullin signed an order so they could obtain the call and cell site records of Camacho's secret phone. And an hour after that, Donnally and Navarro were reviewing them in Navarro's office. They showed Camacho had made a call to Calaca from the area of Hamlin's apartment at 2 A.M. on the night Hamlin was murdered and showed calls from and to some numbers they didn't recognize on the night Frank Lange's house was torched.

Donnally wondered why Camacho and Calaca hadn't started with Lange. After all, he was the one actually in the DEA debriefing room with Camacho when Camacho shamed himself in his own eyes by snitching, and Lange would have been a more immediate target for Camacho's rage.

They also spotted something else: calls a couple of days before Hamlin's murder between Camacho and Ryvver Moon Scoville.

CHAPTER 53

"You've got call records, but the rest is double hearsay, you overhearing Jackson talking to Janie about what Ryvver said to her," Judge Mc-Mullin had told Donnally over the phone. "If you got it straight from Ryvver, then you could draft a search warrant that would stand up."

Donnally wasn't even sure he and Navarro could question Ryvver without advising her of her rights. These days, Navarro knew the law better than he did. He hadn't read a DA legal advisory newsletter since he left the department. Who knew what the appeals courts were saying now as they second-guessed officers on the street whose duty required them to make quick decisions.

He was sure some judge somewhere would say that Ryvver running to a murderer like Camacho, to tell him something she knew would infuriate him enough to kill Hamlin, would make her part of a conspiracy, the death of Hamlin being a natural and foreseeable consequence of her action.

Ryvver hadn't pulled the trigger, but she sure as hell had pointed a loaded and cocked gun.

Donnally didn't like having to do it, but he asked

Janie to come down to Hamlin's office after Jackson got back from lunch and attempt to leverage Jackson's guilt into a means to pry more information out of her about Ryvver.

Janie showed up, but she wasn't happy about it, now uncertain about what her role was. She dropped into the chair across from Donnally where he sat behind Hamlin's desk.

"There's no expectation of confidentiality," Donnally said. "She didn't seek you out in your professional capacity and she didn't ask you to come. You showed up here last time looking for me."

"She knows what I do for living, that's part of the reason why she talked, part of the reason I hoped she'd talk and unburden herself."

"She also knows you're an employee of the Veterans Administration—and no money changed hands between you and her. There's no rational way she can see herself as your patient. At most, as a new friend."

The sound of the opening door drew their attention to the outer office. Jackson looked toward them as she walked toward her desk, then stopped. Donnally rose. Jackson spun away, heading back toward the entrance.

"Wait," Donnally said.

Jackson turned toward him. "This some kind of setup?" she asked, her eyes fixed into a glare as they shifted between Donnally and Janie.

Janie stood. "Only if you treat it that way." She gestured toward Donnally behind her. "He's getting close to the guy who killed Mark and Frank, but he needs your help."

"Like what?"

"I need to see the payment history for the clients who cooperated."

That wasn't all he wanted, but it was a safer start.

Jackson took a step into the office and pointed at Hamlin's monitor. "It's in there."

"I couldn't find it."

Jackson sighed like a frustrated little girl, then walked around the desk. Donnally stepped aside so she could sit down. She tapped a few keys, clicking tab after tab too fast for Donnally to follow until a report appeared on the monitor. He spotted Camacho's nickname, Nacho. Short for Ignacio.

He tapped the screen. "Can you . . . what's the word?"

Again with the sigh. "Drill down. It's called drilling down."

Jackson double-clicked.

A shorter report appeared, showing a deposit of fifty thousand dollars in the form of a check from the U.S. Treasury, marked Rafa.

Rafa was the drug dealer Camacho had rolled on, and this must be his reward, or at least a down payment on what could go five times higher.

Below that was twenty thousand dollars withdrawn in increments and in cash and paid out to Camacho, and twenty more that had been transferred to one of Hamlin's personal accounts.

Hamlin had split the reward with Camacho fifty-fifty, except for ten thousand paid out in a check to Reggie Hancock.

Hancock had gotten a cut because it was his client, Guillermo Gutierrez, who had rolled on Camacho.

"There," Jackson said, her face angled up toward Donnally. "You happy now?"

Jackson was acting like she was being forced to confess a sin of her own, and maybe she was. One of omission.

Donnally pointed at the couch. Jackson rose, walked over, and dropped down into it, arms folded across her chest.

Janie sat at the opposite end, not close enough to make Jackson feel any more cornered than she already was.

Donnally returned to the chair behind the desk and backed out of the shorter report. The routine showed him how to produce more of them. He felt Jackson staring at him. He tried a few.

"Is this up to date?" Donnally asked her, not looking away from the monitor.

"I don't know. Mark entered the data himself."

Donnally found a tab to print out a detailed report of the entire account. He pressed it, and Hamlin's printer activated. He closed the program and swiveled the chair toward Jackson.

"I need you to get in contact with Ryvver."

Donnally watched her right hand tighten around her left bicep, her knuckle skin lightening as it stretched.

"I know you've been in contact with her."

Jackson's head pivoted toward Janie. "Isn't there some rule about confidentiality?"

"I'm not your therapist."

Jackson looked back toward Donnally. "What do you want from her?"

"Probable cause."

"Whatever she can tell you is hearsay."

"I'm not asking her to repeat what anyone told her, just what she said to Camacho. Her own words. That's not hearsay."

Jackson looked down at her forearms, then lowered them and folded her hands in her lap. Donnally could see her eyes moving side to side, as though she was watching a boxing match, but it was all in her mind, and he wondered what the fight was about.

Finally, she spoke. "That might make her a co-conspirator."

"How do you figure?"

Her body stiffened. "Don't play games. You know the law. Foreseeable consequences." More internal boxing. "Let's say I didn't tell her how bad a guy Camacho was until afterwards. Maybe she was just warning him to get a new lawyer, not asking him to do something."

Donnally didn't challenge her. Whatever rationalization she wanted to make, whatever lie she wanted to tell herself was fine with him, as long as it got him to where he was going: his boot kicking in Camacho's front door.

"That's fine," Donnally said. "Then she's in the clear. What do we need to do to meet up with her?"

"Will you put that in your report?"

Donnally nodded. "Just like you said it." As a lie.

Jackson reached into her purse and pulled out her cell phone. She searched the memory, pressed "send," and waited with the phone against her ear.

"It's me . . . hang in there, baby girl. It'll be okay."

Jackson listened. Eyebrows knitted, biting her cheek.

"There's a man who wants to meet with you. The special master . . . No, he's not a cop. He can't arrest you for anything. He needs your help."

Jackson listened again, then looked at Donnally.

"She wants to know about witness protection."

"The program was created so the government could get witnesses to testify against crooks exactly like Camacho," Donnally said. "I'll go to the feds myself. Judge McMullin will help. When can we meet?"

Jackson spoke into her phone. "He can do it . . . Can we get together?" She fell silent, then covered the mike. "She won't meet, but she'll talk to you on the phone."

Donnally shrugged his assent.

"Here he is," Jackson said, then reached out her phone toward him.

Donnally took it, introduced himself, and said, "I don't need much at all. Just a couple of questions." He could hear sniffling on her end. "Don't worry, we'll take care of you."

More sniffling as Ryvver drew in a breath. "What do you want to know?"

"Did you talk to Hector Camacho?"

"A couple of times."

"What did you tell him?"

"Just that Mark Hamlin set up things so a man in LA would cooperate against him—but I didn't know he would kill Mark. I just wanted . . ."

"Wanted what?"

"I wanted him to find out from Mark who he got to roll on Little Bud. That's all."

"Hold on." Donnally walked to the printer and

scanned down the pages. The entries ended two months earlier, just before Little Bud pled out and went off to prison.

"I'll find out and do something about it," Donnally said. "But I won't be able to tell you who it was until it comes out in court."

"I'm done with this. First Mark, then Frank. I didn't think this is how it would end."

Donnally heard her sobbing, so he lied. "Don't blame yourself," he said. "Eventually Camacho would've figured it out on his own. He's responsible for what he did."

Another sniffle.

"Okay," Donnally said, "let's run through it front to back."

Donnally listened and took notes. It matched what he'd overheard Jackson tell Janie, just a few more details about the dates and times of the calls.

"Don't you think you should call your mothers?" Donnally said at the end. "They're worried about you."

Ryvver's voice toughened. "They've always had a crude way of showing it."

"What do you mean?"

"That's between them and me."

And the phone went dead.

He handed it back to Jackson.

"I think I went a step too far. Keep in contact with her. Once we've got Camacho locked up, she can come in."

"What about Camacho's people? They'll be coming after her. I've been around long enough to know what happens next."

Donnally couldn't disclose the federal investigation and the wiretap, but he needed to offer her some assurance.

"The world's going to cave in on them soon enough. They'll be so busy looking out for themselves, they won't have the time or the inclination to help Camacho."

Donnally thanked Jackson, then signaled to Janie to follow him out. She walked with him to the elevator.

"See if you can get Ryvver's phone number from Jackson. I've used up my supply of touchy-feely for the day."

Janie nodded and headed back.

Donnally called Navarro as he rode the elevator down, and then called Judge McMullin and drove to his house.

The judge let him use the desk in his study to handwrite his search warrant affidavit targeting Camacho's house, restaurant, cars, hair, and blood. His fingerprints were already on file.

Donnally had the record of calls between Ryvver and Camacho, Ryvver's own words to Camacho, Camacho's calls to the person believed to be Calaca that bracketed the hours when Hamlin was killed, Camacho's cell site records first putting him in the area of Hamlin's house and then on a trail leading in the direction of the Golden Gate Bridge.

The search was aimed at identifying Calaca and at locating evidence of Camacho's participation in the crime, not just hair samples, but also the rope matching the one found tied around Hamlin's neck or the one Navarro had discovered on the floor between Hamlin's washer and dryer.

Navarro arrived with the court-issued search warrant forms as Donnally was finishing and set them on the judge's desk as he read over the affidavit.

"I've got officers spotting on Camacho's house," Navarro said, "but they can't tell whether he's there."

"We better not go in until we see movement," Donnally said. "If he's not there, neighbors might tip him off that we're on the hunt for him."

Judge McMullin looked up. "I'm glad you aren't asking for an arrest warrant. There's barely enough here for a search. And I need a sworn officer to sign it."

The judge handed it to Navarro to read over. "When you're done, add your part."

Navarro added a paragraph at the start stating the facts below had been told to him by Donnally and he believed them to be true, then moved to the last page and signed.

Then the judge said, "Raise your right hand."

CHAPTER 54

I didn't kill him," Camacho said, looking up from the floor of his living room and rubbing his ribs where Donnally had nailed him.

It hadn't been until 8 A.M. that they spotted a light come on in the house, and seconds after Navarro did the knock and notice, Camacho had run through his house and toward the back door. The wood and glass exploding inward and the SWAT officers marching into the kitchen had sent Camacho running back into the dining room and to the threshold of the living room, where he met Donnally's lowered shoulder.

"I just helped her afterwards. Fuck, man, what was I supposed to do? I had a dozen calls with that lunatic. I had all kinda motive because he set me up and I had no fucking alibi. And she's screaming she did it for me and for some guy named Little Bud I never heard of before. And how she'd just killed her father—"

"Killed her father?" Donnally tensed. "I thought we were talking about Hamlin."

"We are. When we get over there, Hamlin's tied to a chair, dead, a rope around his neck tied to a piece of a broom handle in the back. Like she used it for leverage, to tighten the noose, like squeezing water out of a rag."

"Why do you think he was her father?"

"That's what she said, man. She was bearing down on him and he's saying, 'Don't kill me. I'm your father. I'm your father,' and then the guy has some kind of spasm and slumps over dead."

Donnally backed up a step and pointed from Camacho to the couch. He rolled over onto his knees, then pushed himself up and onto it. Donnally sat down on an ottoman. Navarro stayed by the door.

"I told you the bitch was nuts," Camacho said.

"How do we know that it wasn't her interrupting you killing him?" Navarro said.

Donnally knew the answer.

"Because I wouldn't have strangled the guy. You know guys like me don't do that kind of shit. I would've just kept breaking fingers until I got what I wanted. And how was I gonna get the guy stoned on opium? That's how she got him dazed enough to get him into the chair and tied up."

"And the rope," Donnally said.

"Yeah. That, too. It was a mountain-climbing rope. Where the fuck would I get a mountain-climbing rope? It's not like they sell them at Home Depot."

"Why Fort Point?" Donnally asked. "And why leave him hanging there half naked?"

"Why do you think? We were protecting the chick. No daughter would do that to her own father. No fucking way."

Donnally realized that if Camacho was telling the truth, his theory had been wrong. Hamlin hadn't been stripped down and hung up in order to send a message or to humiliate him, but as misdirection, to keep the police from even starting down a trail that would lead to him.

"I knew she didn't have the stomach for what we needed to do. We left her in the van in the parking lot when we went up with his body. I figure she didn't even find out how we handled it until she saw it on the news."

"Hamlin smelled like lavender," Navarro said. "Why wash him off?"

"Wasn't us. The flake said he'd gone running with some gal after work and they came back to his place and took showers. I don't know if that was true, but he reeked like a fag."

Donnally looked up at Navarro. The detective's eyes hardened against the slur, then he nodded, telling Donnally that he'd figured out the rest just as Donnally had.

Ryvver then went after Lange, blaming him because she'd killed her own father and for Little Bud's suicide. After their argument on the second floor during the party, she dropped Rohypnol into his drink and torched his house.

Ryvver's Mother Number One was wrong. Killing Frank Lange wasn't patricide.

But why would the mothers tell Ryvver Lange was her father?

Or why would Mother Two tell Mother One that it was Lange she'd slept with in order to conceive Ryvver?

Donnally shifted his gaze back to Camacho.

"I had no idea she was gonna kill Lange," Camacho said. "She promised she'd be going away, up north. We're driving away from Fort Point after we hung him up and she starts rambling on about a bookstore someplace. Why somebody would be going to a bookstore after murdering her father beats the hell out of me."

Donnally was almost sure she hadn't done that. Mother One was convincing in her worry, and Ryvver's cell records showed she had stayed in San Francisco, or at least her phone had.

"Where's the rest of the rope and the bolt cutters?" Donnally asked.

"Where do you think? At the bottom of the bay."

Donnally rose to his feet, looked down at Camacho, and said, "Don't move," and then walked with Navarro just outside the front door.

"If he's telling the truth," Donnally said to Navarro, "she's got to be figuring we're getting close. Find out whether she's still using that pay-as-you-go phone. There's one person left on her hit list."

Donnally walked down the front steps to the sidewalk. He called directory assistance and punched in the number.

A voice answered on the first ring, "Law Office of Reggie Hancock."

He identified himself and asked for Hancock.

"I'm sorry. He's not in today. Can I take a message?"

"Do you know when he'll get it?"

"I'm sure he'll call in during the day."

Donnally looked toward the house. Navarro was

on his cell phone and staring into the living room, watching Camacho.

Donnally gave her his number and told her it was urgent, that someone might be aiming to harm Hancock.

She didn't seem to react to the news. Donnally had the feeling that she'd heard threats before. He suspected if he'd called Jackson a month earlier to report that there were threats made against Hamlin, she would have reacted the same.

Donnally thought of a way to get her to take this one more seriously.

"If you have any doubts about me or what I'm saying, do a search of my name on the Internet. Check the *San Francisco Chronicle*."

He listened to light tapping in the background, then, "Oh, I see."

"To verify it's me on the phone, call the San Francisco Police Department and ask to be patched through to homicide detective Ramon Navarro."

Donnally glanced toward Navarro. He was leaning against the doorjamb, arms folded across his chest. Donnally heard her disconnect.

Navarro reached for his phone a minute later, answered, and glanced toward Donnally.

Donnally nodded. Navarro passed on Donnally's number. His phone rang fifteen seconds later.

"I'll call his cell and his house so he'll know who you are," she said, then gave him the numbers.

"And if a woman named Ryvver calls," Donnally said, "I want to hear from you right away."

"But she's already called. Twice in the last few

days. She said she wanted him to represent her in a case in San Francisco."

"Is he on his way up here now?"

"No. The appearance is for tomorrow afternoon, so he won't fly up until the morning. That's what he always does. I made the reservation myself."

"Were they going to meet ahead of time?"

She paused for a moment. Donnally heard a rustle of paper.

"It's not on the calendar, but I have a vague recollection she may have come down here for a couple of hours yesterday. He left and said he had to meet someone, but didn't say who."

"I'll try the number and you do, too," Donnally said. "If he doesn't answer, send the police to check his house. Then call me back."

Donnally disconnected and walked over to Navarro, who said, "I got the news a few minutes ago. There were a bunch of calls from Ryvver's pay-as-you-go cell phone and Reggie Hancock—"

"But none since last night."

"Yeah, but none since last night." Navarro squinted at Donnally. "How'd you know?"

CHAPTER 55

As they drove away, Navarro called Judge Mc-Mullin and got the bail on Camacho for moving human remains raised from the statutory fifteen thousand dollars to no bail in order to keep him locked up and then got another detective to swear out a warrant on the same charge and bail amount for Calaca, whose full name and address they found in the search of Camacho's house.

Donnally tried to reach Jackson on her cell phone. She didn't answer. He wondered whether she'd put it back in her purse and couldn't hear it or was just refusing to pick up.

His phone rang just as he was returning it to his pocket. It was Hancock's secretary.

"My assistant just told me Reggie left a message on the main office voice mail. He usually leaves them on mine, but he knew I had an early doctor's appointment. I just listened to it. He said he's in San Diego and that he'd stop by the office in the morning on his way to the airport."

"How did he sound?"

"Strained. Really strained. And I checked the

caller ID, the phone he called from had a 415 area code, San Francisco."

"We'll start looking for him," Donnally said. "I'll call you as soon as we find him. Let me have the number the call came from."

Donnally wrote it down, disconnected, and relayed the conversation to Navarro, who called the intelligence unit to check the number. It was another pay-as-you-go cell phone. He called it. There was no answer, and no voice mail had been set up. The number seemed familiar, but he'd looked at so many in recent days, almost any number would have.

He glanced over at Navarro. "You have Camacho's cell phone records?"

Navarro thumb-pointed over his shoulder toward his briefcase lying on the backseat. Donnally flipped it open and pulled them out, and there it was.

"Bingo. Ryvver called Camacho a few minutes before he called Calaca on the night of Hamlin's murder."

"Another noose just tightened."

"That's not the only one. Ryvver will figure out pretty soon that Jackson's usefulness has just about ended. And Jackson is our only lead."

"And if Ryvver is as crazy as people think, she may blurt out that Hamlin was really her father, and Jackson will put it all together and figure out that Ryvver did in Lange, too."

"And then Ryvver in her crazy way will start thinking she needs to get rid of Jackson."

When they arrived back at Hamlin's office, they

found that Jackson was gone. Navarro sent area beat officers to knock on her door. They reported back ten minutes later. Jackson wasn't there either. Her roommate let them search the apartment. She hadn't seen Jackson in two days. Jackson had told her she'd be staying with a friend out in the avenues. They left instructions for Jackson to call Navarro if she showed up.

Donnally thought of Ryvver's cell phone calls. Almost all from the avenues. He walked to the window and looked down, scanning the street.

"Mother Two is down there," Donnally said. "Parked in a yellow zone." He turned back toward Navarro. "How about you block her in? It's time we had a talk."

Navarro nodded and left the office first. Donnally waited a few minutes and rode the elevator down. He stopped just inside the main entrance, where he had an angled view up the one-way street. The front of Mother Two's truck faced him. Her visor was down and she had a newspaper against the steering wheel to hinder the view of anyone looking inside. He saw Navarro pull to a stop next to her, blocking the driver's side door.

Donnally watched Mother Two roll her window down and scream at Navarro, then Donnally ran up to the passenger side and yanked the door open and jumped in. Mother Two swung an elbow at him. Donnally blocked it with his left hand, then grabbed her wrist and turned it down. Next came her left arm, roundhouse style. He blocked it with his right, but missed the grab. She drew back, and

Navarro reached in through her window and locked onto her arm. She struggled, twisting her body like a bucking bull. Navarro snapped a handcuff on her wrist, then hooked the other end to the steering wheel. Donnally pulled the keys from the ignition.

"Enough," Donnally yelled at her.

Mother Two was breathing hard through her nose, her nostrils flaring.

"Why didn't you just come up to my window and ask to talk to me?"

Donnally thought of her screaming at Navarro.

"And what would you have done?"

"Found a way to run your ass over."

"What's your beef with me?"

"My beef with you is that you're trying to drag a mentally ill young woman into something she's not a part of. She didn't hang Mark Hamlin out there. She weighs all of a hundred pounds."

"I know she didn't."

"Then why are you hounding her?" Mother Two pulled on her arm. "Let me go."

"You swing at me again and you're going to jail."

Mother Two breathed in and out again, forcing the air like she wanted it to be heard. Finally, she said, "Okay. I won't hit you."

Donnally released her wrist.

She reached over, jerked on the handcuffs, and looked out at Navarro. "What about these?"

"They stay where they are."

"Have it your way." She lowered her free hand to her side.

A horn honked behind them. Navarro held up

his badge. An engine whined as a car accelerated around them.

"Tell me about Ryvver and Frank Lange," Donnally said.

"What's there to say?"

Donnally noticed a calmness in her voice. He wondered whether his saying he knew Ryvver hadn't strung up Hamlin had led her to conclude her daughter wasn't a suspect in anything. He guessed she was about to head down the patricide trail Mother One had already blazed.

"What's there to say is why you lied to Ryvver all those years about who her father was."

Mother Two's head pivoted toward him. "Say what?"

"You heard me, and she knows already."

Her eyes widened and her face paled. She started to speak, more of a gasp, the words trapped in her throat.

"How . . . how?"

"It's not important. But she believes Mark Hamlin was her father."

"Mark wouldn't have told her."

"Let's say he was desperate."

Mother Two snorted. "If he was desperate, he would've said anything. That's the kind of guy he was."

"The medical examiner has tissue samples. We can still do a paternity test."

She raised her fist, held it in front of her face, looking at it like it had somehow let her down, like it was a weapon she had failed to fire in combat. Her head fell forward and she dropped her hand to her thigh.

"My partner hated Hamlin, saw through him from day one, that's how I ended up with the fat pig Frank on top of me day after day. I only found out after Ryvver was born that Frank was shooting blanks. Got hurt as a kid. On his bike or playing football or something."

She looked over at Donnally.

"He just got off on the idea of screwing a lesbian, so he lied to us. I didn't know what was wrong, but I wasn't getting pregnant and wanted the whole thing over with, so I let Mark fuck me a couple of times. And that was it. We got Ryvver."

"And you never told your partner?"

"No. I was afraid she'd always look at Ryvver as a kind of Rosemary's Baby."

"How did you find out Frank was impotent?"

Mother Two looked at Navarro. "Do I have to answer that?"

Navarro nodded.

"The asshole blackmailed sex out of me after she was born. Mark told him about me and him, and Frank used it to make me put out or he'd tell my partner. I told him to wear a condom so I wouldn't get pregnant again, and he laughed and told me. I should've killed the bastard right then."

Donnally didn't follow that with "Instead of later?" for fear of giving her the idea of trying to protect her daughter by taking the fall.

Navarro cut in. "Where is she now?"

"I don't know. I was hoping you would lead me to her and I could . . ."

"Help her get away?" Navarro said.

"Maybe. Frank deserved it."

"What about Mark?" Donnally asked.

Her head snapped toward Donnally. "You said . . ."

"No. She killed him all right. Someone else moved the body out there and hung him up."

"You son of a bitch."

She raised her elbow to strike him.

Donnally pointed at her. "Don't do it." She lowered it.

"I had no choice," Donnally said. "I needed to know the truth."

"Now you know. And now it's over."

"It's not. Reggie Hancock is missing. She was supposed to meet him in LA yesterday. Nobody has seen him since."

Donnally described the rolling scheme, its connection to Little Bud and his suicide, and the call from Hancock to his secretary. He didn't see any risk in telling her. If Mother Two refused to cooperate with them in finding Ryvver and getting her to surrender, Navarro would lock her up for assault so she couldn't do anything to help her daughter.

"She never went to LA. I know. She lives on SSI and her credit card is in my name. If she'd flown or driven down there, I'd know about it. I've been checking her credit card and bank account online. She'd need a plane ticket or gas for the car. Like always, there's hardly any money in there and she hasn't taken cash out for a couple of weeks."

"Maybe Reggie figured out he'd be next," Donnally said, "and came up here to try to grab her on his own terms."

"Where would she try to meet him?" Navarro

asked. "Maybe someplace where Hancock wouldn't think there was any risk."

Mother Two closed her eyes. Donnally watched her thumbs working against her fingertips. Finally, she opened them.

"The place she knew best in San Francisco was Golden Gate Park. The California Academy of Sciences and all that. She spent a summer working as a volunteer at the Steinhart Aquarium. She even had her own key. She liked to hang out there late at night. Just her and the animals."

Donnally imagined Ryvver tying up Hancock and feeding him to the alligators.

"She still knows lots of folks who work there. They're very fond of her and let her do work around the place when she's in town."

CHAPTER 56

"What hat will happen to her?" Mother Two asked.
Donnally, Navarro, and Mother Two were
sitting in a surveillance van outside the California
Academy of Sciences. Undercover officers dressed as
homeless people were hiding in the bushes watching
the front and service entrances. Two others were already
inside, dressed as janitors. All had been given
DMV photos of Ryvver and Reggie Hancock and
descriptions of her hairstyle and likely clothing.

"That's hard to say," Donnally answered.

But it wasn't.

If the mothers were willing to mortgage their
house and business to hire the kind of lawyer
Hamlin had been and the kind of investigator
Frank Lange had been, the worst she would get was
a not-guilty-by-reason-of-insanity verdict.

"It depends on what the psychiatrists say," Donnally said.

"She has a history of violence as a child. We tried
everything."

Donnally squinted at her. "Violence? Your partner
told me as a kid she wouldn't pick flowers for
fear of hurting the plants."

Mother Two took in a long breath and exhaled. "The lies we tell ourselves." She looked at Donnally. "If she was a little boy, nobody would have said anything. Catching and torturing lizards and frogs is what they do. Catch them. Lead them down the sidewalk on strings. Swing them around. Dissect them. She was just a little aggressive on the dissecting side."

"And she was a girl."

"And the child of lesbians. Don't think that didn't play a role in the school psychologist's theories about why she was that way. This was more than twenty years ago."

Navarro's radio clicked, followed by a voice.

"Black male and white female walking close together south along Music Concourse Drive, near the fountain between the palm trees."

"Check."

That would mean the two were behind the van.

Mother Two leaned toward the rear and her body tensed like a sprinter.

Donnally grabbed her arm. "Take it easy."

Navarro turned on the monitor and directed the video camera in the top vent toward the back.

"Cancel that. He's too tall. She's too heavy . . . and they just separated."

"Check."

Mother Two settled back, her eyes moving, seeming to be searching for the trailing end of her last thought.

Finally, she sighed and looked at Navarro. "You know how it was back in those days. You're old enough. I know you called people up in Guerneville to check up on me. They told me. And they told me you're queer. What do you think those same shrinks would've said about you?"

"I know what they said about me." Navarro gave her a hard look, like he was fighting off an invasion that had started at his professional life and had now moved into his private life, then his face softened and he said, "They said I could be cured."

Another click. A different radio voice.

"I just spotted a Toyota Corolla. Dark. Like hers. Two-door heading up South Drive. Two people inside. Can't make the plate yet."

"Check."

"Got the plate. Wrong one."

"Switch to another channel," Navarro said, "and run it for lost or stolen."

The voice came back a minute later. "The plate is clear and matches the car. It's not hers."

"Check."

Donnally thought of Frank Lange. He understood the reason and the mechanism, Ryvver drugging him, then searching his files for proof of the rolling scheme that took the life of Little Bud, then setting his house aflame.

"Did Ryvver have access to Rohypnol?" Donnally asked.

"A generic form. She was prescribed flunitrazepam for insomnia, but it had the reverse effect on her. Made her agitated and aggressive. She went off on my partner the day after Little Bud died. Hitting and scratching. Only after we threw her out did we do some research and figure out it might've been the drug."

Mother Two sighed again.

"You'd think that after all these years, and all the psych drugs she's been given, that we would've checked first."

She looked at Donnally, her eyes seemed to deepen, then went dead, and she looked away.

He knew she'd just hit on the foundation of her daughter's insanity defense: The drugs made her do it.

And he had no doubt that for the right price she'd be able to buy a lawyer like Hamlin and one of his hireling shrinks to sell it to a jury.

CHAPTER 57

Three A.M. and Donnally was still staring at his bedroom ceiling and listening to pounding raindrops that had ridden the squalls up from the Pacific three blocks away and then swept down onto the neighborhood. He was hoping his phone would ring with the news that Hancock had been saved from Ryvver and Ryvver had been saved from herself.

His job as special master was over. He'd sat in the van for two hours feeling his court-appointed identity dissolve and watching himself return to who he was before Judge McMullin had signed the order.

Mark Hamlin's death was solely a law enforcement issue. There was no privilege left to protect, and he and the judge had agreed he should back away. The arrest would be clean, and any admissions Ryvver made would be unimpeachable in court.

And he had realized he was now twice done with San Francisco, each time a decade apart, each time having broken free of the city's vortex of crime and corruption.

Even now, he felt his stomach tighten with guilt when he thought of his pushing Janie out onto an ethical tightrope, pressuring her to extract information from Jackson. That they succeeded in the end wasn't justification enough.

Listening to the crash of distant thunder and watching the ceiling strobe with faint lightning, he wondered whether he could convince Janie to move north with him to Mount Shasta and to take a job in the nearby VA clinic. Maybe that way they could narrow the circumference of their lives and free themselves from the kinds of contingencies that had pulled them into Hamlin's.

Donnally felt a wrenching contraction of the world toward the California Academy of Sciences, then its expansion into the infinity of unknowing. He might be done fugitive hunting, but the fugitive hunter's nightmare wasn't done with him.

He thought about Ryvver's two mothers, now together in the surveillance van praying she'd show up, and then about the girl murdered by Hamlin's stalker client and his nouveau riche parents humiliated by the prosecution of their son, wanting to get it over with. Keep him off death row, but on the shelf for life. Make him old news as fast as possible and make the world forget.

His mind jumped back.

Humiliated.

Donnally sat up. Janie looked over. She, too, was still awake. He said the word aloud.

"You may be right," Janie said. "And she now knows how to do it."

They were in the car in three minutes and pulled into the Fort Point parking lot twelve minutes later. He'd called Navarro on the way. Donnally told

Janie what his route up to the lighthouse would be, then left her to meet Navarro. He wanted to make sure Navarro or another officer didn't shoot him by mistake in the darkness.

Donnally's eyes adjusted slowly to the shadows under the bridge and his ears took in nothing but the gusts shuddering through the Golden Gate and the raindrops exploding on the water-sheeted pavement and the waves crashing onto the rocks below.

As he ran toward the fort he looked up at the dark lighthouse, backlit by city lights reflecting off the low clouds, a mass of black on top of a skeleton of angled steel.

And the bridge high and behind it, another skeleton, another black mass, headlights and halogens illuminating the surface like a sunset.

The two structures looked like dinosaurs. Mother and child.

Now soaked through his clothes, he made his way around the south end, not using his flashlight for fear of giving away his presence. He slowed, searching for the door through which Camacho had carried Hamlin's corpse, feeling along the brick wall. His shoe hit something hard, he pitched forward, then caught himself, one hand on the ground, the other braced against brick, his hip once again torn with pain. He looked up as lightning shot across the sky and lit up a man-sized frame of metal ten feet away. He crept over to it and then reached past the edge, encountering the nothingness of the open door. He slid his hand down, and his fingers touched the hasp holes no longer filled by the padlock.

Ryvver had broken in for a second time.

With the premeditation required to trap Hancock and to again buy rope and a bolt cutter, Donnally didn't see Ryvver—whoever her lawyer was and whatever medication she'd taken—obtaining a verdict of not guilty by reason of insanity.

There was no madness in her method.

Another burst of lightning bounced off the brick wall and the metal door. He ducked as something swung at him. It thunked against the doorjamb. He rushed the moving shadow behind it, hitting it low and taking the flailing body down. He heard a ringing of metal hitting concrete. He expected to hear Ryvver's scream; instead it was Jackson swearing and pounding on his back.

"Let me go, you motherfucker. Let me go."

Donnally got her into a headlock, his arms under hers and his hand braced against her neck.

"It's me," Donnally said.

Jackson stopped struggling.

"Why'd you take a swing at me?"

"I thought you were a security guard or a cop."

Donnally released her and pushed himself up onto his knee.

"Is she inside?" Donnally asked.

He could now make out Jackson in the darkness.

"Her and Reggie. I guessed they'd be here."

"Why didn't you call somebody, clue us in?"

"Because I didn't want some trigger-happy idiot to shoot her."

"Like me?"

"Take it any way you want. And I didn't want her to panic and kill him." She pointed toward the courtyard. "I was just about to go up when I heard you trip and fall, so I came back."

Donnally stood and reached down to help her up. "Show me."

Jackson led him down a short hallway toward an opening into the courtyard. He scanned the three stories of arched walls, looking scalloped in the night. He stayed in the shadows as he squinted up toward the lighthouse. He spotted movement, but not on the ocean side where Hamlin had been left hanging from the walkway with his feet scraping the fort's roof, but on the bay side facing them, above an eighty-foot drop to the floor on which Donnally was standing.

A male voice called out from above, fighting the wind and rain.

"Please, don't. Please."

Then louder.

"Please, I'm begging you."

Jackson moved forward as if to cut across the courtyard. He grabbed her and jerked her back, and then stepped near the curve of the arch and looked up. Now he could make out two figures standing along the lighthouse railing. Neither was moving.

He whispered to Jackson that they should make their way around the perimeter, then up the stairs he'd told Janie he'd use.

Donnally turned back and led her through the vaulted rampart, their footfalls masked by the brick around him and by the rain and wind swirling around the lighthouse. They worked their way along two sides of the courtyard, then stopped at the base of the circular stairway.

Donnally turned back toward Jackson. "When we get to the roof, try to get to the opposite side of the lighthouse and get her attention. Keep her looking your way. Don't react to anything I do."

Jackson grabbed his arm. He felt her quivering with wet and cold and fear. "You're not gonna . . ."

"No. I won't shoot her."

He headed up the steps, Jackson behind him.

Once on the roof, they held back in the shadows. He waited for a lightning burst, then made a curving motion with his hand, indicating the route he wanted Jackson to take, and signaled her to go ahead.

He watched her sneak across the roof and past the crisscrossing metal supports of the tower. He waited until she called out, "Ryvver . . . Ryvver . . . It's me . . ." then he crept along the roof edge.

Hancock started yelling again, now begging. "Please. Please. Help me."

Donnally looked up. Hancock was standing on a ledge, outside the walkway, a noose around his neck, hands bound. The other end of the rope was tied to the railing. Ryvver stood behind him, her hand gripping the knot at the back of his head.

Ryvver screamed down at Jackson. "You're as evil as the rest of them."

"He had nothing to do with Little Bud," Jackson yelled back. "Nothing. It was all Mark and Frank."

"You're lying."

Donnally reached the foot of the lighthouse, then took off his belt, held it in his teeth, and monkey-barred his way up under the wrought-iron stairs and around the walkway until he was just under

Hancock. He could see the tips of Hancock's shoes overhanging the ledge and could see his legs trembling in the wet and cold.

Donnally locked his hand around Hancock's ankle. He felt the man's body jerk in surprise, then shudder in fear. Donnally patted his leg to calm him, then released his grip and pulled himself up farther until he could see Ryvver. She was still holding the rope, but was looking away and down toward Jackson. He slipped the belt behind Hancock's legs just above his knees and around the rail post behind him, then cinched the buckle closed.

Hancock sighed.

Donnally heard it.

Ryvver heard it.

She looked at Hancock, then down.

Lightning flared. Then again. Almost strobing, illuminating her pale face consumed by shock and fury.

Donnally was now illuminated, confronting her like a living nightmare. As thunder vibrated the lighthouse, rain tattooed his face and eyes as he grabbed the railing to pull himself up.

Ryvver shoved Hancock. He rocked forward, against the belt tying him to the railing. He screamed. A rising wail. But it held, and he straightened up.

She shoved again.

Donnally had a leg up to the ledge, now pulling hard. He saw her hand come around Hancock's body. When she extended her arm toward him, he knew what was coming. He ducked just before the bang and muzzle flash.

Hancock jerked back and to the side, trying to butt her with his shoulder and head.

Donnally pulled himself over the railing, then reached around Hancock, grabbed her, and threw her into the lighthouse wall.

The gun discharged a second time. Hancock grunted and slumped forward.

Donnally swung at her, but missed. Her hand came up. He blocked it with his forearm and grabbed the front of her jacket.

The gun fired again. A simultaneous flash, bang, and thunk of lead punching sheet metal behind him.

Now she was flailing, swinging at him with fist and barrel.

He heard running footfalls on the roof—Navarro and Janie—and knew he couldn't risk another wild shot.

He threw her toward the railing, thinking she'd drop the gun and grab for a handhold. But she didn't. The muzzle flamed upward as she fell back and over and she merged into the void.

Then there was just the sound of the wind and the rain, until she struck the floor with a thud of flesh and bone, and a rattle of gunmetal on concrete.

District Attorney Hannah Goldhagen stood on the roof of Fort Point just before sunrise, gazing up at the criminal defense lawyer still tied to the railing with Donnally's belt, his dead body doubled over. She then looked down at Ryvver splayed on the courtyard.

She glanced over at Donnally.

"Sorry," Goldhagen said. "It never crossed my mind it might come to this kind of thing. I thought maybe it would be an angry client or sex that went bad . . . something . . . anything . . . but not this."

Donnally was listening to her, but was replaying in his mind the last seconds of Ryvver's and Hancock's lives.

He'd been surprised by the gun until he'd remembered that one had been stolen from Hamlin's nightstand. Even back then, Ryvver must have known she'd have at least a second, maybe even a third victim.

Donnally imagined Ryvver tying Hamlin to a chair in his apartment, him thinking he could buy his life back by paying with lies, then realizing he couldn't, and the only thing that might save him was what he had never done: Tell the truth.

But it had come too late.

Janie shivered next to him. He reached an arm around her. She had felt for Hancock's pulse in the darkness, checked Ryvver's body, and then tried to console the two mothers in the parking lot when the surveillance crew brought them over from Golden Gate Park.

Navarro had ordered the bodies left where they were until the crime scene crew finished their work. He wanted to make sure he got it right. His career, first tied to Hamlin's, was now also tied to Hancock's.

Standing there, they all already knew the future. There would be questions and press conferences and grand juries, and later, when the rolling scheme was exposed, court hearings and dismissals and reversals, and eventually dozens of crooks would walk back out through prison doors, the Assistant U.S. Attorney would be fired for conspiring with Hamlin and Hancock . . .

Donnally felt his mind race ahead, riding a wave of bitterness and anger, for the thought that had framed his struggles in the last days had been true. The momentum of Hamlin's existence, the chains of causes and effects, of things done and suffered, hadn't ended with his death.

And he was certain Hancock's wouldn't end with his.

"What's the truth?" Goldhagen asked. "Did Hancock have anything to do with Little Bud?"

"Specifically," Donnally said, "I don't know. But generally, yes. He was part of Hamlin's world, what made up his world. There was nothing he could say that would've saved him from Ryvver. As crazy as she was, she understood everything."

Donnally closed his eyes, remembering Ryvver going over the railing, realizing now that she hadn't screamed as she fell, and in those empty moments he'd felt the presence of her mothers. He'd called out Janie's name, fearing a stray bullet had found her, wrenched by guilt until her voice reached out to him from the wind and rain.

Then came the scream. Jackson's. And her sobbing that continued even into the ambulance that had taken her away.

Donnally opened his eyes again and looked up at the bridge, at the spectators gazing down, their cell phone cameras taking pictures and videos.

This time he didn't care what they saw, what they photographed, what they videoed.

Let the facts be known and the truth be seen.

Wasn't that why Judge McMullin had appointed him?

And hadn't the time now come?

Special master.

He did his job and found Hamlin's killer, but he wasn't sure what he'd mastered.

Helplessness sank into Donnally as he realized that all he'd discovered in the end were the steps and the path Hamlin had taken in becoming who he was, but not why he'd chosen to take them. And in his weariness, Donnally found himself fearing he'd simply run up against the limits of understanding human beings such as Hamlin and then anguishing over whether those limits were in himself or in the world.

And he sure hadn't mastered the facts of what had happened soon enough—wasn't sure even now he'd mastered them all—otherwise there wouldn't be two dead bodies in front of him.

He thought of the words Goldhagen had spoken when they last stood in this spot. She'd been wrong. The shortest distance hadn't been a straight line. It had been through a maze that took him not to the heart of the matter, but only back to where he'd started.

"Do you know why Ryvver was so determined to go after Hancock?" Goldhagen asked.

Donnally squinted against the swirling salt wind and looked up at Hancock's inert body, his suit jacket flapping and his pant legs fluttering, the mountain climber's rope quivering, and then he thought of Ryvver tightening the noose around Hamlin's neck and later Hancock's, and confronting Lange in between, drugging him and searching his files.

He realized his theory had been mistaken. She'd scattered Lange's papers not because she was trying to destroy them in the fire, but because she'd been searching for something, maybe something she'd seen while she worked for him that had become meaningful when she'd interrogated and tortured Hamlin.

"I suspect she wanted a final confirmation Hancock was somehow responsible for Little Bud's suicide," Donnally said. "Either directly because it was one of his clients who rolled on Little Bud, or indirectly because he was Hamlin's partner in the kind of evil that made Little Bud's death inevitable."

"But I don't get why Hancock would come up to San Francisco," Goldhagen said. "He must've suspected he might be walking into a trap."

"My guess is something terrified him enough to make it worth the risk."

Donnally thought of Sheldon Galen and Takiyah Jackson, the surviving links in the chains of wrongdoing, and of the Vietnamese holding a gun at his back in the parking garage, and of victims' brothers and fathers, sisters and mothers, and of trials twisted by perjury and corrupted by manufactured evidence.

"It might even be the real reason Hamlin told Jackson to reach out to me if something happened to him. Maybe that's what Ryvver found in Lange's files and became her leverage against Hancock."

Donnally sensed Goldhagen's head turn toward him and felt her eyes lock on him.

His body stiffened. He met her gaze and shook his head.

"Don't worry," Goldhagen said. "I'm not even going to ask."

NOTE TO THE READER

I was surprised one day when an image came to me of Mark Hamlin hanging from the lighthouse on the roof of Fort Point. I had intended to limit him to the part of a role player in *Act of Deceit*, but that still image developed into a moving scene, and that scene transformed that first Harlan Donnally novel from a standalone into the beginning of a series.

Writers know much more about their characters than appears in the book, and often the depth of a minor character is shown only by implication. *A Criminal Defense* became an opportunity to put more of Hamlin, and those like him in the legal community, on the page.

Each Donnally book sets its story in a part of the American criminal justice system. *Act of Deceit* began with a systemic failure relating to how courts deal with defendants found incompetent to stand trial. *A Criminal Defense* deals with criminality on the defense side. And, after having leaned rather heavily on the defense in this novel, book three will rebalance the scales by looking at a corrupt prosecution.

While the particular events that Donnally discovers in *A Criminal Defense* are fictional, in the way of fiction they represent, and I hope bring home to my readers, a disturbing reality. One can debate whether truth, in fact, is stranger than fiction, but one of the advantages of the latter is that you get to push certain kinds of truth a little farther down the road it was already headed. In this book, that road was paved by the fictional life of Mark Hamlin and his overdetermined death.

ACKNOWLEDGMENTS

I have been fortunate to again have had the benefit of readings of the manuscript by my wife, Liz, whose insights have made me a better writer and Harlan Donnally a deeper character. I owe special thanks to my sister Diane Gore-Uecker and my mother-in-law, Alice Litov, ceaseless supporters of my books, to Dennis Barley, whose thoughts about the first draft went a long way to improve the story, and to Myles Knapp, who was kind enough to read the manuscript far ahead of publication and comment on it in excellent detail. As an investigator, I had the benefit of working with some of the best, including my wife, Dennis, Trevor Patterson, Randy Schmidt, Rick Monge, and Nancie Huntington, whose professional and ethical standards were as high as the character Frank Lange's were low. Thanks also to Susan Ryan at the River Reader in Guerneville, who let me rename her store and rearrange the fictional furniture for the sake of the plot, and to Gabe Robinson, who was kind enough to help with translations.

Thanks to my editor, Emily Krump at Harper-Collins, who spotted gaps in the plot and in character development invisible to me that would have been all too visible and troubling to the reader. Thanks also to my copyeditor, Eleanor Mikucki, for her help in turning the obstacle course of my writing into a smoother run for the reader, my publicist, Katie Steinberg, for her enthusiasm and tireless support of my books, and to artist Alan Ayers and designer Tom Egner for the stunning cover. Finally, I appreciate more than I can say the countless readers who have sent such generous e-mails about both the Graham Gage and the Harlan Donnally books.